Macki

The Shuffler Saga:
Macki

Alina Simon

For everyone who feels lost, scared, abandoned, or anything that doesn't feel right.

You're not alone.

--

First of all, thank you. Yes, you. Because you're awesome.

Big thanks to my grandparents and my dad, Troy. My friends – you guys support this borderline insane endeavor and me, and that is just fantastic. J.T.R., thanks for sticking with me. Nicole, thanks for being such a huge inspiration for Latinas everywhere and me. Thank you, Mateo, for listening to my rants about this crazy story I have to tell. Finally, my mom. You are an incredible human being.

Prologue
Macki

As I crept to my father's room that night in my family's ageless brown house, the floorboards creaked with every whispered step I took. I was curious, that was all, and most of all I wanted to see my father after a long day with my mother in town. My sister should have been watching him. Maybe I could stay with him for a while. I crept closer and closer to the door cracked just a little bit. There was a ray of light protruding out as if it opened to a wondrous magical world, but behind that door, I knew was the biggest pain I'd ever endure.

As I got to the door, I put my eye to the crack and watched my sister soothe my father by rubbing his sickly hand from the old rickety chair she sat in beside his bed. His veins protruded from his knuckles. The little room he had been locked away in for the past few weeks consisted of the bed, in which he was lying helplessly in, and was stuck in the middle of the far wall. There was a small bedside table that held a pitcher filled with water, medication, and a candle; two ornate windows spaced perfectly on either side. The constant glow of my sister's candle illuminated the night-consumed bedroom. I smiled.

My father, he was sick, and we all knew he would die, but I trained myself not to think of that, so instead I thought of all the fun times we'd spent together over the fifteen years I knew him. The forest behind our house was our favorite place, a safe haven, especially when he was with me. We would sit in our special tree for hours and hours, sometimes doing nothing but enjoying the wilderness in silence.

I felt bad interrupting my sister, so I just watched.

"I love you," she whispered to his ear.

"I love you, too," he said as he grinned and looked at her. I started crying, of course. We were expecting only a couple more days with him, but that could turn into just minutes, so I decided to sit down, smile, sob, and peer through the crack for a while longer. I have a lot of patience, you see. My long, brown, curly hair was tied together with a piece of ribbon. I traced the curls with my fingers over and over.

When I looked up from my hair, I saw my father up, out of his bed, his eyes red, a mixture of fear and aggression in his eyes as my sister tried to run toward me. I jumped backward. He grabbed my sister's leg and dragged her back toward the far wall. I panicked. My brain couldn't register that fast. What do I do? Try to save her? Or run?

I froze, unable to make a decision, I watched as he grabbed my sister's neck... and a swift, horrifying crack sent a chill through my body from head to toe. He dropped her lifeless, unmoving, awkward body to the floor. Looking unstirred by what he had just done, he turned his head until his stare met mine. I bolted in the opposite direction, hoping I could save my mother… at least.

Oh my God, this can't be happening, it's a dream.

I hurdled down the stairs taking four at a time and then ran through our kitchen, where I saw my mother.

"What's going on?" she asked me, worried. I backed up toward our back door. *Run,* I wanted to say, but nothing came out. I heard thick, loud booms on the stairs. Before I could say anything, she was swept away by the beast. She barely screamed before the second sickening crack came.

I practically fell through the door to our backyard. I didn't bother to close it — I just started running as fast as I could into the trees. I jumped over logs, swerved through trees, and bounced on soggy spots of loose brush and twigs. More footsteps cracked behind me. I kept telling myself that it was all a dream and that I'd wake up on the floor of my bedroom screaming eventually. I tried to jump over a creek but missed the opposing bank by a foot. The water froze my shins and knees, but I had to keep going, so I climbed onto the squishy bank and ran more with soggy, brown shoes, never looking back. My dress bounced and ripped when twigs caught the soft blue fabric. My legs elongated to their limit with every stride. Wait.

I stopped and swiveled around to look back, noticing I hadn't heard anything for a while. The silence was eerie and disturbing. I turned in a full three-sixty and saw nothing moving, nothing breathing, just the soft lull of the wind in the trees.

Then... I looked up.

1
Alex

The air was crisp, and my sweatshirt fluttered lightly in the wind. The moon was nearly full in the star-filled sky that was pasted above us like a sticker. There were a few guiding lights around the school sidewalks that gave us just enough vision to see what was around us.

"Go, Alex," my friend commanded. We'd been playing PIG (the basketball game where you have to copy what someone else does so that you don't get a letter) parkour-style for the last hour or so at our high school. Clint had just gotten out for the umpteenth time, so it was me against Rory once again.

I looked to my right and saw a flat brick wall. In a split-second, I was sprinting toward it. With my momentum going forward, I transitioned to go vertical.

I took one step up the wall and then another, flipping over seamlessly and landing pretty well.

Rory'd been doing parkour-esque things for a long time, and Clint and I were new to it. Unlike Clint, I was naturally athletic. Sports were my life. School was pretty easy, too. I was a junior getting calls from colleges across the country to play football and run track for them.

"Jesus, you like those wall flips don't you?"

I knew Rory could do it with ease, but I just liked that whole feeling of walking against gravity. Rory got a running start and did the exact same thing I had done, his shaggy hair flying around against the air.

"Can we do something else?" Clint asked. I was sure he was tired of us doing all of this stuff over and over, where he couldn't do one pull-up by himself in his measly body. He was one of those guys who probably wouldn't grow until he was in college, if even then.

I looked around, trying to find something cool to end on. I mentally checked off all of the stuff that we'd done while I looked around. Wait, I was missing something. Oh, bad idea, Alex. I looked up at the roof of the building. At one part, it went up three stories. Then there was a gap between it and the two-story building next to it. Bingo.

"Hey, Rory, you ever jumped a gap like that?" I pointed at my finding, beginning to rethink it.

Clint and Rory both saw the gap that I meant, and for a moment they didn't speak, just silently weighed what their responses should be. Finally, Rory shrugged.

"Hell," he said. That was, of course, short for: *I'm secretly scared, but we're idiot teenagers, so why not.*

I immediately headed toward a trash bin by one of the shorter parts of the building that I remembered.

"Uh… guys," Clint said, following us to the

trash bin. "You really think this is a good idea?"

"Stop it, Mom," Rory retorted. Clint shut up, but I knew he was terrified.

The area around the trash bin smelled like, well, crap. I hopped up, and the black plastic lid depressed under my weight. I looked above me and saw the edge of the building. It was higher than I expected. Probably so people didn't climb up there. Rory hopped up next to me.

"Here," Rory said, lacing his hands together. At a little over six-foot-one, I wasn't exactly an easy person to boost up off of the flimsy surface of the bin. I secured my left foot into his hand.

"One, two, three," Rory said. I jumped up with my right foot and felt Rory's feet bend the plastic even more. I reached up with both hands and grabbed the edge of the building. Pulling myself up, I hooked one foot onto the roof, and kind of rolled around onto it. I felt the slight impression of the gravel-like stones covering the roof on my hand as I pushed myself up and peeked back over the edge.

I got onto my stomach and stretched my hand as far as I could, bracing the other one against the edge of the roof. I shook my hand a little bit, signaling to Rory that I was ready. He leaped up, grabbing at my hand with both of his. He connected and I began to lift him up. He was fairly skinny, but still had some height on him, so he was somewhat heavy.

After pulling him up most of the way, he grabbed the roof with his other hand. I brought his other hand up, and he spilled onto the roof.

"I didn't realize you were that strong, Alex," he said, breathing slightly heavier than normal. It hadn't been a strain for me. I lifted a lot and was the best on my football team. No big deal.

Rory looked back over the edge and so did I.

Clint was still on the ground.

"Are you coming up?" Rory asked him.

"Uh…" Clint hesitated. "I don't think so. I'll watch from down here."

Rory shrugged. "Suit yourself."

We turned toward the other end of the roof. Luckily, there was a ladder leading up the next two stories.

Rory and I trod through the stones silently. Rory and I hadn't been friends for very long. He had been really into weed and booze and stuff for most of high school, but then he'd been busted a few months ago, so he left that crowd. I knew he still smoked and dealt, but he didn't want to get caught again, and being around his former group would raise immediate red flags.

So he found Clint and me. I'd been best friends with Clint since I was in kindergarten. He was definitely more of the nerdy type and not at all like most of the kids I hung around with, but he was always there.

"So, Alex," Rory started, "why don't I ever see your parents anywhere? I've seen a kid and some girl, but not anyone else."

"Oh, uh, my parents left after my brother, Joey, was born. The girl's our guardian, Lauren."

"Sorry, dude."

"It's cool. It's been almost seven years since they left."

"And that Lauren chick, how old's she? She seems pretty young to be your guardian or whatever."

"I'm not exactly sure; she's never told us."

"Ah. Is she…"

"Single? Has been ever since I've known her."

We approached the ladder and I grabbed a rung, climbing it quickly. As I rose closer to the sky, I couldn't help but look up. When I looked at the moon and stuff, I couldn't help wondering if my parents were out there, looking at the same sky I was. I never understood how they could just leave ten-year-old me and a newborn boy with Lauren. She was amazing, but… it always angered me.

Since they'd left, I felt obligated to look after my brother. I gave up my dream of going to Texas to play football early because I needed to stay close to Joey. I didn't leave the area unless he was with me, and I always kept close tabs on him. He was always fine, and Lauren kept her eye on him 24/7, but I couldn't risk losing him. Would I feel like that for the rest of my life?

After climbing two stories, I crept onto the roof. It was a little windier on top of the building, but it felt nice. Rory came up behind me.

I went immediately to the edge and looked across the gap to the opposing second floor.

"Dude, there's no way we could make that jump." He spat at the ground. I thought for a moment.

"I think I can do it."

"Are you nuts? That's a lot farther than I thought it was. Let's go." He turned to leave. I saw Clint down below, illuminated by the soft light and looking up at us.

"I'm gonna do it."

"Jesus, you're kidding me."

"No."

"You'll die, seriously."

I went to the back edge of the roof and readied myself to take off. My heart was pounding. Adrenaline was pumping. I was confident I could do it. I was faster, stronger, and smarter than any person I knew. I was somewhat embarrassed to admit it, but I felt like I was superhuman. I could show them what I meant. I could prove it to myself too.

"Tape it," I told Rory.

"Tape your death? I don't think so."

"Rory, do it." He sighed and pulled out his phone. I stared straight into the night, seeing nothing on the horizon. The opposing roof was down below, I knew, but I couldn't see it.

Rory pointed his phone's camera at me.

"Go." I took off at record speed, my feet pounding on the gravel, sliding on it a little more than I thought I would. I reached the side and took a giant leap. Nothing seemed real in that moment. I was floating through the air, awaiting impact, ready to roll like Rory had taught me. I was almost there, floating in time. I put both my hands in front of me and reached out for the edge.

And then before I knew it, my velocity was taking me down, cutting the angle short. I had one second for the fear to shoot through me… before I slammed into the brick side of the building. I felt myself falling down like a rock toward the cement, my head spinning.

I wasn't thinking anything before I hit the ground and all of my senses shut off.

2
Macki

It wasn't an unusual situation for me. There were many times in my past that I'd been left to rot. I paced around my small, moldy-smelling, circular cell that I'd been cordially introduced to around twenty years ago. Or something like that. I had been avid to keep track of the time, but even in a drone atmosphere such as this one, I'd grown bored and given up a few years previous. Like nineteen years and three hundred and sixty-three days ago. Oh well. Time is relative was what I told myself. After all, I was a hundred and sixty-five years old. Although I was "stuck" in the body of my fifteen-year-old self, which sometimes I rejoiced and sometimes I regretted.

I ran my fingers through my shoulder-length hair, attempting to pull out the tangles and knots, but there were way too many for me to handle. My hair was disgusting, as well as my petite body. Zahra would occasionally send some of her goonies to chuck buckets of water on me, which was refreshing. My wrists were chained to the wall in thick, titanium binds, but they gave me enough freedom to roam around and pace. I would often pace for hours on end, muttering to myself, thinking things through, slowly letting myself go even crazier (if that was possible).

Sometimes I'd begin to think about times I'd rather forget in my life, and with that, I shoved the thoughts away valiantly... most of the time. Some thoughts would seep through, especially when I was sleeping (which I didn't do much of). I would think about Asime, mostly. He was Zahra's brother and my lover. That's all I'd say for now about poor Asime Avi.

Zahra also frequented my thoughts – and with thoughts of her, a scowl never failed to cross my face. In the old times, she had been my friend and partner in many things, but more recently she was a selfish, torturous bitch. When I was first imprisoned, she would shoot me at point-blank range with that stupid pistol of hers to get me to tell her the formula – or drown me or tie me up and let some of her larger associates beat me until all of my bones were broken and I was just an oozing ball of pulp.

But I held my tongue.

I will admit, she made it somewhat challenging, but her methods were not even close to what it would take to break me, if anything could. Some of her more peaceful ways also proved ineffective. She sent in one of the sweetest, most caring (but certainly deadly) person she could find. I was very fond of Logan, as she had been one of the first we'd turned – an orphan I had found in the remains of World War Two – but I had to resort to being my asshole self to her to get her to realize that I wasn't interested in any of the crap that came out of her mouth. I admired her calmness and somehow envied her drive for peace, but also her willingness to fight and hold her own if she had to.

I don't know exactly what was going through Zahra's mind when she decided to lock me up in here. She should have known that giving me this much time to myself to think would prove a very grave mistake. She'd been too scared to kill me, though, even if she had had the chance, which she very rarely did.

We'd been training together for many years, recruiting what I thought of as an army of lost souls from all corners of the earth. We had built the Terrene, which my cell was in the belly of. Three of our recruits had proved most triumphant: Logan, Phoenix, and Ella. They were each from very different backgrounds, but all shared one thing: very intense sadness.

Ella was very special to me. When Zahra and I began "parting ways," she came immediately to me. She was a quiet girl, but was wicked with her weapon of choice – a barbed chain – and was quite the asset to have on my "team."

Most of the Shufflers began to really, really hate my guts. They believed that I was destined for tragedy and madness, and Zahra was their savior from that and could keep me soundly under control. True, I had killed many in my time, but never because I was simply bloodthirsty. Mostly in times of war among the humans.

There was one I killed who Zahra would never forgive me for. I had tried to explain to her so many times that it was a genuine accident, but she would never forgive me. And so she decided to get me back, turn against me all of the community that I had created out of my own desperation to help in some way, shape, or form, and exile me to this private hellhole. She spread the rumor that I was going crazy, and I was going to kill all of the humans in order to rule the world. It was all bullshit. Until she did this to me.

It was not my fault, how I thought. It just… happened. I wasn't doing it out of thirst for revenge or anything stupid like that – just because that's where my mind took me and for the first time, I had let it run wild. Then, murdering innocents and those who had betrayed me was the only thought in my head. I craved it. I was addicted to it. So I was anticipating *doing* it. But then I would reel myself in like always and start all over again.

There had been two people that I truly trusted – Karen and Jesse. They treated me like a daughter, even though I was much older and much more established than they were among the Shufflers. Karen had come to visit me once while I had been imprisoned, and I was unhappy to find out that she had sided with Zahra and was abandoning me. A shame. They had been valuable allies.

I found a small pebble from the ground and picked it up, examining it. Then I threw it out of my way, shaming myself for looking at such a mundane thing with any interest whatsoever.

I could have broken out at pretty much any time I pleased, but I had some reservations. If I left, I would have a war to fight. I had fought countless wars in the past, but this one would be different. In this one, I would be the bad guy. I would go crazy. I knew as soon as I got out, I would lose control. Maybe being locked up wasn't such a bad thing for a time. Maybe Zahra was right.

Something pounded on the door. Immediately, I was tiptoeing on my dirty, bare feet to the miniature window built into the thick, metal door of my cell. I peered through it, looking for the source of the noise, but instead I found a sequence of tiny, etched letters in the fiberglass.

Automatically, I translated the small phrase in my mind from Russian to English, knowing exactly where my message had come from. It read: _you have three minutes._ I checked the lock. It clicked open. I smiled in delight, but it wavered. Was that really what I wanted? Was I ready? I hesitated for a moment, counting down the seconds in my head. Then I nodded my head in agreement with myself, snapped the chains off of my wrists, and swung the door open, careful to keep it as silent as possible.

I made my way down the spiraling rock steps until I reached a long hallway. Color streamed in through a number of stained glass windows enclosing the hall. I glanced out the one nearest me. It was raining. Typical of England. But it was nice to finally see something natural again. I admired the noise the soft padding of the rain made... then I stopped myself abruptly. I wasn't out of the Terrene yet. I had a long way to go.

I began going through the path in my head. I knew the place like the back of my hand, and I realized it was going to be even a more challenging trek than I had once thought.

Stop. One thing at a time. I looked to the end of the hallway, where I knew there would be a guard.

The German boy stood where I figured he would be, his back toward me. Normally, he would stop Shufflers from coming to see me, but this time it would be the other way around. I knew this boy as the main medic of the group. He had pink eyes, but was weaker than most his size. My mind momentarily thought of his brother, the hotheaded boy who thrived on death and destruction. He was a bully, but Ryker was – like his brother – not the strongest in a fight. Any of the three girls could defeat him easily. I was still drawn to him, though, as he was drawn to me. His weapon of choice was an interesting one – a chainsaw.

I let the thought of Ryker flee from my head as I slithered up one of the posts leading to the rafters far above. I wrapped myself around the beams and silently began making my way toward the unsuspecting boy below. It felt nice to be able to move freely again, and I made the most of it by flipping and tumbling from beam to beam, landing as softly as I had trained to do all those years ago.

Once I was above him, I took a breath. I didn't think he heard me or saw me – but he sensed me and turned around, alarmed. He stood no chance. I jumped down and landed on top of him, wrapping my arms slyly around his neck and pressing as much as I dared to without breaking his spinal cord. What fun would it be if I killed all of my competition off?

"Miss me, Quinn?" I sneered. He desperately tried to grab for the bolas held on a carabiner around his waist. His arm fell as his strength gave out, his bright pink eyes staring widely at me. I got up, carefully allowing his unconscious body to slide to my feet. I unclipped his bolas and took them in my own hands, swinging them around a bit. They would do for a while. I'd worked with the weapon before, but it had never been my strength by any means. Quinn was much more experienced than I in that matter.

I slinked away from his body, making my way into a more compact hallway. This was the hard part I'd been thinking about.

I came to a door and stood near it, out of sight, listening to what was coming from inside. It was Zahra's office.

"I am sure Ryker is just joking with your brother, Phoenix," Zahra said in her stiff, African accent I knew all too well.

"You think it's funny to make jokes about killing humans?" I heard Phoenix say. I recognized her strong voice instantly. She probably hated me more than Zahra did.

"No... of course I do not," Zahra replied.

"You think it's funny when Ryker talks about Macki coming back?" Phoenix pressed. Thatta boy, Ryker! I was trying my best not to giggle at Phoenix's frustration.

"No, Phoenix, you are missing my point. Ryker does not know what he is saying. He is irrational and immature," Zahra stated.

"That's not what Quinn thinks. He's concerned. The reason Logan isn't with me right now is because I was going to, once again, point out Ryker's extreme obsession with Nazism. Isn't that a little worrying?" Phoenix argued. "Shouldn't the Core at least talk to him, Zahra? He'll break under pressure if he has anything to hide."

"I will think about it," was all that Zahra said, indicating to Phoenix that she was not to take the matter any further with her.

It was as good a time as any to make a move; otherwise, Phoenix was going to see me as she left. I readied myself... then took off at a sprint, which was faster than any human would even have a chance of catching up to.

As I passed the threshold, I saw a blur of Zahra's dark skin and Phoenix's blonde-gold hair and eyes, uttering out a quick, "Good afternoon, Zahra" as I passed.

"What was that?" I heard Phoenix say as I rushed away. She'd obviously not comprehended who I was. Then she realized. "No way," she said in disbelief. She scrambled out of the room, taking off after me.

Even though I was almost out of range, I heard Zahra yell an angered and shocked, "Dammit, Mackinley!" from inside her office, slamming a fist through her desk.

I raced through the hallway until I came to a door. I burst through it. Suddenly, I was in the greenhouse, a place I had cherished, and where I (and many other Shufflers) could find temporary serenity from all of the chaos of the Terrene.

God, Phoenix was fast, I realized. She was catching up with me. She was strong, too, and stuck at the prime age of 21.

"Logan! Pilot!" she cried out. "Jesus Christ, it's Macki!" I hadn't noticed the pair at first, but then I saw them in the tree ahead of me. Logan immediately slid her metal staff from a sling on her back, Pilot taking out his pair of metal nunchuks. I thought I would beat them, but...

Logan fell down right in my path, Pilot slightly behind her, guiding her with his hand. At the last moment, I flung the bolas at Logan's feet, hoping I'd get lucky, but her hands were too quick – unnaturally quick, even for a Shuffler. My bolas bounced harmlessly off of the thick metal of her staff and fell onto the dirt path.

"Great," was all I could say as I dodged Logan's swinging staff. I managed to get a swift kick in, knocking her enough off-balance that I could pass. Pilot's nunchuks were swinging savagely in front of me. For a moment, I thought I was screwed, but adrenaline was really pumping and my eyes and hands were working in overdrive. I caught them both – one in each hand – and slid between Pilot's legs, pulling myself off of the ground and back into a running motion in one move.

They took off after me, realizing I had gotten

through their barrier. I shoved another door open, which led to a dimly lit dirt tunnel. Almost there. I heard a faint whizzing sound and instinctively jerked my head to the side. Sure enough, a "preypin," as Phoenix called them, flew past my head. It was a cross between a nail and a needle, steel feathers pressed against the metal, ready to spring open and dig into the enemy's flesh on contact.

I couldn't believe Phoenix was still using those ridiculous weapons.

"Really, Phoenix, preypins?" I said. "Thought you'd be over those useless things by now."

With that, Phoenix pushed Logan and Pilot out of her way.

"Watch out you two. I've had enough of this crap."

Logan and Pilot listened to Phoenix's command, stepping off to the sides of the tunnel, letting her go ahead. They knew she was in a blind rage and didn't want to get mixed in with that. I knew what was coming next. I had been waiting for twenty years to see it again. I looked back just as Phoenix flipped, transforming mid-air into a brilliant cheetah. She sped up in her pursuit of me, reaching speeds not even I could match.

"Okay. I can play that game," I proclaimed, smiling as I did. I planted a foot on the side of the tunnel, pushing myself off of it, flipping into the center of the tunnel. I felt my body shift, the molecules rearranging to create a new form – a form I had missed for a long, long time.

I landed as a white tiger – my mold. I felt my paws pushing against the dirt, propelling me forward with incredible speed. If I hadn't have been so busy running from Phoenix, I would have stopped to roar just for the hell of it. But, unfortunately, I had a cheetah on my tail, so I had to scoot.

Shufflers were shape-shifters basically. We could each turn into one animal that was chosen for us by a, well, it's complicated. Imagine all of the incredibly strong, fast, vicious animals you can and then picture them with a brain more developed than any human. Yes, that would be us. Sounds like fun, hm? And guess what? I was the only one who knew how to turn people into Shufflers. It's a long story of how that came to be – but, in short, I'm very smart and so was my father.

Finally, we came to the vestibule, where I was glad to see a fiberglass bulb built into the side of a hill waiting open for me. I got my first glimpse of the sky, which was still gloomy, but a beauty all in itself. I could also see the tips of the green hills waiting for me outside this wretched place. This would be a long jump...

I jumped, barely clawing myself up onto the English landscape. I looked back again, seeing Phoenix struggle with the jump, but she eventually made it up, continuing to pursue me as the fastest natural speedster on the planet. Too fast for me.

She grabbed the back of my foot, which was enough to bring me down hard on the soft dirt. I rolled for a ways, and decided – as I was being flung from the top of a hill – that I should mold back to my human form. I did so as I was tumbling down the hill. I popped up as fast as I could, turning to face Phoenix. She changed back to her human form, and I got to fully see all of her features. She was nearly six-foot (much taller than I was) with a long braid of golden hair wrapped around her, rage and hatred burning through her golden-inflected eyes.

She was charging toward me, raising a fist to punch... but my reflexes didn't fail me, and I was able to stop the attack and counter with a quick kick to her stomach. She stumbled a bit, but it wasn't hard enough to do much damage. She came at me with full force, trying anything to hit me. I hadn't had much practice fighting in a while, but I was glad to see that I was at least holding my own against my experienced opponent.

Whack! Phoenix's fist connected hard with the side of my face.

"Seems I'm a little rusty," I sputtered out as I blocked her next attack. Phoenix had a problem with getting a little too agitated, and when that happened, often it would make her easier to fight because her head wasn't clear enough. I played on that observation and eventually began to attack rather than defend and counter. I was right. She couldn't keep up with my quick moves and eventually I got a good one to her face and her nose began gushing out blood, making her turn away for the split-second I needed to make my escape.

"Dammit. Cramp. Should have stretched before I did that," I said as she struggled to recover. I started laughing a bit. And by the time she looked up...

I was gone.

3
Alex

Before my eyes were even open, I knew my head hurt. It was pounding. When I opened my eyes, I just saw lights at first. When they finally adjusted, I looked around. I was in a hospital room. Everything was sterile and looked way too clean, of course, and there was an IV going into my arm. A computer ticked nearby.

I sat up a little and heard some people talking just outside my door.

"Ma'am, we highly advise that you leave him here for a few more days. His whole right arm is shattered. We need to go in and do reconstructive surgery on it, otherwise he could lose full operation of it. On top of that, we need to do a psychological exam. He did jump off of a three-story building."

"I'm telling you, not asking. He was just being a

dumbass," someone said back. I knew that voice. Lauren.

Everything hurt, but my arm did the most. It was held in a splint at my side. My fingers were an eerie bluish-purple and tingled. I tried moving them – and I could, barely. My shoulder hurt really badly, too; maybe I'd dislocated it or something.

I heard new footsteps come toward the group talking outside.

"We got a call about a disturbance up here," a man with a deep voice said.

"A disturbance?" Lauren said.

"Yes, this woman wants to take a child out of our care. He's in critical condition."

"Miss, are you on any sort of thought-impairing substances?" the man asked.

"No, of course not. I'm sorry, guys, but I just need my kid."

"He's too weak right now." A pause.

"Just please. I don't want to fight you to get in there, but I will if need be." Another pause.

The door to my room opened. It was Lauren. Her hair was pulled back in an auburn ponytail and her hazel eyes looked angry.

"Alex, you're awake. Finally. We're leaving."

There was a doctor, a nurse, and two security guards standing in the hall, watching us.

"Why?" I asked. "Shouldn't I stay and– "

"Listen to me, Alex. We're leaving," she said. She was hardly ever this serious, so I knew my trust had to come before logic, even through my foggy brain. "Take this out, please," she said to the pair standing in the hall. The nurse hurried in, obviously frustrated, and slid the needle out of my arm, covering it with a cotton ball and finally taping it up.

"And either I can carry him, or you can take

him down for me," she told the nurse. The nurse clenched her teeth. Lauren was the nicest person I knew, but when it came to protecting Joey and me, she was a mother bear.

But what was really up?

--

"Where are Clint and Rory?" I finally asked, breaking the silence of the car ride home. It was eight in the morning, and the sun was already up. Apparently, they'd flown me to a hospital in Newark, so it was a bit of drive to our house. I'd fallen asleep for a while due to the sedatives and pain meds that were still streaming through my body. Neither of us had said a word since we left the hospital.

"Well, Rory's in jail for breaking his probation. And Clint's with his mom, probably crying his eyes out."

"Why's Rory in jail?"

"Trespassing and breaking curfew. You and Clint have fines to pay as well."

I leaned my head back and sighed. Crap. I turned my head over to look at her, silently asking if she was mad.

"I'm not mad. I don't really care, actually. I mean, you're an idiot, of course. But at least you're safe."

"Why didn't you let me stay at the hospital?" I knew that was the elephant in the room. But I wanted to know.

For a few moments, she didn't say anything, keeping her eyes on the road.

"How's your arm?" she asked. I kind of picked it up, feeling it.

"It feels fine. Maybe it's just the pain meds

kicking in or–"

"No. It's all you. I didn't know it until you about killed yourself last night, but it's you."

"What's me? What are you talking about?"

"I don't exactly know yet. But you're special."

I looked out the window, watching the countryside fly by. Wait.

"Lauren, where are we?" She didn't want to talk, so she didn't say anything. *"Lauren."* She hit the wheel.

"I'm sorry. I'm a little stressed out right now. Bear with me."

I looked in the side mirror. The right side of my face was purple, red, and scraped up. Through the heavy medication, I started to actually think. My thoughts started racing. I was anxious. I realized that something big was going on… and I had absolutely no idea what it was or what piece I played. Was Lauren in trouble or something? I couldn't fathom her doing anything illegal…

Lauren had never acted like this before, that's for sure.

"Where's Joey?"

"He's with my sister."

"What? You have a sister? Why didn't I know you have a sister?"

"She's been really busy the last few years."

"Older or younger?"

"Neither really. I mean, I'm older by a few minutes."

"Twins?" I asked in disbelief. "You have a *twin?"*

"Yes, Rachel. My identical twin. She's a little more… intense than I am, I guess. They're heading west as we speak." She turned onto a dirt road, and the car rocked uneasily on the ground. Up ahead was a small wood. I knew this place. I definitely knew this place.

"Is this Kaley's place?" I asked her.

"Yep," she said. "We need a place to crash away from home for a while." The sun hid behind the trees as we drove up to the house beyond. I'd been up here once a few summers ago. It was a big house built like a modern log cabin. Huge stones and painted wood with big sliding doors in the back led to a pond hidden in the forest.

As we drove up to the entrance, I saw someone sitting on the porch steps. My heart skipped a beat. It was my girlfriend, Kaley. Her wavy blonde hair was down and green eyes sparkling. The car stopped and I opened the door, eager to see her. We'd been dating for all of high school and the end of eighth grade. She was always there for me, and I loved her with all my heart.

She walked toward me, crushing leaves as she came.

"I'd give you a hug, but that might not feel good," she said.

"Yeah… guess so."

She ran her fingers lightly over the side of my face that'd been damaged. A frown crept across her face.

"Wow," she said, "Lauren wasn't kidding." Lauren came up behind me, a duffel bag around her.

"I didn't have time to pack much," Lauren said as she walked past us up to the house. They'd given me my clothes back at the hospital, so I'd changed into them earlier, but that was all I had. I guessed my cell phone was smashed too.

"Let's go inside," Kaley said. "It's really cold out here." We walked up to the house, and the glow inside made me feel warm automatically. Of what I understood, the place was Kaley's aunt's summer house. She was a writer from Manhattan and liked to come down to write in the summer away from everything. Sometimes, other family members would come and visit from the New England area; that's why I'd been there. Fourth of July maybe? I thought so.

Kaley made sure to walk on my left side so that she could hold my hand; a sling held my right arm up. Her hand was cold. She must have been waiting a long time for us. She opened the door and I walked in, the warmth instantly making me melt. Straight in front of me was a staircase and to my left was the kitchen. She took my hand again and led me to the right. It was the great room – the back all windowed sliding doors. There was a grand stone fireplace and comfy couches that looked like you'd just sink into them. In the corner was a black grand piano and a guitar hanging on the wall. It was definitely the home of an artist.

"I remember now," I told Kaley, referring to being here once before.

"It's hard to forget. The pond out back is frozen this time of year, too, and the woods usually has the brush of snow on it. Very beautiful."

We walked to the giant windows and looked outside. It looked like one of those nature backgrounds that people had on their computers. The lake was frozen around the edges, but still soft in the middle, and a circle of lightly dusted trees surrounded it.

"Wow," I said. "So… what are we doing here?"

"Honestly, I don't really know. Lauren asked if I could come down here and let you guys stay for a while and it seemed urgent, so I said that was fine. When you hurt yourself, I drove to the hospital, but Lauren called and told Clint and me to leave before you woke up. She also made us swear not to tell anyone about what happened. She even talked to Rory before the cops took him, destroyed his phone, gave him a couple hundred bucks to replace it, and made him swear not to tell. So none of us did."

"What... God, Lauren. Okay. Well... I'm glad you came to the hospital to see me. Who told you?"

"Clint. He called me crying. On my way to the school, I had to stop him from hyperventilating over the phone."

"Sounds like Clint," I said. "I'm getting really tired again. You want to put in a movie and I'll drift in and out?"

"Sure. Which one?"

"Something cheerful." Kaley grabbed the remote and sat down next to me. It was really nice to be with her. Seriously. She found a movie on Netflix and clicked it on, then chucked the remote down and snuggled into me, making herself comfortable. I put my good arm around her as the movie started.

What a nice ending to what could have been a nightmare.

4
Macki

I woke up remembering how much I hadn't missed hay for all those years. I mean really, I'd slept in a countless number of barns, and those ungodly bales were in every single one of them with their pokey-scratchy quills of death. Just enough to always annoy me.

The sun had already been up a while on Iceland's southeastern coast, and I didn't like that either. One, my eyes hadn't adjusted to the light of day yet because I'd stuck myself in the bottom of a ship on the way here. Two, I liked the cover of darkness so I could sneak around with a lesser chance of humans noticing me. Luckily, the barn didn't have any window-like things open, so a single dull, buzzing bulb hanging in the center was easy enough on my eyes.

I sat up from the hay and looked around. It was

a barn, but there weren't any animals, just equipment for tending fields. What kind of fields? Hay fields, of course.

It was cold inside, but last night when I'd gotten in, it had been *freezing*. I had to find somewhere to crash, at least until it got above freezing and/or I was wearing something other than shorts and a T-shirt. Shoes would also be nice.

I'd found the barn on the outskirts of a tiny village the boat had docked in. I crawled in about one or so in the morning and was completely exhausted. Hungry. Tired. Aching. Brain hurting. Despite how worn I was, I couldn't sleep. It just... there was too much going on. I didn't even know where to start. I managed about thirty minutes of decent rest, which was weird for me. Normally – meaning before I was thrown in a hole for twenty years – I could sleep like a rock anytime, anywhere.

I jumped down from the bale of hay I was on, which was five bales up, and landed on the cool dirt of the ground. The ground felt weird on my feet.

It kept slapping me in the face over and over... I was out and this was real. The world was real. Dammit.

I snaked my way around the farm equipment, the sharp chill of the air still biting at me. I passed tractors and the like and came to an old car that looked like someone had been planning to fix it up, but gave up fifteen years ago. The wall next to it was covered in hanging tools and a workbench with old nails and miscellaneous parts strewn across it, covered in cobwebs and left to rust.

I went over to the workbench and looked at everything more closely. Seeing nothing of interest, I then looked up at the wall of tools.

And *oh*, how I'd missed that stuff. An axe, a

machete, a chainsaw on the end... and a knife propped up against the wall. I picked it up, and in my hand it felt cold and instantly familiar. It was old, with a blade that desperately needed to be sharpened and a hilt wrapped in leather. I tossed it around a bit, getting a feel for the weight. Everything was coming back now. Everything from before.

And my mind started racing. A grin spread on my face unlike any I'd sported the last twenty years. It was of power. Of life. Of opportunity. Deep inside, I knew there was still the feeling of insecurity, anxiety, and fear that I'd felt about being free boiling and trying to get the best of me. It wanted me to hide forever. To wilt. It was too late to save the image of a gracious, kind Macki, but instead I could fade into the background of time and be forgotten as someone who was a false threat.

That was not going to happen.

I spun around suddenly, flinging the knife across the barn with impeccable form that had come back to me in an instant. The time and practice I'd put in learning the art of attack and defense seemed only as rusty as maybe a week. The knife hit the other side and stuck itself in the wood, perfectly level with the ground.

Beautiful. I felt like my blood really started pumping. My body was rejuvenating and forming into the Macki I had known twenty years ago. I stretched my arms all the way up and shook the kinks out of my neck. I bent over and let my spine crack all the way down. I knew I still had some wounds that were healing up, but they should be all closed up within a few days or so.

Two of my fingers had been crushed on my right hand not too long ago, and that would probably take a bit longer. Luckily, I'm ambidextrous as far as most things go. I turned again to search the bench for some tape. I shoved some things out of the way and, after a few moments of shifting things around, found a roll of duct tape that was almost down to the rind. I peeled off a piece and ripped it off, chucking the tape back onto the workbench. I wrapped it around my right pinkie and ring finger, so that they'd stay upright together.

I still looked like shit, though. And I was disgusting. My hair was knotted, an ewwy dark brown color, filthy, and longer than I liked it. The clothes I was in had been stuck to my body for the last year or so and were basically falling apart. Probably a good plan to get new ones, although streaking was definitely on my bucket list. My feet had a layer of filth on them and my toenails were all disfigured and weird. Jesus, yeah, I was a wreck.

I jogged over to the opposite side of the barn and quickly unpegged the knife, sticking it in the band of my shorts right where my left hand would normally hang in case I needed it right away. I doubted I would; I was in Iceland, for Christ's sake.

I walked toward the door and hesitated before walking out. I started whining in my head 'cause I knew it would be cold and bright and there'd be people out there. Finally, I shoved the big wooden door open and found myself blanketed in the white light of snow and the sun.

I was temporarily blinded, and immediately started getting a headache. Once my vision was restored, I saw I was on the edge of hay field. Not too far in front of me was a small house where the farm owners lived. Down to my right was a path to the heart of the village.

I stepped out onto the slushy snow toward the house, and my feet felt like they were stepping on a giant snow cone. It was squishy but the sting of the cold on my feet felt nice. The wind was blowing, but thankfully it wasn't snowing. I looked around the property as I made my way to the house. Behind the fields was a picturesque view of snowy Icelandic mountain peaks. They looked a lot closer than they probably were, but they just made the whole place seem so much more serene, even in the torrent of the icy winds.

I got one last look at the mountains before I stepped onto the small porch of the house and surveyed the area. I looked inside one of the windows by the door and didn't see any lights on or people mulling around the outdated kitchen inside. I scooted back a bit and looked up to the second floor. The roof was pointed, and near the top was a window. I noted that it would be my point of entry if the back door wasn't open, which I suspected it would be.

Out in the middle of nowhere, people don't typically expect any sort of crime. And especially on a farm farther out from town, I was almost positive they'd leave a door open. I turned the knob to the front just to see, and it was locked. I could've easily broken the door down or popped the lock, but it would be more work if people heard me.

I hopped off the porch onto to the chilling snow again and jogged around back with my arms crossed. The house was long on the side and painted a mustard yellow color that made me think of Cheerios for some reason. I turned around to the back of the house and spotted a screen door protecting a thick wood one behind. I turned the handle to the screen door, and it flung open with a high screeching noise. I stepped in front of it to hold it open and turned the rusted gold knob to the next door and it opened.

I stepped inside, the screen door slamming loudly behind me. I shut the other door and the cold was instantly blocked out. The house seemed a lot warmer than it probably was, but my bones started warming up regardless.

The hallway in front of me was dark. I crept toward it like a moth to a light. Again, I was used to the dark and I knew a wicked sunburn would be coming my way if I stayed outside too long.

The walls were covered in old-fashioned floral wallpaper. At least, I thought it was old-fashioned. That stuff couldn't be coming back, right? The first door I passed was open, and I took a brief look inside. It was a couple's room for sure, the bed made neatly and little decorations you'd expect in a grandma's house. This was definitely a farmer's home.

I continued on, just to see what else the house contained. The next door I came to was closed. There was a sign on it written in Icelandic that I didn't understand. I knew many languages, but not this one. The only things I could say would get me slapped by any decent person. The sign was definitely written in a girl's handwriting, though. I could tell by the curves and overall neatness. The door was dark brown with visible strokes of paint. I took the door handle in my hand and twisted it. It caught a little bit on itself and made a series of clicking noises, but eventually I pushed it open.

Beyond was a small bedroom that had definitely been decorated by a teenager. A bundle of handmade bracelets sat on the dresser. The shades were drawn, so I flipped on the light and again was temporarily blinded. This room was not nearly as orderly as the other, with clothes strewn all around like someone took them all out of the drawers and tried to cover everything like a tarp.

I stepped in and immediately eyed a blue hoodie lying near the twin bed in the corner. I bent down and picked it up from under a pile of mixed garments and saw that it had some sort of logo on it. Ah, perfect. The sweatshirt was definitely a little big, but it would work.

The next thing I scanned the room for were some pants. *Pants.* It's kind of a funny word if you really think about it. I spotted some over on the other side of the room and picked them up. Going to be a little long and baggy, but at least they'd stay up and keep me warmer. They were black (yay, my favorite color) and obviously designed for cooler temperatures.

I added them to my growing clothes rack on my left arm and looked for a fresh shirt. There was a plain black athletic shirt with long sleeves basically right under me, and I grabbed it up.

After a few more moments of searching, I'd found some thermal socks, a few hair ties, and some pretty fancy snow boots that laced all the way up. I looked around one last time, just to see if anything else caught my eye. I noticed that the only organized thing in the room was a short bookshelf near the bed. I stepped over to it just to see what young kids were reading nowadays.

A lot of them were in Icelandic (of course), but there were some in English. Some of the classics, of course. Then one with a seriously damaged spine. Obviously, it'd been read many times, so I pulled it out.

To my utter disappointment, there was a dragon on the front of it. Another fantasy novel. I could only take so many of those.

I dropped the book, not bothering to put it back, and trekked back out of the room.

I remembered all of the books I'd read and how they'd made me feel and all that stuff.

Books and dreamers can be a deadly combination.

5
Macki

I practically inhaled everything in the house's kitchen. It was mostly fresh stuff – fish, eggs (not gonna lie, I felt like a badass eating them raw), bread. I chugged an entire gallon of milk to top it all off. I could check food off of my list of necessities.

I chucked the milk jug aimlessly, and it fell to the floor. At the same time, I heard the hammer of shotgun go back in the hall. I looked over and saw a big, burly man in full winter gear had a shotgun trained on me. I'd known he was coming since he came to the back door. I was just too damn lazy to leave.

When he saw my young face, he relaxed a little bit.

"Havatyuhayerayer," he said. Whatever that meant.

"I don't speak Icelandic," I said, deciding to use

my English accent with this dude. It was easy for me to turn it off or on depending on whom I was talking to.

"Oh. What are you doing here?" He gained a little bit of confidence, and clutched the gun tighter.

"I, uh… I'm an orphan," I said. Advantage equals me looking fifteen. "I was hungry." He lowered the weapon finally. "And now," I continued, "I'd just like to use the phone, if you'd excuse me for a while." I kind of did this weird hop thing over to the landline hanging on the wall.

"You're quite the fiery one, aren't yah?" he asked. I was perplexed by the question.

"Yes. Very much so actually. How can you tell?"

"Marching in here, taking my daughter's clothes, eating all of our food, and demanding to use the phone in the presence of me with a gun. That's fire." Oh, that's how he could tell. I looked around the kitchen, and saw that the floor was covered in food wrappers and eggshells and all kinds of shit. I hadn't realized that before.

"Take your time," he finally told me, turning away from the kitchen. "But not too much time. I don't allow thieves in my house on a regular basis. Especially ones that can eat that much food." He left the kitchen and I heard him walk out the front door. Nice man. Considering the circumstances.

I dialed the phone to a number I knew by heart… used to know by heart. I took a few moments, straining to remember.

Ah, got it. I dialed it and listened to it ring once before someone picked up.

"Macki," I heard on the other end. It was a girl's voice, one that I knew pretty well – Frost. She'd been one of my top soldiers since I'd brought her to the Terrene. Her hair was a different color practically every time I saw her. She must have a suitcase full of dye or something. Speaking of dye... I really wanted some black. My hair was still poop brown.

"Tell me you're where I want you to be."

"I am."

"Now tell me you know where she is."

"I do. But–"

"But what?"

"Rachel's here, too. I couldn't keep track of both. Ryker, Bull, and Humvee are on their way now to help."

"Fantastic. The three stooges to the front lines again," I said then thought for a moment. "Wait. *Both?*"

"Both kids."

"Jesus Christ, I see Karen and Jesse have been busy. How old's the second one?"

"Six or so."

"I figured after the first one, they'd try to be all goody-two-shoes like they usually are," I sneered. "Wait. I sent you to spy on Lauren, right? And so now you're telling me Karen's kid is with her?"

"Yeah. One kid's with Lauren and the other's with Rachel, heading west. How'd you know about the first one, anyway? I didn't think anything got into that cell of yours..."

"Sixteen years ago. Karen was pregnant. I never actually got to see the kid. I don't think she ever told Jess that I found out."

"You... never mind. Zahra wants to bring them in for observation. I mean, they have to be special somehow, right?"

"Not necessarily, but I'm sure you don't want to hear my long, ungodly spiel about genetics, now do you?"

"I'm good."

"Figured. I'll be there soon."

"Where are you now?" she inquired.

"Uh, a place with food. Sorry, I was really hungry – now I think I'm going into a mini food coma." She laughed a little. "I have to go now. I'll call you when I'm closer. I'll be in contact with the Terrene as well."

"All right, bye."

"And Frost." I always hung up first, so I knew she'd still be on the line.

"Yeah?"

"Thanks."

"Thanks for what?"

"Being loyal."

"Well... you're welcome, I guess. I'm so glad you're back. I'm *so* glad you're back, Macki." I knew she meant it by the tone in her voice.

"I'm glad too, Frost," I said, trying not to waver to the point where she could recognize my hesitation. I hung up with that. Took a deep breath. Then dialed again. This one I really did know by heart.

"Hello?" I heard on the other end. It was a dude, a young dude.

"Hey, get everyone out." I knew I had to keep this call brief, no matter how much I wanted to draw it out. The Terrene was crawling with Zahra's bitches, and if anyone overheard me having a long, lovely conversation with someone, one of them was bound to pick up.

"What?"

"It's Macki, dumbass. I need all of my people out. Now."

"Okay."

"Now shoo. Go tell them." I semi-slammed the phone back on the receiver. I had no idea how effectively that message would spread among my followers. Oh, well. I'd figure it out. I always did.

I heard someone at the back door again. This time it was a girl, presumably talking to her father.

"No, I want to see. I'm fine," she said as she stomped down the hall. She came around to the kitchen. She was tall – taller than me, for sure – with white-blonde hair put in a messy braid, a coat, thick pants, and boots. I stood there like an animal on display for a moment as she looked around the kitchen. Her father came up behind her, his gun slung around him.

They spoke to each other in Icelandic.

"I guess I'll be leaving now," I said awkwardly.

"Would you like to stay for the night?" the girl asked, their bickering stopping.

"I should probably go."

"No, please stay. You can help me on the farm to repay what you... ate, mostly."

I thought about it. Could I waste another day? I'd already taken a detour here.

But the thought of staying... with this nice family... for a night in a comfy, warm house. It was getting to me. What if I just stayed here forever? In the middle of Iceland, just me hanging out. It was peaceful here, away from everything. They'd never find me either. I could maybe venture even further in the mountains and build myself a big house. It sounded nice in theory.

I snapped out of my reverie. "No, I have to go," I said.

"Shame," the girl said, looking down in disappointment. The thought came back one more time of staying... I mean, I could just–

Oh, not again. Everything inside me froze and that all-familiar chill ran all the way through me. I started shaking, my hands unable to keep still. I clutched the table. I thought this was gone...

The next thing I knew, I had molded. I roared

and my claws went nuts, ripping the kitchen to shreds. I heard the girl scream. I was finally able to control myself and molded back, that fast. Just a few seconds. I calmed myself down in my human form. A bullet hit me right in the chest, the man panicking. He looked mortified.

"Be careful or you're gonna end up hurting someone with that," I told him. Now, I had a choice. Kill them and cover my tracks or run and leave them be. The door was right there. So were they.

"Get out of here," I heard. "Just go." It was a voice I knew too well for anyone's good – Asime. My dead boyfriend Asime.

You see, this can all be explained by the formula. It screwed me up. Sometimes... I can't control my molding. And other times, Asime comes to visit. Until he died, it was my sister, Samantha, who haunted me every day of my life. Now, it's him.

He was behind me, trying to get me to leave, trying to usher me toward the door. I walked forward and looked at the man again. He had the barrel pointed down, obviously getting the message that a bullet couldn't penetrate my advanced skin. He'd have to get closer than he was, and if he got that close... psht. He wouldn't get that close.

I couldn't leave tracks. I couldn't.

I ran at the man and shoved him over, raising a fist in a flash as his gun flew off the sling and crashed to the ground.

"M! Contain yourself!" I looked back at Asime, who was looming over my shoulder. The girl was crying.

Yeah, see, here was the problem: my dead boyfriend talked to me.

"Don't hurt us, please!" she cried.

"Oh, Christ," I said and got off of him, finally

41

beginning to contain myself.

"Thank you," Asime said. "Focus, M." I took a deep breath and folded my hands. "Remember what Kai taught you. Breathe."

My mind went back and forth and back and forth. How much I began to want to kill them. But I also wanted to leave and forget it all. I could take out some of my anger on these dumb, worthless humans. I raised a fist again, the man trying to cover his face.

"M! Cut it out! You don't want to kill these people. They're harmless!" Asime yelled at me.

Kill. Leave. Kill. Leave. Kill. Leave. Kill. Leave.

6
Alex

I strummed the guitar on my lap as softly as I could. The cover of the trees cast shadows on the backyard that made the pond look like a pool of God. I hadn't slept at all last night, so I was pretty exhausted. I was anxious, very anxious, therefore my body felt tense. It sucked.

Lauren sat in the chair, reading one of those cheesy adult romance books. Every few minutes, she'd look up as if to check on Kaley and me. We were literally five feet away on the couch. She was definitely not herself. Normally, she was very uncontrolling, kinda go-with-the-flow, and now she wouldn't let me out of her sight. She wouldn't let me go outside either. The worst thing is that she still wouldn't tell me what was going on.

Kaley lay with her head on my shoulder,

listening to the soft sounds the guitar made. It was pretty chill. Last night, she'd crept into my room, and we just laid there all night together talking about everything. No sex – otherwise, Lauren would have gone ballistic. And although she was pretty even-tempered most of the time, she wasn't shy to go off when she felt she needed to.

Apparently Kaley's dad was out of town for a few weeks, so she was able to come down and hang out here, but she was leaving soon. I didn't want her to leave. In fact, I wished that we could just stay here forever, just the two of us. Out in the middle of nowhere in this nice house with a pond in the backyard. It was a nice fantasy to have – and a simple one, I thought.

"I should probably leave now," she said finally, getting up off my shoulder. The warmth immediately left my whole body. I sat down the guitar on the couch and got up with her.

"You're sure you have to?" I asked again.

"Yes, Alex. My dad will be home in a few hours, and I have to beat him back."

Lauren got up, too.

"Thank you so much, Kaley," Lauren said.

"Any time, Lauren. How much longer do you think you'll stay?"

"Not very long at all. We won't be too far behind you, I'm guessing."

"Great. Well…" We walked toward the front door, and Kaley grabbed her bag from the stairs. She opened the door and turned to me. We hugged. Tightly. I sighed and she reached up to kiss me.

"I love you, Alex," she told me. That wasn't a normal thing for us.

"Love you, too, Kaley," I said, my heart starting to sink a little, anticipating her departure. She took her bag, got out her keys, and walked out the front door. Lauren and I stood by the doorway. It was still cold outside, and Kaley crossed her arms as she went to her car and got in.

Our eyes locked for a few moments before she finally drove off down the rocky path and behind the timber.

"Can you tell me one thing?" I asked Lauren.

"Possibly," she replied.

"Will I see her again?"

Lauren took a long pause, and I knew her answer.

"Possibly," she said again. It was doubtful, then. I thought about grabbing the car and going after her. I wanted to so bad. Just hop in and go, be together with her forever. Boom. But another part of me knew it wasn't that easy. Someone or something was out there looking for Lauren and me – I'd figured out that much. And my arm felt fine, so obviously there was something up with my healing ability. Unless it was magic or something, but… God, I didn't even know anymore.

"What's going on?" I pressed. "You won't let me go to school, Joey went with your sister I never knew about until yesterday, and you haven't been acting like yourself. Seriously, Lauren."

She was calm as she said, "Just trust me. Please, Alex." And gave me a hug. I must say, it did calm me down. And I knew she meant what she was saying. Again, it wasn't the answer I'd hoped for, but I was more confident in just letting this whole thing take its course than I had been before.

"Hopefully Zahra will be here soon to explain everything. Just hang tight," she told me mysteriously.

Who was Zahra?

I plopped onto the couch and took a desperately needed nap.

About three hours later, I woke up. Lauren was still sitting in her usual spot, this time reading a different cheesy adult romance novel. Great. She got up and set the book on the chair.

"I'll be right back, I just have to grab something from upstairs," she told me.

"Okay," I said groggily. I sat up a little and looked out the window. *Holy crap!* I was up faster than I thought possible, and then I just stood there in shock, unable to move. A girl was standing near the pond. She was smiling devilishly with a submachine gun slung around her. Her hair was purple, and she looked about eighteen or so, but something about her scared the crap out of me. I was sure she wasn't on our side.

Finally, I sprinted up the steps to Lauren, nearly knocking the door down when I got there. She was unpacking some odd things, but I didn't have time to take a closer look.

"Lauren," I said.

"What's wrong?" she asked me, very alert.

"There was... backyard..." I couldn't spit it out. My mind was going a hundred miles per hour faster than my tongue, but I said what I could. "A girl... with a..." That was all she needed to hear. Immediately, she pulled out a shining gold and silver dagger with a strange symbol on the handle out from around her waist. I'd never seen it before, let alone known she'd had it on her this whole time.

She sprinted down the stairs, taking at least four at a time, and I followed. I didn't remember her being that fast. She turned to me.

"Stay right next to me," she said. I nodded. We got down the stairs, and she peeked around the corner cautiously.

"What's going on!?" I asked for the billionth time, but my question was cut short when the front door crashed in, bringing much of the wall around it with it, throwing me violently backward.

It took me a while to regain my senses. I was sure I had a concussion, and my vision was slightly blurred. I was in a heap of siding, wood, and other debris. My left ankle hurt really badly, too, like it had bent beyond its limits. I finally looked up, my vision clearing.

A full-size bull was the culprit of the crash, his nostrils flaring as if he was ready for more. I was surprised to see Lauren already up, dagger in hand, ready to face the beast.

"Alex!" she screamed, making sure I'd hear. "We need to get outside! I'm no use in here!" No use in here? What... never mind. I had no time to ponder what Lauren meant this time. I simply had to follow directions.

"Okay, okay, okay, Alex. Get up." I pulled myself up and out of the debris and searched for a path. The front door was covered in a pile of rubble that I was pretty sure I couldn't get over with my ankle. The back door, then. It was a straight shot, and nothing was blocking it. I saw the bull charge at Lauren, but she had been anticipating the move and slid under its stomping feet, coming back up from behind it to swipe at its eyes with her blade.

Adrenaline kicked in. I took off sprinting toward the exit, but something dropped in front of me. It was the girl from the backyard, the one with the purple hair.

"Where are you running?" she said slyly, her tone alluring and mysterious. "The party's here, you know," she taunted. I took a step back, careful not to trip, keeping my eyes glued to the purple-haired girl. She simply took a step toward me and trailed her fingers around my chin.

"What's the matter, baby? Scared?" she asked. Then chuckled.

"Oh, come on, Frost, he's all mine," someone from behind me said. I swung around to see the most beautiful girl I had ever seen in my life. She was really tall and would easily pass as a supermodel in any circumstance.

"That's disgusting, Ryker," Frost said dully.

"I know," said a male voice. I was startled to realize that it was coming from the could-be supermodel. I stole another look at Lauren, who'd made a series of deep gashes all over the bull, but none of them were significant enough to bring it down.

I looked back to the supermodel and saw that it was no longer a she, but a merciless-looking he. He had a buzz cut and a glinting silver earring pierced through one of his ears. He looked slightly younger than me, but very strong, with a sleeveless shirt on.

"I was never much for Americans anyway," he retorted, grinning. The two had sandwiched me between them. Frost turned me back around to face her and let her hand fall down my chest uncomfortably. I felt my hand hit something and lifted it up – a fire poker.

"Macki has quite an interest in you… I think I do, too…" Frost said seductively. I brought the fire poker around as quickly as I could, hoping to connect with the side of Frost's face, awaiting the impact… but it never came. Her hand had stopped it effortlessly. What the…

"Nice try, hot shot," Ryker jibed. Frost hit the fire poker out of my hand with a shot to my wrist. She backed away, and when I thought she was simply going to leave, she sprinted back toward me. Ryker shoved me to the ground harder than I thought anyone could. It wasn't normal. I hit the ground and felt my eyebrow bust. I looked up from the ground just in time to see Frost flip in the air, and when she landed, a Siberian husky was running in her place. Ryker laughed.

I rolled onto my back and she approached me, teeth bared. I braced myself...

But in a whir of a moment, something swept me off of my feet, and I had broken through the glass of the living room. Once I was outside, I swiveled up through the small hole in the trees and up into the clouds. I didn't understand what was happening until I looked to see who – or what – was carrying me.

It was Lauren.

She had brilliant, black wings and they were thrusting up powerfully in gigantic swoops.

"Oh my God. You... you..." I began, flabbergasted.

"I have wings, yes. I'm a Ndege and those are Shufflers. They shape-shift. I don't have much time, so I'm going to drop you off. If you see a girl in all black, run and don't look back. Zahra's team will find you. And – shoot." She dropped sharply, making my stomach go up to my ears, just missing the rabid claws of some enormous eagle.

"Humvee," Lauren said to herself. She dived toward the ground, dropping altitude rapidly. I saw the green of someone's backyard getting closer and closer, suddenly fearing that Lauren would smash right into it.

"Let go when I say," she said decisively. She pulled herself upward with all of her might and glided just above the grass, racing toward a fence.

"Now!" she exclaimed. I hesitated... then let go, tumbling hard in the grass. I got a last glimpse of her as she spiraled up, pulling out her dagger and chasing the eagle into the clouds.

I sat in the lawn, dazed, the yard torn up all around me. My arm started hurting like crazy again, and my head pounded with my heartbeat. I looked up a little and saw two people standing above me. I hadn't even noticed them come up. One was tall and looming, a girl who was at least six feet tall, with a long, golden braid that wrapped around her and golden eyes to match. The other was shorter with dark hair and eyes so blue they were almost white.

"Sorry if you were becoming emotionally attached to the grass, but we have to go. I'm Phoenix, and this is Logan," the tall blonde one said. Logan smiled sweetly at me.

"Are you with Zahra?" I asked before letting my guard down.

"Yeah. Now let's go." She put a hand down for me. I grabbed it and heaved myself up, favoring my hurt arm. My ankle still hurt, too, but at least I could walk. Phoenix grabbed a cell phone out of her pocket and dialed a number, pressing the phone to her ear like she was calling someone important.

"Yeah, we've got him… yep, heading back now… where are you?… All right, bye," she said and dropped the phone back in her pocket. Phoenix started walking toward the front of the house out to the street.

"Are we just going to leave Lauren? You said she's in the sky, right, Phoenix?" Logan asked softly.

"We're going to have to. We need to get Alex out of here. Lauren can deal with it. Come on," she said. I hadn't moved. She came back and (thankfully) grabbed my good wrist, pulling me along with incredible force. I tore away.

"We can't just leave her," I said.

"She'll be fine. I promise, now let's go," she told me. There was just something I didn't like about Phoenix. When Logan smiled at me reassuringly, I decided – reluctantly – to trust them.

"Fine," I said as I followed.

A gray truck was parked halfway in the driveway. Phoenix hopped in the driver's seat, Logan in the passenger. I got in the back.

"How'd you know where to find me?" I asked them as Phoenix revved the engine.

"It was our backup plan in case you had to vacate the house," Logan answered.

"Where's Joey?" I asked. Phoenix took off down the street, really picking up the speed along the residential stretch of road.

"Human in the car," Logan reminded. Phoenix backed off the gas pedal a little bit, but was still cruising. "Zahra and some of the Core are going to pick him up. It shouldn't be a problem because Macki doesn't know where he is."

"Who's Macki?"

"Macki…" Logan started. "Someone will explain later. The bad thing is that she didn't attack with the others at your house."

"That's a *bad* thing?"

"It means we have no idea where she is or what she's doing."

"And that's bad?"

"Very bad."

"Okay. Well, as long as my brother's okay."

"I'm sure he will be."

"He better be."

"Did you book the tickets?" Phoenix asked Logan.

"Yes, I did. We leave from JFK at nine."

"Where are we going?" I asked.

"It's twenty questions here, isn't it? Why don't you cool it, buddy," Phoenix retorted.

"He's totally confused, Phoenix. He's allowed to ask questions," Logan said, helping my cause against Phoenix. There was already friction with this girl.

51

"Just as long as he asks the right ones," Phoenix said threateningly.

"We're off to London," Logan said, answering my question.

London?

I'd never even been to Canada.

7

Macki

I had officially graduated from the middle of Iceland to the middle of Indiana, United States, where I had memories of the grand cornfields and unrelenting mosquitoes. I'd dyed my hair at a truck stop a while back, so finally it was black – cat-like again, like I liked it.

I left the windows down in the Volkswagen bus I'd found at a campsite with a bunch of kids in it and let my newly rejuvenated hair flutter in the cool Midwest air. The only problem with the damn bus was that it went a max speed of, like, seventy-five or so. On the country road, I was really starting to wish I'd found at least a… I realized that I didn't even know what kind of cars they had nowadays.

I figured that I'd barely be beating out Zahra

and whoever was coming with her to the house, but I didn't need long. I knew the house well enough. It was my only hope of finding one of the Keefe brothers. I figured that Karen and Jesse would have been smart enough to abandon it, though, after I turned "rogue." The couple had only let certain people visit them in their home, and I was one of them. Another was Lauren – the leader of the Ndege – and, on occasion, her twin sister Rachel. Apparently they hadn't remembered that I'd been there, though, otherwise they wouldn't have decided to hide their younger son there under the protection of a devoted, yet relatively weak guardian.

Ah, there it was. I saw the small farmhouse sitting in the middle of an array of high-grown fields. I turned onto the dirt road, slowing a bit so that I didn't do a complete doughnut. She'd probably hear me coming anyway, so I raced down the dirt road and parked almost on top of the porch.

I hopped out and started whistling. I walked up toward the country-style porch, looking around, taking my time. There was snow on the ground, and I took some in my hand. It reminded me of the ash in World War Two, but it was much cooler, more pure. I squished it, letting it drop back onto the sidewalk and went up to the house.

I made my way up the creaking porch and kicked the door in with ease, continuing to whistle. Rachel was a fighter, but she was smart and I knew she would've hidden. Zahra's forces were close behind, I was sure, so I had a limited amount of time to find Rachel and the kid. I always enjoyed a good game of hide-and-go-seek.

The house looked like it had been neglected for a while, with cobwebs haunting the corners and dusty floorboards. Lucky for me, it was a ranch, so no second floor to go through. And it was a pretty small house, with French-style furnishings and classic artwork. The window panes were too small for Rachel to fit through and there was no broken glass, so she was still in the house.

I punched a hole in the wall nearest me and tore through the length of it with my hand. I had a suspicion she might be hiding in the walls. But I had no such luck. I stuck my hand in the next wall and did the same. Nothing. Was there an attic? Too obvious. I looked around the living room, trying to decide where to search next. Then I saw something.

I made my way over to the fireplace, smiling. A single piece of soot had floated into the hearth. I peeked up into the chimney. Sure enough, I saw two pairs of feet. Rachel scrambled to get to the top. I knew that if I let her get to the roof, she'd take off and be gone, so I took one giant leap up. I grabbed onto the sides of the chimney like a spider.

Rachel threw Joey onto the roof, pulling herself up. I thought I was too late, but in one last act of desperation, I flung my hand up. It reached her foot, and I pulled down hard. She didn't move much, but it was enough for me to reach my other hand up and get a grip around her ankle. I tugged on her ankle as hard as I could, and I felt her bones pull apart, dislocating it. She screeched.

I climbed up until I could pull down on her shoulders and did so. Ndege had strength beyond humans, but she was no match for a Shuffler, especially one of my standing. We both came crashing down into the hearth, her landing on top of me. I pushed myself up and slammed her into wall of the small space. She kicked back, hitting my shin. My leg gave way enough for her to dive out of the fireplace and pull out a dagger.

She stood facing me, ready for a fight. By the look in her eye, she was ready for a fight to the death. Ndege were very devoted. If someone gave them a task and they accepted, they were to complete it or die trying. I shrugged to myself as I stepped out into the living room that I had torn up earlier.

I wouldn't mold during the fight, to stay classy and give her a fair shot. She had a weapon, whereas I didn't, but it was no matter. I'd dueled many with nothing more than my bare hands and stunning sarcasm. I got into a fight stance and bowed my head. She attacked, attempting to bring the knife down on my head, but I blocked her arm and kicked. She flew back, hitting the wall, splitting the drywall and a watercolor painting into a crater around her. She fell out of it on her hands and knees, but quickly jumped to her feet.

We circled for a few moments. I knew she wanted me to make a move on her now. I decided to accept the challenge and charged, trying to swipe her feet out from underneath her. She jumped over my swinging leg. I swiveled up and tried to get in a few punches, which she blocked. I did a backflip and kicked her upside the head. It took her a moment to come to, but she did and again attacked me with swings of her blade. I caught her arm as it thrust forward toward my face and gave it a forceful twist. I heard bones crack, and she let out a short scream.

I then used my weight (and her arm) to flip her over so she was on her back in front of me. I kicked the dagger out of her hand with my boot. Then I kicked her side pretty hard, so she stayed down. I was sure I cracked some ribs. She gasped for breath at my feet.

"You've been trained well, young Rachel," I complimented sarcastically. She spat at my feet.

"Go to hell, you worthless piece of scum," she

growled. I kicked her hard in the ribs again, and broke a few more.

"Ah," she said in pain. I took off the jacket I was wearing and began ripping it into the long strips.

After I'd finished doing that, I tied them tight around her hands and feet as she tried to wriggle out of my way. I put my boot on her throat, and that was the end of that. I lifted my boot off and she coughed. I shoved another piece of my jacket into her mouth and tied another around the back of her head, securing it in. I picked her up and she groaned as I did, trying to fight through the pain. I sat her in the corner and pulled out that ratty old knife I'd forgotten that I had with me. She closed her eyes. She thought I was going to kill her. Silly girl.

I grabbed her bound wrists and sliced one open. She screamed through her gag and began crying.

"Oh, shut up," I snarled. I soaked my fingers in her blood that was pouring out and began to paint on the wall. I made it as big as I could, even standing on a few pieces of furniture to reach as far as my short arms could.

When I was done, I stood away and looked at it, hardly noticing the shaking, flushed body of Rachel in the corner. It was my symbol. The same one I had tattooed on my arm after I realized I wasn't aging.

At first, it was the sign of the Shufflers, but Zahra soon turned it on me, so it was my symbol now. The Core had come up with a different one just to piss me off. It was beautiful to see again. I was standing there admiring my work when I realized I had to capture the boy before Zahra got there. I walked over to the chimney and dragged myself up.

When I got there, Joey was sitting on the roof, crying his little eyes out, his cheeks red. I approached him carefully, not wanting to startle him too badly.

I reached an arm down to grab him… when he tried to whack me away. So much for that plan.

I grabbed him up anyway and slid back down the chimney with him securely in my arms. No matter how much I wanted to drop the screaming child down the chute, I kept my cool and made it to the bottom. Once I got there, I turned down a hallway to go to the room that had been his for the last few nights.

The blinds were open, letting in checkered light, but the overhead light was off. I left it that way and set the distraught boy on the bed. He continued to try and bat me away.

"Hey, hey," I said, attempting to calm him down. How the hell do I get a kid to settle down!? I'd never had any experience with such a phenomena.

"Kid. Shut up. Come on, please," I pleaded. "Shut up please?" Maybe that would work…

It didn't. He was trying my patience. Like I said, I couldn't hurt him, otherwise I would have. I needed him.

I looked right at him.

"It's okay," I said. "It's all right." He finally stopped crying and was just staring at me with his big, round eyes. I gave him a crooked smile in return.

"Where's Rachel?" he asked.

"She's uh… she went for a walk," I said.

I heard the door break in. They were here.

I quickly swiped up the kid and stood at the end of the room, letting him stand next to me and take his hand in mine. I imagined Karen and Jesse snaking their way through the house with their weapons of choice – hatchets and a slingshot with spiked metal balls respectively. They'd probably already found Rachel in the other room. Knowing Rachel, she probably pleaded to go help her sister, even in her condition, but they wouldn't let her. I was awaiting the arrival of one particular Shuffler.

The door flew off of its hinges. "He's quite mild-tempered. Unusual for a six-year-old. It's almost *unnatural.* Curious, hm, Zahra?" I lied, trying to stir the pot a bit. Zahra stood across from me, her pistol out defensively in front of her. Pilot was with her, his nunchuks hanging at the ready. Zahra flipped on the light.

"It's amazing what some parents will do for their child and what others don't…" I said matter-of-factly. Pilot rushed at me – I had never seen him so mad – and I simply pulled Joey close, sliding out the knife and pressing it to his small throat. In reality, I probably wouldn't have killed him under any circumstance. He was too valuable for that, but they didn't know that. They merely thought I was a bloodthirsty monster… which was by no means a complete lie. Pilot stopped his assault mid-stride. "It's also amazing what I can do with sharp objects. Come on, you got the older one, can't I have a share?" I jeered.

"Screw you, Macki," Pilot said coolly.

"Ouch," I said sarcastically.

"Macki, it's four on one. Give us the kid," Zahra demanded.

"Oh, hm, I don't exactly feel like it. Although, it would be quite entertaining to see your nifty elephant mold, Pilot. It's been a while," I challenged. He took a step forward.

"Eh, eh, eh. Any closer and we'll be packing you both in the same body bag. Reducing the use of plastic one body at a time. Oh, Macki, who knew you'd go green?" I played. "Anywho, unless you have some ingenious plan that'll completely catch me off-guard, Zahra, I must be off."

"What are you trying to do, Macki?" Zahra

asked. She couldn't have seriously thought I was going to answer her fully. I thought for a moment how I wanted to answer.

"You didn't punish me for twenty years in that damned hellhole of a cell, Zahra, no, no, no. You gave me twenty years to think of the perfect plan to finally kick your ass. Yes, it will take a certain formula. And, yes, I will get that formula put together soon enough. I'm sorry, Zahra, but you and the Core are a little overrated for Macki. Bye now," I said, happy with my vague and (hopefully) misleading answer.

With that, I hopped out the window with Joey and took off. By the time Pilot rushed to try to catch me, I was out of sight, on my way to who knew where to surely get myself into even more trouble.

8
Alex

We'd been trekking over the gloomy, rainy English hillside for what seemed like forever. The train only went to the nearest town, which had to be at least twenty miles away. Phoenix and Logan walked pretty quickly, Logan guiding herself with a metal staff. She let me hold it on the way over, and it was pretty damn heavy, even for me. It was amazing how fast she could move it around. I'd figured out that Logan was blind after a very awkward conversation. She just moved around so well, it was hard to tell. Of course, as I was figuring it out myself was when Phoenix had to pipe in.

Logan was super cool and laid back, though, and I was really happy it wasn't just Phoenix. The air was always tense with Phoenix. The plane ride had been a nightmare. Apparently she hated flying, so she decided to get in fights with people instead. Logan and I talked the whole way, and she really helped me calm down and begin to organize all of what was going on. She still didn't give me some answers to my questions like "Who's Macki?" and "Is my brother okay?" and she only half-answered "Shouldn't we give Phoenix a sedative or something?"

Oh, and she really didn't explain what Shufflers were exactly, although I guess it was pretty self-explanatory. But apparently my parents were Shufflers, too. Now it made them seem like science fiction characters rather than uncaring, boring parents. And I felt a little bad.

"Always the damned rain here," Phoenix complained. She'd been complaining the whole time about how she had to walk to the Terrene instead of turn into her animal or whatever and run. Logan had told me that she was a cheetah mold. I couldn't even begin to imagine that.

To my left, I saw a series of jagged cliffs that I hadn't noticed before. I figured the dark ocean would be at the foot of them. When I listened harder, I heard the soft lapping of the waves.

"Ah, finally, home sweet home."

I didn't notice anything different among the rolling hills, and I wondered what the heck she meant. Then I saw it. There was a large fiberglass bulb hidden by the fold of a hill with metal bars crisscrossed over it.

We walked up to it and there was a boy below. He had disheveled, dirty-blond hair with a bluish tinge to it, and looked pretty scrawny. I was surprised. I figured most everyone here would be like Phoenix and me – tall, strong-looking, and my age or older. This kid was probably around thirteen. He had his feet propped up on a control pad and sunglasses over his eyes. He was sleeping.

Phoenix knocked, annoyed.

"Jesus, Falcon. The whole Terrene's in a state of panic, and he's sleeping. Glad he's a reliable one," Phoenix said. She knocked again. "Falcon!" she yelled. Falcon jerked awake, flinging off his sunglasses. Then, he hit a button on the control pad, and the bars drew back. The fiberglass opened, folding into the hill. We jumped in, trailing in plenty of water along with us. Thankfully, my ankle was healed and I felt great, really – except for being exhausted. I'd been running on adrenaline for so long, my body finally wanted to just collapse, curl up into a ball, and die.

"Took you long enough," Falcon huffed.

"Well I guess we're even then. It took *you* long enough to wake up down here," she retorted.

"Okay, fine. You know my immature mind can't take the torture of sitting still and thinking about meaningful things for very long. I could never be Zahra," he explained. Then he looked at me. "And this must be the famous Alex, huh? The Shuffler baby. So what does he do?" he inquired curiously, acting as if I was majorly inferior to him.

"We don't know yet. That's why we brought him here, dingbat," Phoenix said, thumping him on the side of the head (almost) playfully.

"How about you show Alex around, Falcon? Phoenix and I have some things to do," Logan said.

"Things to do?" he said, complete with full air quotes. "Okay, then. Whatever." Phoenix rolled her eyes. The girls exited to a tunnel winding up and out of the vestibule. I watched them until they were out of sight. Falcon shoved me.

"Dude, stop checking out my sister and my honorary sister," Falcon said protectively. Was he serious? I honestly couldn't tell.

"I definitely wasn't," I said truthfully. "Besides,

I already have a girlfriend."

"Of course you do, hot shot, but just to warn you, beware of the girls around here. Last boyfriend Phoenix had ended up half naked on a cow farm in Fiji. And I don't even want to know what happened to Zahra's. If she ever had one. Anyway, I wouldn't try anything."

"This... has been one hell of a day. That almost sounds normal," I said. We both stood there for a moment, silently making our first few judgments about the other. "Are you a Shuffler, too?"

"Heck yeah," he said, surprising me. "One of the best. Let me show you around a bit."

After walking through a maze of dimly lit underground hallways and tunnels (which I thought I'd never figure out), Falcon introduced me to the Quarters hallway. On either side of a wide, rock-embedded path, there were cube-shaped rooms stacked on top of each other, curtains of varying colors covering each. One on the very top in the corner was blocked off with duct tape. I wondered why.

"And that," he pointed out, "is my room." He ran to the wall and jumped, grabbing the edge of the cubby he pointed out as his own and pulled himself up to it, throwing back the curtain. "What are you waiting for?" he asked me. I stared at him blankly, waiting for him to understand.

"Oh, yeah. Sorry, I forgot. Here," he said as he laid down and held out his hand for me. Luckily, it wasn't any higher or I wouldn't have even had a shot at making the jump. I jumped up and grabbed his hand. Despite how much more I must have weighed than he did, he flung me up with minimal effort.

"Wow," was all I could squeak out. The walls of the small cubical were covered in posters and flags. I noticed the South African flag, soccer logos, maps of the world and other varying places, pictures of athletes, and plenty of selfies and pictures with his apparent sister, Phoenix. There was an old, comfy reclining chair in the corner, but no bed. I figured he just preferred a chair. After all, it looked super comfy.

"A lot of Shufflers' rooms here are personalized like this," he explained to me.

"You're South African?"

"Born in Cape Town. I moved to the countryside after my parents died."

"Oh."

"Doesn't bug me. I was only like a year old. Pretty gruesome though."

I noticed a well-drawn pencil drawing of a lynx hung up.

"A lynx?" I asked.

"It's what I mold into."

"I thought… because of your name… that's pretty ironic. Did your parents have a thing for birds or something?"

"Falcon's a nickname. I picked it up when I became a Shuffler. I grew up with a peregrine falcon that I trained. Beats me why that's not what I mold into. You can't choose, you see. No one – except maybe Macki – knows how it works. Considering she's the only one that actually knows the formula in the first place."

"What are my parents like?" I asked. My conversation with Logan on the plane had somehow skipped over the answer to that question.

"You mean Karen and Jesse? I'm not gonna lie, they're pretty beast. Karen's a jaguar and Jess is a gorilla. They're friends with the Ndege and Zahra and Macki. That's tough to do." I'd learned the Ndege were, well, winged people like Lauren. Macki hypothesized that whatever made them like they were was like a descendent of what made Shufflers, so they were like half-Shufflers. The Ndege had also been around a lot longer than Shufflers.

There were also Serpents, which were snake people, basically. They had some attributes of Shufflers, like increased strength, vision, hearing, and speed, but not as much as the Shufflers did. I couldn't believe that Lauren had been hiding that secret for six whole years. It was mind-blowing. And she was their leader – along with Rachel. Leaders. Of, like, an ancient mythological-style race. Taking care of my brother and me. God.

"So you think I might have special powers or something?"

"No idea. Maybe you're just a human dude. Maybe you're a Shuffler and you don't know it yet… maybe you're something else. Wouldn't it be cool if you were, like, a Shuffler that molds into a jagilla or something?"

"That doesn't sound too pleasant," I said, thinking momentarily about what that would entail. I decided to change the subject. "So do I get a room?"

"No, of course you don't. You get to stay in a cozy hole I dug for you earlier. Kidding. Let me show you." Falcon opened the curtain and jumped back out. I liked him. I felt like if I hung out with him, he'd get me into a lot of trouble, but he wasn't such a bad introduction to the crazy world I was entering. Phoenix had scared me a bit with her… sternness. Logan was nice, but she was too involved in everything that was going on to hang around with me all the time.

I jumped down next to Falcon in the hallway, and I heard someone's voice echoing down the hall, coming closer and closer.

He sung, "Holy mother of God, we're all gonna die. But who the hell cares 'cause we freaking won the

World Cup. If I'm gonna die after something like this…" I finally got a good look at him. He was tiny and even younger than Falcon by at least a year or two. He had dark hair and emerald-green, *sparkling* eyes. Yes, they were literally sparkling, no joke. He was swaying as he made his way down the hall, an English flag draped around him, pants tucked into patterned knee-high socks, chunky, cheap, plastic beads strung around his neck and a tall, striped hat on his head to top it off. I realized he was very, very high.

"Glad to see my favorite twelve-year-old drug addict is doing just swell," Falcon greeted him.

"Well this must be the twinky-lipped hamster-hugger himself. *Hola, chico.* I'm Maverick. Mav for short. Or That Little Asshole seems to be a favorite," he said, some of his words slurred. He was speaking with all sorts of accents that I couldn't place, and probably didn't even exist.

"England won the World Cup?" Falcon asked.

"Offfff ccccooouuurrrrsssseee," he slurred.

"Maverick… you do know the World Cup isn't on yet, right?" Falcon logically replied.

Maverick slapped him, just enough to be supremely annoying. "Don't say that. You'll hurt its feelings," he said possessively as he stroked the flag tenderly. Falcon pulled out a grenade from around his waist that I had noticed while we were walking here, curious and slightly alarmed that he had them…

He handed the grenade to Maverick. "Here. Just hold this and you'll feel great… after the explosion burns your face off," he said threateningly. A man (in his early twenties I thought) strode down the hall, obviously frustrated. He had shoulder-length, thin hair, and gray eyes like Falcon's, but they were different in a way. Something looked like it was hiding behind them – sadness maybe? Worry? It was definitely something, and I couldn't shake the thought of what it was exactly as he picked up the grenade out of Maverick's hand and passed it back to Falcon.

"Pilot," Falcon said to the man.

"Have you seen Logan?" he asked Falcon, his voice anxious.

"She and Phoenix are around doing something hypothetically significant, why?"

"I just…" he started. He relaxed. "Never mind. Anyway, Zahra wants Alex in her office," he said, then turned his attention and sad gray eyes to me. "I'm Pilot, by the way." He shook my hand firmly. Maverick tipped over, falling on his side. He didn't bother getting up.

"Pilot?" I asked, making sure I was registering his name correctly.

"Yes," he confirmed, "Pilot, like the people that fly planes."

"Got it."

"Don't worry about it. Falcon, Quinn's pretty upset about Ryker. Will you go talk to him with me?"

"Yes, of course, because I'm a fantastic counselor," the seemingly mischievous boy said. That kid spoke fluent sarcasm.

"And Maverick," Pilot continued, "don't bug anyone. Especially Phoenix or Zahra. This is really not a good time for you to be like this."

"Aye-aye, Captain Pilot!" he responded. He gave a fake salute then started to crack up. "Captain Pilot. That's great."

9
Macki

I spun lazily on a swiveling barstool inside the modern, mountain-like kitchen of my new temporary place. No one was home and it was in the middle of the Rocky Mountains, so I figured we'd crash here for a while. There were walls full of windows where the sun was pouring in, a spectacular view of the snow-filled hillside beyond. It was the middle of the day, and we'd just arrived. I hung out in the basement for a while before I finally addressed the others.

The ceiling was arched high above my head, and I stared up at it, still trying to calm myself down enough to talk to (and not attack) four of my most loyal followers.

Then I looked at them.

They were across the room from me, hands behind their backs, eyes wide, anticipating what I was going to say or do to them. Regardless, it was nice to see them again. It was nice to talk to anybody, let alone people who worshipped the ground I walked on. I knew their strengths and weaknesses. I knew their pasts. I knew their desires and their fears. I'd recruited them all for a reason. I wanted all of them to be stronger than most… but not stronger than me, just in case they decided to get cocky one day.

I could change people as I pleased and turn away people I didn't want (as I was the one that controlled the formula, may I remind you modestly), so I chose carefully. I wanted to be able to get the best of any of them, no matter how fast, smart, or strong they became. I would always have an advantage over them mentally. *I* was the one who saved each and every one of them from their pitiful, wasted lives. *I* was the one who gave them the hope that they had a future as a Shuffler. *I* was the one who gave them a family. Their pasts were fragile, and (if I needed to) I knew exactly how to break them.

That went for Zahra's followers as well as mine.

And then there was the fact that somehow it seemed that the formula I'd taken was slightly different than the one I gave everyone else, which made me naturally stronger and smarter and faster on its own. So maybe it was impossible to beat me. There was only one person who could beat me in a fight, and that was only about half the time.

Bull and Humvee weren't the sharpest tools in the shed. They knew how to smash and destroy and that was about it. Bull was a short, overly muscular Haitian dude with scars up his arms from years of fighting. Humvee looked like a stereotypical surfer dude. He had dirty-blond hair and… poor Humvee. He just… most of the time he had no idea what was going on. To put it nicely. He was the tallest of the bunch at six-foot-three or so and had a pretty gnarly Australian accent.

Frost and Ryker, however, were some of my dearest… assets, I guess I'd call them. They were both ruthless, savage beings who loved to play games (not like I didn't, too, or anything). Quinn was always trying to get Ryker to "take the good path" or whatever, but being the badass Ryk was, he hadn't given in over the last, like, fifty years or so. And Frost… dear Frost. She had been a wreck when I found her. But she was ecstatic that I was finally out. The others were, too, don't get me wrong, but they were all a little… apprehensive, I guess, to go along with it. They knew what I could be like.

When I finally felt ready to deliver my long, thought-out, terribly boring speech on why they were wastes of space because they couldn't defeat one Ndege and bring in one boy when it was four on one, I decided to change course. Plans weren't really my thing.

"You're telling me that one Ndege took on all four of you and won, correct?" I began. They all nodded slowly in response, evidently ashamed. "Well, then," I said as I got up and slid one of my throwing knives into my hand. I targeted Ryker first, hoping to get a rise out of him. I got into his face, but only his lip quivered as I spoke, trying to keep his brave face on.

"We can't continue like that, can we? One Ndege? You need to know what it feels like to kill something without a shred of mercy," I said. Then I skipped away from Ryker, disappointed that I hadn't gotten him to break. I stopped and swiveled on my foot, turning back to face my worried troop.

"I need to be able to rely on you to…"

I said some downright nasty things that should never be repeated. Ever.

"How about we do a quick reflex check, hm?" I sent a knife sailing straight at Frost's face. She caught it at the last millisecond by the blade. Her hand began to seep out blood, her eyes wider and more alert than ever. She dropped it.

"Frost, you pass," I declared, disappointed yet proud at the same time. I pulled out another knife from a sling around me and twirled it oh-so familiarly between my fingers, looking at all of them, playing. I raised my knife... "Humvee," I said plainly as I flung it at him.

At first, I thought he'd caught it cleanly, his hand on the handle. But then I noticed it had pierced his eye. That was exactly what I had been looking for: proof of their weakness. He screamed and fumbled with it, trying to pull it out. He then dropped to his knees and gathered all of his strength to slide it out. I never really got to see what his eye looked like because he covered it with his hand right away. He dropped the knife and sat on his knees, breathing hard.

"Ah, the numbskull," I concluded happily. "It'll grow back together, don't worry about it. Do we get the point?" I was serious when I said it would grow back, because it would. Huzzah for rapid healing! It would still take a while, but hey, what were a few years when you had an unlimited amount?

Ryker, Frost, and Bull nodded obsessively at my inquiry. I knew they genuinely got the message this time.

"I need you to be trained killers, not my prissy goonies. Work on it. Toot-a-loo," I said as I gave a quick, warped wave. I was happy with my performance, and left my little band of soldiers to ponder their actions. My other followers would be joining us eventually; I was just too lazy to go and round them up. So... I guess that was the plan. They were somewhere. I was somewhere. My plans were great, huh?

A few moments later I was back in my cave – the basement. I'd passed Joey on the way down. He was sitting in the living room watching some cartoon on TV and he didn't even notice me due to the focus he had on all of those little idiotic characters dancing across the screen. I figured he'd be watching quite a bit of TV based on our babysitting abilities. Oh well.

Unlike the rest of the luxurious home, the basement looked more or less like an endless pit of doom. Perfect for me. I shut the door and entered, pulling the long string hanging from the single light in the middle of the dark, cement room. It flickered on and my wall covered in journal entries, pictures, drawings, and calculations was illuminated, bringing it to life.

It looked like a train wreck, but it was really organized chaos. I'd kept those papers for a long time – ever since I was human (some were even my father's). That array of glorified wood was the key that everyone was searching for. Among those ripped, torn, and beaten papers there was the Shuffler formula and a few others I had that were… in development. I sat there and looked at them pinned up on the wall, admiring my beauties.

At first, I never thought that I could keep them out "in the open" like that, but I eventually came to the conclusion that if someone was smart enough to find me, gutsy enough to break into my lair, and strong enough to take me out in a fight, they damn well deserved whatever I had to hide. I also knew that my members weren't spies. I made sure of that. Zahra had sent spies out on me before, and let's just say it didn't end well for them or their commander.

I heard a buzz in my pocket and pulled out my

phone, looked at the number and answered it.

"Hello there," I greeted my friend.

"I'm worried," a girl with a thick, dry Russian accent said.

"Nice to talk to you, too," I said sarcastically. We hadn't talked for twenty years. She might as well take her own sweet time.

"Sorry. You know how it is around here." And I did. "How... are you?"

"I'm swell. And you?"

"Decent."

"Okay, continue." Oh, the joy of overrated conventionality and proper greetings.

"Zahra's been threatening me. It's not awful yet, but if something does come up, I don't want you coming near here and there's no one else to—"

I cut her off. "Just watch the kid. I'll take care of the rest, I promise."

She hesitated. "Okay."

"Okay?"

"Okay."

"I have more control than you think."

She was still worried, and I hardly blamed her. I knew how merciless Zahra could be. But I thought I could handle it. And she would trust me, I was sure, no matter how much she wanted to run and never look back at the Terrene. I couldn't screw this one up, that's one thing I couldn't do.

"I have to go," she said hurriedly.

"Bye." She hung up. Someone must have been coming right then or something. I felt a smidge nervous. Just a smidge.

I smiled. Then I laughed. I was taking things too seriously again.

I was excited for the future, ready to watch it pan out like some sort of game.

And ready to watch chaos erupt.

10
Alex

Zahra made me feel like I was in the principal's office. Or on trial. Or something of that nature. She was extremely intimidating. A tall African woman with black hair sculpted close to her scalp and a permanent stressed and pissed look plastered to her face, she made me feel instantly inferior and want to... I don't know, repent my sins or something. She was definitely the one in charge here.

Her eyes were the only things that would tell me she wasn't exactly human. They were kind of like Maverick's – emerald-green – which contrasted a lot with her skin. They didn't sparkle, though, like Mav's did, and it made them look dead in comparison. But they still shined brighter than any human eyes I'd ever seen.

"We were not able to get Joey out with us," she confessed in a thick accent.

I rocketed up, alarmed, throwing my hands on her desk, staring her down with every ounce of anger I could muster. "What!?" I exclaimed.

"Macki beat us there and threatened to kill him. You are lucky I did not go after her anyway, I almost did. Rachel and Lauren are both injured. The Ndege are angry at your parents. And now Macki has a bargaining chip. Sit down," she said plainly. She seemed indifferent, and that angered me. Everything was a giant mess all of a sudden and the supposed "leader" of this whole thing was talking like she was teaching a math class.

I didn't sit down. How could I sit down? Seriously? "Who is this idiot Macki anyway? Huh? Everyone told me you'd explain, so explain."

"You know what Shufflers are, correct?" she asked me.

"It's pretty self-explanatory, isn't it?"

"Macki was the first Shuffler. Her father created the original formula, which she adapted to become the formula that does the transformation. Now, she's a raging psychopath." She opened a drawer to her desk and I noticed that a piece of it over to the side was splintered, a hole going all the way through the wood. I hadn't noticed it before, but it looked like something hard had gone through it. She pulled out a picture of Macki. She was, wait... what?

"Is that a Nazi uniform?" I felt compelled to ask, no matter how much I hated my newfound enemy.

"Macki is one hundred and sixty-five."

"So... so you... live forever? Like... vampires or something?"

"All we know is that we stay the age we turned at for a longer period of time than humans. That is all.

We are a young species. We do not know exactly how it all works yet."

I finally decided to sit down, talking as I sunk into the chair. "Why did this all happen right now? I mean, why didn't this Macki character come after Joey and me sooner?"

"Well, Alexander, we have unknowingly been protecting you since you were born and even before. Macki was imprisoned here at the Terrene for twenty years. She finally broke out and came after you. The peculiar thing is that none of us knew you even existed, but she did. That is… of concern."

"First of all, call me Alex please. Just 'cause you're old-fashioned doesn't mean you can call me by my full name." I was setting this record straight, standing up to this Zahra lady. "And apparently you guys suck at your job, then. Losing Macki and my brother. Especially you." Yeah, I told her.

And she laughed a little bit – a really dry, rigid, weak laugh.

"That is exactly what Macki wants you to think." The room went silent for a moment as I thought that over. Had Macki really done it on purpose? She couldn't know the chain of events that far in advance, could she? I decided to change the subject and think it over later.

"What about my parents? Where are they?"

"They are not going to give up on your brother, so they left to hunt down Macki themselves. Which should be impossible unless she wants to be found, which I do not believe is the case this time."

"Great, let me go with them."

"You are so, so naïve, Alex. You are not ready to fight anyone, let alone Macki or any of her rats. You would be an extremely unnecessary nuisance. If you are a Shuffler, it has not shown itself fully yet, and if it does, you will need to train hard to even come close to any other Shufflers. Do not get a big head."

"I need my brother back," I told her firmly, my thoughts still stuck on him. "He's my responsibility."

"He was never your responsibility. He was your parents, Lauren, and Rachel's. They are much more qualified than you for the job."

"I don't care!" I yelled, letting a little bit of my anger out. "He's my brother. He's my brother, and I want him safe with me so he can live and get old and die on his own goddamn terms."

"We will do our best," was all she could offer me. "If Macki creates the formula, she will build an army and we will have much bigger problems. Now go. Falcon will finish your tour."

I shoved my chair back and got up. I was done with this fool.

I headed toward the door, wanting to rip the head off of whoever this "Macki" idiot was. I put my hand on the doorknob, but in my other I felt something similarly chilling. I pulled my hand up, looking at it. It was a small, shining, black stone. I tried shaking it off, but it stuck to my hand against the laws of gravity.

"What is this?" I asked.

"Impossible."

"What? What *is* this?"

Zahra just stared at me for a moment, deep in thought. All of a sudden, the stone dropped to the floor.

"Go. Start your training immediately with Phoenix, Logan, and Ella," she demanded. I hesitated… then left, shutting the door behind me. Then, I swore I heard something above me, in the rafters, almost like a slither, but I saw nothing. It pushed to the back of my mind and I soon forgot about it all together.

I started down the hall. But wait. I wanted to

know more; I was too curious. I turned back as quietly as I could and pressed my ear to the door. I heard Zahra open a drawer and pull something out.

"Like Asime, the Mono," I heard faintly as she whispered to herself under her breath. "It cannot be." I heard her slam the drawer shut, shove her chair out of her way and stride toward the door. Crap.

I darted down the hallway and turned into the first corridor I came to, being careful to make sure I didn't breathe too hard. I waited there for Zahra to pass and sure enough she stormed past me, not even noticing my presence. Geez, some people and their temperaments around here.

I should leave. I should go back, find Falcon, and be done. I walked out of the corridor and formed a mental map of where I was supposed to go in the maze of hallways that made up the Terrene.

But then I turned back, immediately my legs taking me toward Zahra's office. I was going to trash it... just kidding. I had to look around. I had to.

I put my palm on the cold door and pushed it far enough in so that I could snake into the room. Once I was inside, I raced over to her desk and looked at what was left on it. The picture of Macki still sat out, worn and tearing, but there was something new that caught my interest – an old, roughly-bound journal. I opened to the first page, careful not to tear it. It read "Part One – The Beginning of Forever" in scrawled handwriting and below was a name: Asime Avi. I fanned through the pages, noticing that some parts were in English and others were in something else that I didn't know.

I looked at the desk and noticed a key sitting on a stack of papers. I grabbed it and tried it on the first drawer. I turned the key and it satisfyingly turned. I set the key carefully on the desk and flung the drawer open. It was littered with pictures. They all seemed to be of a pair – one of which I immediately recognized as Macki, only she seemed a little different. Still no remorse.

The other was a dude, an African dude. I assumed it was Asime, the one Zahra said I was like a few moments ago. The two made an odd couple (Macki looked at least ten or fifteen years younger than him), but they both seemed happy in all of the photos. They were taken in all parts of the world, I could tell by all of the backgrounds – the London skyline, rainforest, desert, kissing in front of the Eiffel tower. Hm.

I heard footsteps coming down the hallway. Uh-oh. I panicked, slamming the drawer a little too hard and twisting the key in as fast as I could, not bothering to put it back where it'd been. I thought about taking the journal, but decided against it. Zahra didn't seem like someone I'd want to upset this early in the game.

I scrambled out of the office. When I stepped in the hallway, the footsteps stopped, and I waited for Zahra to confront me.

But it wasn't Zahra. It was a girl. She was standing right next to me, lavender eyes trained on me curiously. She was remarkably pretty with long, really blonde hair and a slender figure. Her purple shirt made her eyes even more pronounced. I was still nervous that she'd be mad at me for poking around Zahra's office like that, but all she did was bring a finger to her lips as if saying, *I didn't see anything,* and continued on down her path.

I stood there, still stunned that I wasn't currently getting yelled at. I watched the mysterious girl until she disappeared down the hall. I took that as my cue to finally leave the office and go find Falcon.

11
Macki

It'd been an exceptionally long time since I'd walked the streets of Geneva. The air was brisk and felt great to inhale. Ahh... I took a deep breath and stretched my arms a little bit. I was sitting on the edge of a fountain, tourists and other blundering idiots mulling around and taking pictures and such. I got up and looked around, my eyes shaded by some sunglasses I'd picked up a while ago. If I wanted to blend in with the humans, covering my eyes was key. Oh yeah and not molding into an enormous cat. That always seemed to help.

I walked down the street, my mind automatically taking me back to 1965 when I'd picked up one of my most valuable recruits. I'd been so many places in the world. Therefore, it was hard to go anyplace without memories rushing back to me.

Luckily, the ones here were good ones. As I thought of my recruit, I altered my course. I took an alley down to a few streets over.

I was glad to see the bar was still standing, the sign in front teetering in the light breeze. I'd found Pilot practically drinking himself to death there. I walked over to it and the bell rang as I entered. Laws were stricter than they were in the '60s, but I could pass for sixteen and be served almost anything I wanted. I called over the bartender and ordered a beer in French.

When I had entered this bar decades ago, Pilot was already here, downing drinks like they were water. I hadn't been expecting to recruit here, but young Pilot had caught my eye when he got into a drunken fight with a significantly larger dude. Even though he was heavily under the influence and had angered the man by insulting his mother or something like that, young Pilot won the brawl. He then continued to drink, the rest of the bar leaving him alone after that, even though he made rude jokes and continued to annoy the shit out of them.

Knowing me, of course, I had to butt in and ask what his issue was. In my experience, it wasn't ordinary for someone like him to drink so much unless they had a damn good reason for it. I tried to talk to him, but his mind was gone for the night. I scolded the bartender for serving him so much, so he stopped. Pilot begged for more. I "gently" told him that he needed to go home and sleep it off. That's when he finally noticed I was there and swiftly blacked out.

I found that he was my responsibility then, even though I hadn't really found out the true reason for his obsessive drinking. I found a hotel room, tucked him in, and wandered the rest of the night. I came back early the next morning, eager to see if his head had cleared yet. I hadn't been expecting to spend so long in

Geneva, but hell. Plans, plans, plans…

He was awake when I got back, rubbing his head, moaning. I'd said good morning, and he was about to question who I was when he ran to the bathroom and threw his guts up. It took him nearly all day to get over the worst symptoms of his hangover, in which we didn't have time to talk in between puking sessions, so I waited another day.

That had been when it got interesting. He was finally able to talk to me, although he still had quite the headache. He wasn't scared of me – like others in his position had been – but more on the curious side. I'd told him that I was an orphan wandering through town, and I was celebrating because I had just gotten a job at a local factory. I wasn't ready to tell him the truth yet. He believed me, and, in turn, told me his story.

Janik Eder was born to a wealthy Austrian family. His father was an air pioneer, taking part in creating one of the world's first airlines. Janik had learned to fly and was an excellent pilot. His father had expected that (once he was finished attending boarding school) he would return to be a pilot for his company.

But Janik had no interest in working for his father. In fact, he despised his father. It sounded like his father was a real jerk. Janik left his family at the age of nineteen and immigrated to Switzerland. He found work as a bartender and made a fair living. Blah blah. Then was the interesting part.

His life was changed when he stumbled upon a gorgeous girl at a bakery in Geneva. Her name was Emily Victoria Adams, and she was a year older than he. They both fell in love with each other and dated for a long-ass time. When Janik was ready to pop the question, he did so in a park and she happily accepted. They prepared for a life together. Janik liked his new father and mother-in-law, and his fiancée's father soon became the surrogate parent that Janik had yearned for in his youth.

One night, Janik was preparing a romantic dinner for himself and Emily in his home. As he eagerly awaited her arrival, he lit candles and warmed the food. It was raining outside, but it would be ignored once they were together. Just as Janik was lighting the last candle, his heart full of joy, the phone rang. He answered it.

He couldn't bear what was said from the other end.

It was one of his fiancée's best friends. They'd been out shopping for a wedding dress earlier. In the rain, a car was unable to stop at a stop sign and slid into a walker, killing Emily on impact. Janik was devastated. She was his life.

(I had felt like a psychotherapist or something, listening to this story.)

So, he reasoned that he had nothing left. He quit his job, became a drunk, and gambled away all that he had. He cut off all ties with his former fiancée's family and friends and committed himself to a life of suffering, solitude, and pity. That was when I found him.

I finally explained to him what I was and what I wanted to do with him (I'd already tested his DNA while he was half-dead, and it would work with the formula). At first, he wasn't so sure of the idea. He thought he just wanted to let himself rot, but I reasoned with him, and he finally accepted. I always got their permission.

I turned him into a Shuffler, and his eyes turned stone gray. I wasn't sure why Shuffler eyes turned the colors they did, but I felt like gray matched him. I encouraged him to change his name and leave his old identity behind him, and he did. He chose Pilot. Although he was special, I took on very few to train beneath me, so I passed him off to Karen.

Silently, I rose my glass and toasted to Pilot. I felt the need to, as I was in his old homeland. I chugged the beer and decided that I'd had a surprisingly nice time reminiscing, but I needed to move on. He was a traitor now. And I had bigger plans for the evening.

I chucked some francs that I'd pick-pocketed off of some oblivious tourists at the bartender and got up to leave. Just as I was walking out, my cell phone rang.

"Hello there," I said.

"Hi, Macki. I have some news," my friend said. Her name was Ella.

"What is it?"

"It's Alex."

"What about him?"

"I was watching him today, and the Onyx stone just came to him.

"Oh, really? This isn't a little illusion of Zahra's is it? To make her think she's more important than she is. A confidence booster for her little... never mind. Continue."

"What do I do?"

"Listen. Work your 'magic' on him and whatnot. He'd be a nice asset, considering Zahra probably has no idea he's the most powerful person in the world." I let that sink in for a second.

"So you think he really is the Mono?"

"I don't think, I know. Now go. Be a teenager again."

"I'm in my seventies."

"That's okay. I'm in my hundreds and I've still got it. Get with it, kid."

"Bye."

I hung up and smiled. Then, for some odd

reason I started laughing. "Leave it to my favorite airhead to make things entertaining," I chuckled to myself. Seriously. Fifty-fifty chance, and I got the short straw once again. Well, damn, guess it'll make it more interesting.

I got up to a run and planted a foot on a bench, flipping myself over effortlessly just for fun. I had stuff to do, but I could take my time. I walked off down the street, happy as a clam and smiling like an idiot.

Oh, the love of the game.

12
Alex

When I found Falcon, he was sitting on the edge of his room with his feet dangling off the edge. Maverick was sitting next to him, his lofty hat now removed to reveal a head of messy black hair. He looked like he'd calmed down a bit, but I couldn't be sure.

"What'd Zahra have to say?" Falcon yelled down. Maverick's sparkling eyes were trained on me, somewhere between curious and hostile. It was weird. Falcon hopped down, landing a few feet in front of me.

"She, uh, she said I need to start training," I said hesitantly, like that might mean something to him.

"With who?"

"Phoenix, Logan, and Ella," I said, recalling the names.

"Phoenix, okay. Logan, okay. But Ella... what the hell is Zahra thinking?"

"Who's Ella?" He leaned in a little closer, whispering.

"She's Macki's right hand. Says she's not anymore, but everyone thinks she still is. Gives me the creeps." He leaned back. "Phoenix's worst enemy, too." I thought about that for a moment. Maverick hopped over to another room (his, I assumed) and disappeared inside.

"What's Maverick's problem?" I whispered. I didn't know if he could hear me or not because of the Shufflers' advanced senses or whatever, but I really didn't care. Falcon looked back at Maverick's room.

"He basically thinks you're bringing on the apocalypse. I can't believe that got through to him – it's only the most talked about topic here nowadays. Sheesh."

"And this is my fault?" I asked, astounded that someone would actually think that.

"We've pointed our fingers enough at Zahra. Some blame Lauren and Rachel for not... well... just killing you guys. Some blame Karen and Jesse for 'doing it.' And then people like Maverick blame your existence and naïveté that personally I know you couldn't help. Here, let's go find Phoenix." He started walking toward a tunnel, and I followed. It felt like every moment, I had more and more questions to ask.

"So what do Shufflers do when they're not here? I mean, you guys don't just hang out here all the time, do you?"

"We take shifts holding down the fort. Before this, I was here with a few others, and we guarded the Terrene. Sometimes I'd be able to get out and explore the world, but not too often. As a thirteen-year-old superhuman slash animal thing, it doesn't give me many options. It can get pretty boring sometimes, actually. Phoenix gets to do more of the traveling. She occasionally works for the police or whatever in different countries and does some diplomatic crap. I don't know exactly. A lot of us join militaries, though, and fight.

"As long as you don't draw too much attention to yourself in the human world, nobody cares what you do. Zahra's the only stickler. If you're too noticeable, she'll pull the plug on whatever you're doing." He paused. "So what's new in the human world?"

We turned down to the vestibule with the big dome leading outside. It was actually clear out.

"Uh… I don't know…" What kind of question was that?

"You play videogames, right?"

"Yeah."

He got visibly excited. "A bunch of the guys here play Call of Duty religiously. You should play with us sometime."

"Are you good?"

"Good… yeah. Dude, we tried playing in leagues once and we got to the number one spot, so Zahra made us only play locally."

"I'm not *that* good."

"Then we'll have our fun slaughtering you repeatedly."

"Great."

Phoenix and Logan stood against the wall behind the control pad of the vestibule.

"Hey, dipshit, what's hangin'?" Phoenix asked Falcon.

"Shuffler baby needs some training."

I really didn't like them calling me that, but what was I going to do about it?

"Ah, I see. I'll take him first, Logan. This should

be fun. Could you grab me a staff, Falc?"

"All the way over with the weapons? No. Get your own."

"Then you get to man the hatch while Logan gets me one."

Falcon huffed.

"Not my fault," Phoenix sneered as Falcon turned to leave. "Let's go, Alex," she commanded me, opening the dome. She hopped out, but I took the ladder. It was too big of a jump for me.

The wind picked up and whipped my hair around a bit. I heard the waves hitting the cliffs not too far away. The grass was wet, but it was some of the greenest I'd ever seen.

Phoenix walked toward the cliffs, and I followed. Finally, she turned around to face me.

"I want to see what you're made of first," she said, changing into serious mode. "Come on." She put her fists up and started bouncing back and forth like she was in a boxing ring. I shadowed her, putting my hands up into fists. I felt confident. I could hold myself in a fight with any of these guys. She relaxed and put her hands to her sides, but I kept tense.

"Hand-to-hand combat," she began simply enough. "Concept one: Shufflers move fast. Really fast." She flung a hand up exceptionally quick. "Concept two: offense is the best defense. Be aggressive. Concept three: opponents will mold whenever they feel like it. Be prepared. Now, attack me."

She stood there passively in front of me. I gathered my strength and threw a punch. She dodged it with ease. It was embarrassing, but all she said was, "Harder."

I punched again, really focusing on myself and my mechanics. This time, I noticed I was a hair quicker. She still dodged it with relatively little effort.

And again she commanded, "Harder."

This next time I really tried as hard as I possibly could. I was determined that I could hit her. I felt her arm lead my fist off-course. It was an improvement, at least. She wasn't fast enough to dodge, so she had to block. It was a small success, but I cherished it.

"Good," she reinforced. I think that was the first positive thing I'd heard her say. A wooden staff flew out of the dome, landing a few feet away from us. She picked it up, focused. "That's more like it. Now, this next task is simple. I want you to stop this staff from hitting you, okay?"

I nodded. It did seem simple.

But it quickly proved not to be. With a flick of her wrist, she thrust the staff forward, moving it every few milliseconds, hitting me every. Single. Time. After about a half-a-minute, she stopped.

"Again," she said. This time was the same. She still hit me every time, as I struggled to stop her. She only hit me lightly, though, never enough to cause me much pain.

"Again," she repeated. I tried again, expecting the same results. It didn't seem like I'd ever get the hang of it. I was losing hope fast. But one time I managed to block it, returning a little bit of confidence to my withering ego.

"Again," Phoenix said.

13
Alex

The next day... I was exhausted. Completely and utterly exhausted, a feeling I'd never really felt before. Phoenix and I'd practiced hand-to-hand all night. I got about an hour of sleep before she woke me up again to go eat, then go to my next lesson. My muscles were so sore, I could barely move without wincing. Even the muscles in my fingers hurt.

I walked into the cafeteria with Phoenix and there were only a few people in it. Giant stone pillars that looked like they were supporting the weight of the room loomed; the walls made of packed dirt. Circular tables with benches were scattered around the fairly large room.

At one end, there was a buffet of food with the youngest Shuffler I'd seen yet behind the bar, filling it. Her hair had strands of different, vibrant colors, and she was super small, like a child. I figured she couldn't be more than eleven.

Immediately, I knew where Falcon was. He was cracking himself up by looking at me standing there like the hunchback. I half-walked, half-dragged myself over to the table. There was a group sitting there, each with a plate stacked so high, it looked like they were all just going to fall over. Apparently no one really slept around here either. It was like four-thirty in the morning or something.

"Ha-ha," I said, glaring at the group. Pilot was there, sitting with his arm around Logan. And then there was a man I didn't recognize sitting with his leg up. He was really tall with short, white-blond hair cut very specifically, and pink eyes. It was wild, all of these peoples' eyes. Mine were just plain old brown. I wondered if they'd change eventually or not.

"Oh, this is Quinn," Falcon said after he'd finished his laughing fit. "Quinn, this is Shuffler baby – I mean Alex." Quinn looked upset. He gave me a slight nod and I returned it. Phoenix abandoned me to go get her own food.

Falcon put both of his hands out, as if the buffet was a shrine. I walked over to it and looked over the choices. Of course, my eyes went straight to the desserts. They had, like, every sweet you could imagine. Candy of all sorts, cake, cookies, cupcakes, soda in the old-fashioned bottles.

"No one can agree on what to get, so we get everything," Phoenix leaned over and told me. Made sense, considering all of the different countries and such that everyone was from. I grabbed a plate and filled it with an array of things (fruits, veggies, meat, the usual… and, of course, a section of gummy bears) then headed back to the table.

"I would get a giant falcon all over my back," I

heard Falcon say as he walked up.

"Like you're patient enough for that," Phoenix chimed in, coming up behind me and plopping down at the table next to me. Great.

"I wasn't asking," Falcon snapped back. Apparently Phoenix had been listening to the whole conversation. "What about you, Pilot? What tattoo would you get?"

"Me? I would get…" He thought. "A giant pink doughnut on my face." Everyone at the table laughed. Seeing Pilot with a giant doughnut tattoo was really a funny (and very strange) thing to picture. The laughter died down and we sat in an awkward silence. I continued to eat like a pig, my mind barely able to comprehend anything but *food!*

"Anyone hear anything about Macki?" Quinn asked the group. The air immediately got serious. No one wanted to answer.

"Not me," Pilot chimed in finally. He rubbed his chin, tense and anxious. "It's a terrible feeling, isn't it? Not knowing?"

I tried not to think about Joey. But it was hard. I was left completely in the dark when it came to him, and it was horrifying.

"What do you guys think about Ella? Traitor or innocent?" Phoenix asked. Phoenix was obviously on the "traitor" side, so I wondered why she even asked.

"Traitor," Quinn said in disgust.

"Damn traitor," Falcon spat.

Pilot and Logan seemed hesitant to answer as the rest of us stared them down in curiosity. I really wondered who this Ella chick was. I'd heard enough about her already.

"I think she's easily influenced – not one or the other," Pilot said, trying to remove himself from the conversation with a neutral position.

"Hm," was all Phoenix said. Surprising once again.

"Do you think by staying here… we've made a death wish?" Logan asked. It was weird of her to ask something that made everyone seem so… vulnerable, I guess. I mean, they were these cool superhuman/animal things with crazy strength and shape-shifting abilities and for that to all be in the hands of one Shuffler… it was crazy.

"I think Alex is a blessing and a curse," Falcon piped in. I looked at him, astonished that he was actually talking about me like that, like I wasn't even there. I was obviously out of place in the conversation.

"How so?" Quinn asked.

"He's aggravated Macki, but he could be worth something, meaning he could be as strong as Macki. So he could help us fix a problem or he could have created a problem that won't get fixed and we'll all die. It could go either way in my book. Quite a load, buddy, sorry," Falcon said to me. "But whatever Macki has in store will definitely be lethal. She already has a mini-army, too, with all of her 'followers' leaving the Terrene."

"Wait, if all of her followers left, then how could this Ella person be on her side?" The words came out of my mouth before I even thought about what I was saying.

"As a spy, of course," Quinn answered.

I heard the doors to the cafeteria slam open and instinctively turned to look and see who it was. It was Maverick and what looked like a very small, Asian friend of his.

"Wazzup!?" Maverick yelled over to us, waving a hand.

"Oh, great. Serious conversation equals over," Falcon said. Maverick was wearing a vest over a washed-out green T-shirt, a beret, long plaid socks and falling apart Converse. Interesting.

"God, I wish this mess wasn't happening," Maverick said as he approached us. He went over to Falcon and ruffled his hair. Falcon batted him away, annoyed. "I was really looking forward to winning *les* Games this year."

"Oh, bull," Phoenix said. "Like you'd have a chance, you little moron."

"Ooh, of course I would. Ella said she'd take me." He started laughing, even slapping his knee. I was kinda lost.

"Yeah. Of course. That would totally work considering that I've won the last ten," she said sarcastically, agitated at Maverick's mere presence. Phoenix, Falcon, and Maverick continued bickering, but I kind of zoned out. Maverick's little friend stood by his side, silent.

The door squeaked open again. This time, everyone stopped completely in their tracks when they saw who walked in (even Maverick). They tried not to make eye contact, keeping their heads down, expressions of disgust spread on their faces.

I took a stab in the dark and guessed this was Ella.

Ella. The one I saw outside Zahra's office, the one who pretended like she hadn't seen anything. Finally I could put a name to that mysterious face.

I tried to see the hostility and mercilessness that everyone was talking about, but she looked vulnerable… harmless.

She just stood near the door, looking at me, not wanting to come any closer to the group. Amidst the silence, I found that was my cue to get up, so I did. I tripped getting over the bench and the clatter rang throughout the whole room.

I walked over toward her, and before I could

get there, she was already out the door. I went into the hall and saw her standing there, waiting for me anxiously, her big lavender eyes staring me down once again. We stood there for a moment, taking each other in for the second time.

She half-smiled. "Let's go," she said.

Phoenix had told me earlier that Ella would be teaching me weaponry and Logan would be teaching me how to mold, so I was prepared for guns. Lots and lots of guns. I mean, shape-shifting was crazy, but how crazy could *weapons* get with these people?

Again, we set off down a maze of hallways. Eventually, she turned into an opening and we were in an even darker room. Rows and rows of weapons lined the walls. Some I hadn't seen before, but most I had. There were big, locked (from the inside) doors marked with white, sprayed-on numbers leading into other rooms.

Curiously, there were also shoes placed outside the occupied ones. Every few moments, I heard a loud thump radiate from inside them. I figured they were practice rooms. We walked to the room labeled "3." She opened the thick metal door.

"Take off your shoes," she said, her voice much quieter than I expected it to be. I expected her to be loud with a commanding, leader-like presence – more like Phoenix or Zahra. Not meek like she seemed. Although, I considered, Logan wasn't exactly a Phoenix or Zahra either. Thank God.

"Why?" I asked, simply curious.

"It's tradition. Zahra probably came up with it."

"This is the fun part, right? Weaponry?" I asked as I slipped off my tennis shoes, anxious to know if it'd be any less tedious than Phoenix's workout.

"I guess," was the only response I received.

Inside, it was a circular room, the walls covered in cobblestone, the floor and ceiling made of compact dirt. In a strip in the middle of the walls was a ring of candles covered by fiberglass so they wouldn't be hit. The cool dirt felt strange on my feet.

"Dirt?" I inquired.

"Some Shufflers drench it in water and make it into a mud pit to make it more interesting," she explained. "Here. This is yours now." She pulled the little stone that had strangely attached itself to my hand in Zahra's office out of her pocket. "The Onyx stone." She handed it to me.

"This is a *weapon?*" I asked, perplexed, trying to figure out what sort of trick she was playing on me. Was she trying to make me look stupid? The stone wasn't much bigger than a pebble, and it was black and smooth, the sheen on it almost making it sparkle. She handed it to me.

"Not just a weapon," she said, "but every weapon. If you really are the Mono, it should work."

"What is a Mono exactly?"

"For one, they're supposedly stronger and faster than normal Shufflers. But the real catch is that they're supposed to be able to mold into any living thing they want. It's a human mutation, I guess. It's natural. All of us... we're synthetic."

"Are there any others like me?"

"There's only been one. Zahra's brother, Asime."

"And I'm assuming..."

"He's long dead."

"Great." I paused, switching subjects in my head. "So how does this work?"

"I'll show you. Close your eyes, Alex," she half-whispered to me. Her voice was so calm, so serene. Especially for around here and what she was going through. I closed my eyes like she asked, and I heard footsteps softly padding around me.

"Are you familiar with any weapons?" she asked.

"Just an old slingshot my dad gave me when I was little." I had been pretty damn good with it, too.

"Of course he did," she said, and I sensed she was smiling. "Now, I want you to remember that slingshot. Everything about it. The way it felt... the way it looked..." Her voice got slower and even softer yet, a slight whisper. "What it felt like to pull it back and release whatever you had in the sling... the force of it flying away from you..."

I felt her stop directly in front of me, her lips gently whispering near my chin. I couldn't help but think it *was* pretty sexy.

"Feel it in your hand, Alex... feel the shape of it... now open your eyes," she finished. I opened my eyes at her command, and for a subtle moment, I was lost in a puddle of soft purple. She looked back at me, no expression on her face. She looked angelic. Then, she gestured toward my hand and stepped away. "It worked," was all she said.

I was about to ask what she meant, but then I looked at my hand. In it was a shining black slingshot – the same material the stone had been made of, although it looked like carved black wood, the sling hanging limply as if it were rubber. I held it up, analyzing what I'd created. I felt really tired, like all of the energy had been suddenly drained from me.

"That really takes the energy out of me," I said, hoping to find out if that was normal or not.

"Wait until you're the one molding." She paused and looked around. "That's enough for today."

"So I can really make it any weapon I want?"

"Anything you can visualize. We'll go over

different types of weapons later."

Our conversation paused as I thought of what to say next. I felt pretty comfortable with Ella already.

"I've been hearing things around the Terrene about me being this great Mono or whatever. What is everyone expecting me to do?" She sighed.

"They... they think if you grow strong enough, you'll be able to defeat Macki. The Terrene's about split in half – half think you'll be able to do it and half don't."

"Which side are you on?" I inquired.

"Me? Oh... I'm kind of on my own side. I think it could go either way depending on... well, depending on whatever Macki wants it to turn out as." She walked over to the side of the room and picked something up from the ground – a journal. It was the journal I'd seen in Zahra's office. I knew it was Asime's. She handed it to me.

"I assume this is what you were looking at in Zahra's office, huh?"

"Yeah," I said, looking at the worn notebook.

"Keep it safe. It's the original copy. Zahra would be beyond furious if anything happened to it. It's all she has left of him," she warned. I knew that wasn't the whole truth. She had all of those pictures of him, but I wasn't about to bring those up just to be jerk. I worried about Ella's warning. I had a way with losing things and spilling fluids. I made a mental note to keep it away from water.

"I meant to ask if he had more. I saw this one said 'part one,'" I told her.

"No. He never got the chance," she said bleakly. For some bizarre reason, I felt as if Ella was the first Shuffler I could trust. I mean, I trusted Logan, but she was so close to Phoenix, it'd be hard to keep more serious things away from her.

"With my brother gone, I'm going to fight for him. Zahra knows that, right?" I asked, promptly regretting it.

"Yes," she again answered transparently.

"Do you have anyone like Joey to me? That means the world? I couldn't live with myself if I let my own brother get hurt."

"I do actually, and I really need to get going." She turned to the door, unlocking it. I put my hand on her shoulder.

"Who is it?" I asked, being no more than curious; I felt that it wasn't my place to go digging around in a Shuffler's life if she didn't want to reveal anything. She opened the door, and I didn't think she was going to answer me, but she did, very quietly.

"The person who saved my life."

14
Macki

The alarms of the Swiss research facility were really beginning to really annoy me. There were keypads at every thick, locked door (though I was able to break into them all), locked coolers of mysterious chemicals, cameras everywhere, computers installed in every wall and counter. The corpses of the scientists lay strewn around me, as well as the security team. They'd been an easy takeout. I twirled one of my slick, black, perfectly weighted throwing knives around my finger.

I spotted what I needed on one of the walls. I walked toward it, stepping over each body. I tried to be careful, but I did trip over one of their heads, revealing the long, bloody rake across his face and neck. One of his eyeballs was nowhere to be seen. Oops. I tried to remember seeing his face before he died, but it was all a blur.

Once I got to the safe, I noticed that it too had a keypad next to it. I'd always absolutely sucked at opening stuff like that. It had been a struggle to even get into the lab in the first place, so I decided to use my brute force to remove it instead. I pried the safe out of the wall with a bit of concerted effort. My cell phone rang. I set the safe down on a counter and answered it. Then, I picked the safe back up and continued out.

"*Hola,*" I answered.

"Zahra wants me to train Alex," Ella said.

"Train him how?"

"With the Onyx stone."

"Okay... uh... congratulations!" I said sarcastically, wondering what her point was. I was sure they'd have military and police here in a very short amount of time, so I quickened my pace as I walked. Frost and Ryker had gone to fetch weapons for the group. Bull was waiting outside in case I needed any assistance (basically he had nothing better to do). Humvee was taking care of Joey somewhere in the city. Probably shouldn't have trusted him with a kid, but what else was I going to do?

"What do I do?"

"What do you mean?"

"I mean... if I train him with the stone correctly... won't he get too strong?"

"Yeah. That's the point."

"You don't care? It's like... I feel like I'm betraying you."

"Oh, sweetheart, trust me. Just do what Zahra asks or you'll be scalped."

"All right. I will then. You're sure—"

"Of course I'm sure."

"Okay. Bye," she said meekly.

"Bye." I shoved the phone back in my pocket. The facility was underground and made up of a plethora of illuminated tunnels. One of the lights was hanging down. I batted it out of my way. Sirens in the distance grew louder and louder. A *lot* of sirens.

I ran through the rubble of some broken doors. Finally, I got to the staircase leading all the way up. I tripped a little bit on one of the white tile steps and almost ate it. What was up with my coordination? Hmph.

I heard a platoon of footsteps on the platform above me. I had a few seconds before they saw me…

"Freeze!" the leader of their group yelled in French. They were in all black with helmets and masks and the whole bit. All of their guns were trained on me. Some were semi-automatics and others shotguns. I stopped where I was, just for fun. Role play, you know.

"Get on the ground!" he yelled again, moving toward me at a painfully slow pace.

"Fine," I said under my breath. I set the safe down carefully and laid on the landing. It was cool and hard. I should have expected it'd be like that considering… well… it was the floor. Anyway.

I really wanted to have fun with these people. After all, I had nothing better to do, really. They converged on me as soon as I hit the ground. One yanked me up, securing handcuffs on me way too tightly for anyone's good. Once I was upright, two of them pretty much dragged my small body up the stairs. I pressed a little bit of weight on my toes, but basically they were carrying me.

The setting sun made me turn in adjustment, and I let out a slight "ah" as they opened the door. In front of me was a barrage of cop cars, trucks, news crews, and vans. The news crews stood on the other side of the caution tape, fighting to get a view of… well… me, I guess. I would have waved, but my hands were still pinned behind my back.

We were just outside the city with no other buildings around, just the fenced-off research facility I'd just raided. Nobody would have noticed him, but for me, it was easy to spot Bull on the horizon, watching over the scene. He looked angry. But he always looked angry. Such a downer. I smiled at him and started laughing. It was all a joke and nobody even knew it yet. It was always weird how serious people were. It was like they were stopping World War Three or something.

We were almost to one of the cop cars. In one fluid motion, I snapped the handcuffs in half, brought my elbow around to hit one of the men in the face, and swung a fist around at the other. I saw the news people stop, staring in awe. After taking a moment to recover from the shock, everyone who had a gun had it glued on me.

They yelled in me in French to "get down." The two people I'd hit were down for the count. I guess I'd hit them a lot harder than I thought. I put my hands halfway up in the air, excited.

I felt a slight pinch as a bullet hit me. It was a pretty bad shot, honestly, right in the meaty part of the shoulder. Everything stopped once again. I probably just could have made a semi-dramatic exit right then and there and no one would have tried to stop me.

Then the bullets rained down on me. The whole fleet of people were shooting and yelling at me. My skin felt like it was crawling, little pinches hitting it pretty much everywhere. I kept my hands in front of my eyes so I wouldn't be blinded. Through the cover of my hands, I found the nearest barrel to me. I reached out and grabbed it from the dude, just ripped it out of his hands. He looked at me, terrified. I half-ass kicked him and he hit the ground. A little too hard. His head snapped back.

Not again.

By this time, the bullets were winding down, people stopping to reload or just plain giving up. Some were running. Some just standing in shock. So vulnerable. So, so delicate. Just creatures yearning for their lives to be sucked away...

No. No, Macki. Don't do it.

I raised the gun. It was a semi-automatic and a new type of gun that I didn't know. I wasn't much for guns.

I got someone in my sight, staring at her right down the top of the barrel. It was a female police officer. Green eyes, blonde hair pulled up into a tight bun. She had a shotgun and continued to shoot at me, panic and adrenaline taking over. Time seemed to slow down.

One shot. One shot was all it would take.

I squeezed the trigger until it was halfway down. The lady let her gun drop, desperation and fear now moving into her expression.

I dropped the gun and it clattered to the ground. The woman ran off.

I couldn't... I couldn't do it. She reminded me of someone. Someone very important.

Ella.

Time seemed to pick back up, bringing me back to the realization that I was getting peppered with news crews taping it all. A few choppers were circling as well.

"Enough!" I yelled in French. Everyone stopped. I pulled two of my throwing knives out of their sling, twirling them in my fingers. I motioned to one of the news crews on the other side of the fence. "Bring me a camera." Hesitantly, one of the camera men walked around to the opening in the fence. He walked toward me and gulped.

"Is this live?" I asked. He nodded. Perfect.

"Zahra," I began with a smile. "When you see

this, I'd just like you to know that... well..." I made a face like I was going to cry. "Well... screw you." I chuckled. "Keep playing my game, little pawn." With that, I punched out the camera's lens. Bull came up and stood beside me, arms crossed. Zahra *hated* being known to humans. And I knew that. I also knew she hated being a piece in my game and that she'd never admit she was.

I liked it that way.

15
Alex

I stood against the wall of a hallway, awaiting the big double doors at the end of it to open. This morning, Falcon had come into my room (made quite the entrance) and told me that I wouldn't have any training for a while today because there was an "emergency Core meeting." Apparently there was an . elite group of Shufflers here that were part of the Core. Ella, Phoenix, and Logan were part of it, so they couldn't train while they were in session. It sounded like Zahra was the head of it (of course). Pilot and Quinn were in there, too, I thought. They had two people missing from it today, though.

My parents.

Nobody had heard from them since I came. Was I worried? A little bit. Was I still angry? Yep. Why didn't they think I could handle the truth? I mean… it was going to come and bite them in the butt sometime, wasn't it?

I heard yelling coming from beyond the doors.

"What are we supposed to do then!? Just wait for Macki to kill thousands of people and take over the world! Are you guys insane!?" That was definitely Phoenix.

"Phoenix! Enough!" rumbled out the doors. I'd never heard Zahra raise her voice like that. I'm sure it was enough to shut Phoenix up. A few moments later, a quiet boom radiated from inside the Core room. The doors at the end of the hall slammed open. Phoenix came storming out, her golden eyes tearing through me like fire. She slammed the doors behind her, closing off the Core room. Leaving me alone in the hallway with her.

"What are you lookin' at? Huh?" she grilled me. Uh-oh.

"Nothing, nothing…" I said and looked away sheepishly.

"You're gonna get us all killed, Mono. I know it," she spat back at me. Her hands were made into fists.

"I… I…" No words came to me.

"You what? You're weak, you're dumb, and you're naïve. That's not a good combination for a supposed 'savior' of our kind." She pushed me, my shoulders hitting the wall. She was so strong. Even a little push like that could have snapped a bone or two in any normal human. "You know what? Maybe I should teach you a lesson right now. Teach you how to fight when your life is on the line, huh?"

I looked right back at her. I was seriously scared for my life. She grabbed my collar, pulling it upward. My heart was about to thump right out of my chest.

"You little piece of–"

A hand laid on her shoulder.

"Nix. It's not his fault. Calm down now," I heard a soft but stern voice say. Phoenix looked at Logan, the fury still in her eyes. After a few tense moments, she relaxed, jerking her hands off of my collar in a huff. With a scowl on her face, she stormed down the hallway, away from Logan and me.

Geez.

"I'm so sorry, Alex. Phoenix can get a little... riled up sometimes," Logan told me.

Really? Wouldn't have guessed.

"I thought... I thought she was going to kill me," I sputtered out, adrenaline and fear still running through my body.

Logan gave a slight smile.

"I would have fought her myself if she didn't lay off of you. Come on, Alex. We have some training to do." Logan took off down the hall at a steady pace, her staff on her back, unneeded in the halls she knew so well.

No one else came out of the Core room, so I assumed they were still attempting to figure things out. All of us had seen the video of Macki in Geneva. The rumors spread like wildfire around here. Rumors that she was going to build a Shuffler army and attack. Rumors that she was going to kill us one by one. Rumors that she was going to enslave the human race.

It sounded pretty serious, but it was so hard for me to imagine her doing any of those things. I mean... they all sounded so... so evil.

After some light talk to get my mind off of things, we arrived at the greenhouse. The first thing I noticed was the door. It was intricately engraved with silver vines that almost gave the illusion of movement. I didn't think they were. I didn't *think* so...

Once she pushed open the door, my breath got away from me for a moment, not gonna lie. There was a stream flowing through the giant room with plants in planters and growing from the ground all around with patches of perfectly green, low-cut grass separating them. I could see sections of trees and heard birds tweeting rhythmically. There were some dirt paths twisting their way around the enclosure. The ceiling was glass, sunlight spilling in.

It was amazing, really. Spectacular even. Something I wasn't expecting. Something I *would* expect to be right out of a movie. We walked down a squishy dirt path that ran parallel the crystal-clear stream, a waterfall at the end of it. Finally, she turned off the path and sat down on a perfectly groomed hill.

She sat there, eyes closed, silent. I stood there like an idiot, unsure of what I should do. The waterfall roared softly in the background, the sound of the stream flowing right next to us calming.

"Sit down, Alex," she told me as she patted the ground next to her. "Just... take a moment."

Take a moment? I could go for that right now. I sat down next to her and closed my eyes.

It was a nice feeling. I'd been going, going, going since I'd been here. I'd slept (a little bit), sure. But sleep was always uneasy and I woke up every few minutes, unable to turn my brain off.

I sat there thinking of absolutely nothing. It was great.

Finally, I felt a soft tap on my shoulder.

"All right. Let's get to work," she said. I opened my eyes and hers were already open, her gaze lost forever in the distance. I forgot she was blind sometimes. "What's the first animal that comes to mind? Anything at all." I thought for a moment, but I already knew my answer.

"A tiger," I answered. I'd loved tigers ever since I was little. I remembered Lauren taking me to the zoo and I would watch them for hours, my face smashed against the glass. It'd even gone so far that I'd wanted to become a tiger trainer for a circus. When I was around ten, I packed a bag and wrote a note to Lauren detailing why I had decided to run away with the circus, although I hadn't executed. Obviously, that was when I was little, but I still thought they were pretty awesome creatures.

"Interesting," was all she said.

"What?"

"Never mind. This is going to be a lot like the Onyx stone. Close your eyes and think of a tiger. How it moves, what it looks like, what it would be like to actually *be* a tiger."

I concentrated, really trying to dig deep. I waited for something to happen, but nothing came, so I asked about it.

"Is something supposed to happen?" I asked, worried I wasn't going to be able to do it or something.

"No, now get up," she instructed. I got up, and Logan instinctively grabbed her staff, leading herself up with it. "This is the part that will take some practice. It's easier to mold when you have a large amount of kinetic energy, although once you have enough practice, you'll be able to do it from a standing position. Run as fast as you can, and when you feel ready, flip. Concentrate on what you want to change into."

"Okay," I told her, but it was mostly for my own sake. I got up and half-jogged over to the flatter grass. I readied myself to run, a long belt of grass in front of me, and just beyond that, a group of planting beds (which I was sure I wouldn't run into). I was trying to really get myself into it, but I had some reservations.

"Are you sure this will work?" I asked, hoping

her answer would reassure me.

"Nope," she replied simply.

"Perfect. Okay, here it goes." I took off running full speed, which I guessed was a bit faster than any (human) sprinter would be. I was waiting for something (I had no idea what) to tell me when I should flip, but nothing did, so I had to pull the trigger myself. I leaped, my feet leaving the ground and tucked my head downward, pulling my legs over...

When my face hit the soft grass, tumbling forward in a way that was out of my control. I felt myself hit some of the planting beds, snapping the wood, soil seeping under my clothes. My head was spinning, but once I regained my senses, I saw that I'd left a huge dirt hole in the previously perfect grass and crashed into a group of raised planting beds, the plants tumbling out of their binds around me. What did Logan think was going to happen?

She came over and stood above me. "Not even a Mono can do it the first time I guess," she revealed.

"Thanks a lot," I spat out. I was just slightly pissed off.

"Now you get to clean that up," she informed me, smiling. Oh, come on.

I heard laughing coming from near the door as I struggled to orient myself and get up. My head was spinning. I looked over to see who it was. Maverick and Falcon stood by the doors cracking up like they'd just seen the funniest thing in the world. I glared at them.

"Way to go, Alex!" Falcon yelled over in my direction.

"Really, an audience?" I said only so Logan could hear. She tried to keep back a smile, but it didn't work.

"It was pretty funny," she said.

Ha-ha. Yes, of course it was hilarious.

Finally, I smiled a little bit.
I mean, after all, I did have some serious hops.

16
Macki

The old floorboards creaked under the weight of my boots. The place looked awful; they'd really let it go. The windows were boarded up, walls covered in peeling, white paint. Like a snake's skin almost. Some of the rafters above were dangling by a thread of wood, ready to snap and break off at any moment.

The pews of the church were about the only thing that made it resemble a church. That and the giant hanging Jesus covered in a layer of dust at the front. I walked down the row, hands neatly behind my back, inspecting the place. Frost, Ryker, and Humvee were behind me. I'd left Bull on babysitting duty this time. Luckily, the kid had survived a day with Humvee, so I figured Bull would at least keep him alive.

I walked up to the front of the church and

wiped a line of dust off of the table. I wiped it off on my pants and continued around the table, keeping my ears and eyes open.

I heard a loud crash behind me and a body hit the floor. I turned around, hoping to find who I was looking for.

"Sorry," Humvee said as he got up from the ground, an eye patch still covering his split eye. His clumsiness was going to get him killed one of these days.

"Shut up, idiot," I commanded him. He pulled himself up by the edge of a pew and kept his mouth shut.

I turned back around, looking to the front of the church once again.

Wait.

A slither. I swiveled around to face my left. I swore I saw something.

Then again. I saw it again. A small shadow at the side of the church. I ran over toward it. It disappeared down an old, caving in hallway.

"Hey!" I yelled at the shadow. The others came clambering behind me. I slowed to a fast walk, determined to stop whoever was there. I got to the end of the hallway and looked around. There was only a boarded-up door leading out.

But wait. There was more. There was a door behind me left cracked open.

I burst into it, the door flying off of its hinges from the force. It was an old office, barely any light coming in. There was a giant hole in the wall… a hole big enough for who I was looking for. I slinked past the dark, damp, termite-infested desk and poked my head in the hole. It was in between the drywall, just boards holding everything somewhat together.

I focused, looking all the way to one side. It was

117

dark, but my enhanced vision picked up a shape among the shadows – a young boy curled in the corner. I could only see his outline, but that was all I needed.

I walked into the space between the drywall, heading deeper into the pitch-black belly of the church.

"Macki…" I heard Frost say weakly. I kept going anyway.

Finally, the boy was within reaching distance. I grabbed his arm, and he squirmed out of my grasp. I wiped my hand on my pants. He was slimy just like a snake. I grabbed him again, this time getting my arm around his neck. He gasped for breath as I dragged him out of the hole.

I threw him onto the floor of the office.

"Ryker, lighter," I told him. He reached into one of his pockets and tossed me a small lighter. I turned it on, illuminating the boy's terrified face. His face was blue. Not like blue when you lose your breath for a few moments, but literally blue. Well, I guess it had a greenish tinge to it if I wanted to get specific. His hair was blue as well, cut roughly on his head. The rest of his body was covered in blue-green skin and… well… scales. He looked repulsive, his whole body inflating when he breathed.

"Where are the others?" I demanded, the lighter right in front of his long, narrow, snake-like eye slit thingies. He looked at me, unable to comprehend what I was saying for a moment. I assumed out of shock. I grabbed his collar forcefully, taking a wad of his shirt in my hand.

"Where?" I asked again, trying to get through to him.

"Uh… uh…" he said, his tongue flicking out as he talked. "They're gone."

"Gone? Gone where?"

"They split up about seventeen years ago. Uh…

uh… who are you looking for?"

"Mavril."

"Mavril? Uh… uh… sheesh. Well–"

"Do you know who I am, kid?"

"I don't… I don't believe so." I noticed he didn't hiss with "s" sounds. Strange. Most Serpents did and it pissed me off. I shook him around a little bit.

"What happened here? I thought this was the Serpents' base."

"I know, Macki," I heard Humvee pipe in. I looked back at him. He didn't say anything after that, so I raised my eyebrows.

"Speak."

"Oh, yeah. Okay. Right after they locked you up, the Ndege and Serpents had a big fight. The Serpents were driven out of their base. Then they all split up."

"Why didn't you bring this up before we came? Huh?" I looked at my group. They all kinda shrugged passively. Nitwits. "What happened to Mavril?"

"He was captured by the Ndege," the boy said. I sighed.

"Really, guys, you couldn't have piped in when I said we were going to find Mavril?" I looked back at them again.

"Sorry. We thought you knew," Frost said sheepishly.

"We'll talk about it later," I said. I'm sure that made them all panic. I turned back to the boy. "What are you doing around here then? Just out of curiosity."

"They left me behind."

"Why?"

"Because," the boy said.

"Because why?" I insisted. He tapped on my hand and I realized he was telling me to let go. So I did and he got up. I flicked the flame closed.

He stood there and shook out a little bit. Then, to my astonishment…

He opened his wings.

"Jesus Christ. People are really getting inventive when it comes to the whole baby thing, huh?"

"Half Serpent, half Ndege. My god," Frost said. We all stared at him. He blushed and pulled his wings back in self-consciously.

"They couldn't stand to be around me. So they dropped me off here and left." A silence for a moment as we all let everything sink in. "You're *the* Macki, aren't you?" he asked, staring at me with his freaky eyes.

"I am."

"You escaped?"

"I did."

"I've heard stories," he said. "Are they true?"

"What kind of stories?"

"They talked about you being mad."

"Mad? Me. No. Wrong person," I said half-genuinely and half-pretending-to-be-serious.

"Then you'll help me?" Uh… how do I put this…

"I can't do that. Sorry." With that, I got up and headed toward the door, the gang following behind me. "But thanks for the information that I should have—" I glared at the group. "—already had." I walked out of the room and back into the hallway.

Wait. I could use him. I stopped in my tracks.

I pushed past my goonies and stormed into the room. He was still standing there, a tear on his cheek. Oh, please.

"Come," I told him, motioning with my finger. "Let's go. We don't have all day." He hurried toward me.

"We can't seriously take a kid, can we?" Frost

whispered to me.

"Frost, piss off. I know what I'm doing," I replied. She went quiet. We walked out of the hallway and back to the church. "Everyone out," I commanded. The group walked out, leaving me alone for a moment.

I stood in the middle of the church. This had been the Serpents' base – their home – for so many years. I'd visited on many occasions, always being welcomed warmly. I could use that kid. I could. They'd all see.

I flicked open the lighter.

Then I lit the floorboards on fire. The old wood caught on fire easily.

Somewhat ceremoniously, I walked out, leaving the place to burn until there was nothing left.

17
Alex

I threw my arm up in front of my face as fast as I could. Phoenix's staff hit it, bouncing back toward her harmlessly. She brought the other end toward my right thigh. I thrust my other hand down as fast as I could... but I was too late. Before I could dwell on my miss, she brought the other side back at me again, which I blocked once again. I was left-handed, so my right hand wasn't nearly as strong. It became habit that I missed on the right side. She was just too quick. I'd definitely improved though, blocking about 50% of the strikes.

"Better?" I asked Phoenix, hoping her answer would be a positive one.

"Getting there. Again."

She came at me again. Block. Miss. Block. Miss. She swiped at my feet unexpectedly and I face-planted into the moist grass.

"Get up," she commanded. She'd been in an awful mood ever since the Core meeting yesterday. My shoulder and some of my ribs were already bruised from training today with her. I hoped a few bruises would be the worst of it. I got up slowly. It took all of my strength to push myself up.

I got up and immediately she was coming at me again. Only this time it was harder than normal.

Miss. Miss. Miss. Block. Miss. It hurt.

Finally, I stepped away, out of her reach.

"What are you doing?" she questioned angrily.

"It hurts."

"Boo-hoo." She took a step forward and came at me again. Only *harder* this time.

I tried to stop it more out of desperation than practice. Finally, she hit my rib and the staff split, the wood breaking completely apart. I fell back. Something was definitely broken. I lay on the ground, holding my aching rib, and rolled around like a baby. I felt like I was going to throw up as I gasped for more air.

Phoenix turned around and strode toward the cliff. She stood above the water, arms crossed. I gathered my strength, determined to get up one more time. I took my time, getting up extremely slowly, one little bit of energy being released at a time. Finally, I was all the way up.

"I'm tired of you pouting," I told her. She turned to me, shocked at what I'd just said. Wait, maybe I hadn't thought this all through...

"*What* did you say?" she said.

"You heard me," I said. She stormed back toward me. "I'm not some little toy you can just take all of your anger out on."

She grabbed my collar. "Didn't you hear me yesterday?"

"You didn't mean it. You were angry," I said, hoping she would find that the case.

"Of course I meant it, you little worm." She pushed me backward and I fell once again.

"I'm sick and tired of you treating me like a pile of crap, Phoenix. You need to learn to control yourself. Logan's not always going to be there."

She crossed her arms and looked down at me. And... wait... was that a tear? She turned away. I really was tired of it. She wouldn't stop pouting and it about drove me nuts.

"I'm sorry I have such a temper," she said, her words quivering. She put her face in her hands, and I saw tears drop down. I mustered all of my strength one more time and got up. I dragged myself over to her. She pushed me away, not wanting me to see her cry.

"Piss off," she commanded me, wiping away the tears shamefully.

"No," I told her. She turned to me, shocked.

"No? *No?*" she challenged me.

"What's wrong?" I asked, trying to be sympathetic. Maybe if she could just get it all out she'd be fine.

"I'm serious. Get out of here right now, Alex."

"I'm not going anywhere," I retorted. "What's wrong?" I asked again.

"Nothing. I'm fine."

"Really?" She looked straight at me, making a decision internally.

"I'm just... I just..." she stuttered, more tears crawling down her face. "My hunch is that Macki's going to build an army. And you know what happens when she builds an army? People die. And I'm scared."

I took a moment to think. "You're not scared for you though, are you?"

She wiped more tears away on her sleeve. I

wouldn't have thought she ever cried. Hm.

"How do you know that?" she inquired.

"Because I feel the same way."

"About who?"

"Joey. It's my job to protect him."

"Alex…" she began, "Falcon's all I have left."
She started crying a little bit harder with that. "I just
want to get out there and hunt that freak down so that
Falcon's safe. So that everyone's safe."

"She could be anywhere."

"I know, but… God, you're right, I don't even
know where to start." She put her head in her hands,
the tears starting to disappear.

"Maybe Karen and Jesse will find her. You
never know."

"Maybe. But that doesn't take away from the
fact that I really want to punch Zahra in the face."

"Yeah. I think we'd all be appreciative of that
actually."

She laughed a little bit. "I'm sorry, Alex. I really
am. I didn't mean to… you know… hurt you," she
said.

I let that sink in. Maybe this conversation really
was getting somewhere with her. I was still angry,
but… I didn't know. We both had the same goal, so we
couldn't exactly be enemies. We needed to all work
together if we were going to take out Macki.

And we were going to take out Macki.

18
Macki

From my perch, I looked out over the vastness of the Alps. It was a wonderful sight, it really was. Except, I was cold. That sucked. The soft snow came up to just above my boots, so it seeped into my socks and chilled my feet. I was right above the entrance to one of the Ndege "sanctuaries," as they called them. Basically, they had bases all over the world where any Ndege could go any time. Safe houses.

The boy stood below me on the ground. The path he was on was carved out of the mountainside and was, of course, covered in a layer of snow. I looked to my left and saw Frost sitting there, waiting to pounce like me.

"Go," I told the part-snake, part-bird, part-human boy. He walked up to the huge, locked door and knocked. A little peephole opened and an eye peeked through, looking at the boy.

"What do you want, Serpent?" the guard said from inside.

"I need somewhere to stay. Please," he said, just how we had practiced.

"We don't allow Serpents here anymore. I'm sorry."

He was about to shut the peephole.

"Wait! I'm not all Serpent," he said. "Look." He opened his wings just how he'd showed me. They were magnificent. A deep purple color, almost.

"Oh my," the guard said. The kid recoiled his wings. "Well..." He didn't know what to say. "Well... any Ndege is welcome here. Come on in." I heard a series of locks click before the big door was heaved open by three guards.

This was my ticket. I jumped down. Frost did the same. It was probably a forty-foot drop, but it didn't bother me in the slightest. I pushed past the boy and walked through the door. The guards didn't even realize Frost and I were standing there until they looked over. Their eyes got wide in fear. I chuckled a little bit.

"We'll just be a minute, boys," I told the guards. They got into fighting positions, unsure of what to do now that we were inside. I took out a throwing knife from around me and felt the blade. "You can either direct us to Mavril or we can have ourselves a little fight, hm?" I spun the blade between my fingers. Frost had an Uzi strapped to her back, and she got it out, pointing it at the guards.

"We'll never let you through," one guard said confidently, stepping forward. I kicked him hard in the stomach. He doubled over, coughing. Not such a tough guy, huh?

"Mackinley. Stop it. Don't hurt the Ndege," I heard over my shoulder. Asime.

"Go away," I told him as I pushed the guy back hard against the wall and put my knife to his throat. "It's okay to kill birds every once in a while."

"M!" he yelled at me.

"Tell me," I told the guards, "or this guy won't make it."

"Fine, fine," they both said, trying to get me to calm down. "He's in the basement." This place had a basement? Funny.

"Let him go, M," Asime commanded. I moved away from the guy, taking my blade with me.

"Just having a little bit of fun," I said. I looked over to see Asime's face, but he was gone. Hm.

"What's going on here?" a voice boomed. I saw the boy still standing there, scared. The door to the place was still wide open. I turned around so the voice could see my face and laughed.

"Good morning to you, too, Lauren," I told the auburn-haired girl. She looked like a Greek goddess or something. Her clothes were white and gold, hair pulled up into a braid. She stood about five-seven or five-eight I guessed. A good few inches taller than Frost and me. Lauren stopped in her tracks when she saw my face and immediately grabbed a dagger out from around her waist.

"Macki. What are you doing here?" she asked.

"Just passing through," I told her, smiling. "We found this kid and he needed a place to crash, so we figured we'd come drop him off like responsible people."

"Bull," she said.

"Put that blasted thing away, Lauren, there's no need." She looked at her dagger. Hesitantly, she put it back in its sheath. "I didn't know you were here."

"Just passing through," she said, mimicking me.

"How about we go to the Pillar and have a nice

chat? I think your guards have had enough of me already."

She sighed. "Take the kid to Mark, please," she told the guards so nicely that I wanted to slap her. They nodded a little too much. Slowly, they pushed the door closed. "Come," she told Frost and me.

We walked down the carved mountain hallway until we arrived at the Pillar. I'd never been before, actually, only heard about it from Karen and Jesse. Lauren pushed open the glass door and we walked inside.

Giant pillars (duh) supported the place, each intricately and differently designed. On the other side of the room were enormous windows looking out over the rising sun above the Alps. In the room were long tables carved out of stone. Rocks jutted out from the other walls.

"Where's Rachel?" I asked.

"In Thailand, I believe," she said, clearly not wanting to say more. She found a table and sat down. Frost and I sat down across from her. It was creepily quiet in the giant room, my foot tapping on the marble flooring the only thing I could hear.

"So, how have you been, Lauren? It's been a while," I said. She glared at me.

"Is this really an appropriate time for small talk, Macki?" she asked me. I shrugged. Okay, if she wanted to get to the point, we could get to the point.

"Where's Mavril?" I asked.

"Mavril? That's who you want?"

"He's a good friend."

She half-laughed. "Mavril is past his prime. The Serpents already have a new leader. A leader that's brought peace between the Ndege and the Serpents."

"Who?" Frost asked curiously.

"Erin."

"Erin? Good lord," I said. Erin had almost ripped the Serpents apart. She was some weird naturist cult leader snake thing. "Well there's no way I'll be getting along with her. I need Mavril."

"I can't do that," she said.

"Sure, you can. You're the Ndege leader. You can do anything you want."

"No, I can't, Macki. My position has to be earned, not abused. If I let Mavril go, it could start a war between us again."

The Ndege leader was chosen by the other Ndege. If everyone agreed that someone was a good and noble person, they'd promote him or her to leader. There was really no pattern or system. That's why Lauren and Rachel were both chosen. I figured Lauren would lose her position when she chose babysitting for two Shufflers over her own clan. Mark really should have taken it. If I were him, I would have fought for it, but I guess that wasn't "their way." Anywho.

"Would you rather start a war with me or the Serpents?" I asked seriously.

Lauren looked down uncomfortably. "Macki, please. I'm begging you. Don't make me do this."

"I won't make you, no. It's totally up to you, Lauren."

"What? Then no."

"Okay. You get Mavril and I get to kill Joey. Fair?" I raised an eyebrow, knowing she was about to explode. Ndege didn't do it very often, they're usually very sweet and blah blah blah, but she was pissed. I could do that to people. She rocketed up, waving a finger at me.

"Macki, you lay a finger on the boy and I swear I'll rip your head clean off," she threatened.

"Settle down there, feisty. I won't kill him if you give me Mavril. That's all. It's up to you. I really don't care either way."

She looked at me right in my eyes. I could see the internal gears shifting, turning, trying to weigh the consequences.

"Fine. You can have him. But keep my Ndege out of whatever you're doing, you hear me? We don't want any part of it. And give me the boy. I'm sure by now you've figured out he's useless to you."

"Joey? But he's my little buddy."

"Mavril for Joey. And a truce between us."

"Deal. But…" I began, "you can't tell the Shufflers you have him."

She looked at me, thinking things through carefully once again. "No," she finally said. I raised my eyebrows. "That's torture to Alex."

"Exactly," I said.

She glared at me then rubbed her chin, thinking. Then, she looked out over the mountains. "Fine," she muttered, grinding her teeth.

"Huh? Did you say 'fine'?" Frost asked, just to make her face us.

"Fine," she said louder as she faced me. "Keep us out of it," she commanded.

I put my hand out for her to shake as I smiled smugly. She glared at me. I didn't know whether she'd accept it or not.

After a long pause, she did. It's part of Ndege culture to keep promises and be nice and stuff to everyone, but she struggled with me.

"I'll go get him," she said. "In the meantime, I want you out of my sanctuary."

"All right. We'll meet you out front." We got up and walked toward the glass doors.

She opened it for me and I went through, not bothering to say thank you. Frost followed my lead. Lauren turned to go a different way.

"Hey, Lauren," I said.

"Yes?" she asked, turning around. Still pissed, I was sure.

"Take good care of the kids," I told her. Her face relaxed a little bit as she nodded and headed back on her way.

At least someone knew how to make a deal.

19
Macki

Oh, sweet Jesus, my feet hurt. I swung my knife up to whack a giant leaf out of my way. If I knew how far into the rainforest we were going to come, I would have at least rented a… I don't know what. I guess the only option was by foot, but I really wished it wasn't. Nothing I could do about it now that we were almost to the Serpents' lair.

With Mavril in front of me and my little mini-gang behind me, we made our way through the dense rainforest of dah-dah-dah-dah… Cambodia! Yes, Cambodia. Apparently where Erin, the current Serpent leader, had made her base.

She was a bitch. Seriously. Back in the day, she was just starting to break off from the rest of the Serpents and she was all like "Earth this" and "natural that." She wanted the Serpents to "reach into our past and find peace with the world."

Bleck. I really didn't understand how she'd become their leader.

"How much farther?" Humvee asked. We were all just waiting for someone to speak up.

Mavril barely looked back over his shoulder. "Not too far," he said quietly. Humvee huffed. A leaf swung back and hit me in the face.

"Hey, Mavril, how about *clearing* a path, huh?" I shoved him so he'd get the message. He stumbled forward a little bit but kept going, keeping his head down. He slinked forward at a steady pace, his feet seemingly gliding across the forest floor. All around me, I saw green. Lots and lots of green. So much green in fact, that I didn't think I could get back out if I wanted. That made me uncomfortable.

I mean, I'm Macki, I don't need to ask for directions. Like ever.

Another giant leaf hit me in the face.

"Hey, snakeballs." I sped up for a moment and grabbed his shoulder, making him turn to me. His eyes were green and staring at me almost like a cat's. Creepy shit that was. "What's with you? Huh?"

"How did you feel when you got out?" he asked me.

"Like I had to get the hell out of the Terrene. That's how." Our whole group stopped, Mavril and I staring at each other for an uncomfortable amount of time. I was looking straight up. He was literally a foot taller than me. His skin was dark green and his scales had a goldish tinge to them. They looked like they were sparkling when we were in the sun. His forked tongue flicked out a little.

"After that," he said. Oh.

"Well after that… after that…" I looked back at

my little group. Ryker, Frost, Humvee, and Bull all looked at me, apparently anxious to know the answer. "I uh… I…" I knew exactly what I'd felt like. I'd felt so… perplexed by the whole situation. I had this annoying little feeling that kept slapping me in the face telling me… telling me that it wasn't worth it. That everything wasn't worth it. That *I* wasn't worth it. That I was washed-up old Macki who nobody gave a goddamn *crap* about, so why continue when… when the end could come so swiftly?

Everyone was staring at me. I had to say something.

I looked all the way up at Mavril and folded my arms, glaring at him, telling him silently that *I* was the leader here. *I* was the stronger one.

"I felt like a god," I said with no waver in my voice. He looked down, ashamed. I shoved him again. "Now stop this bullshit and get a move on." He turned back around. Then looked back at me, whispering.

"You know exactly what I mean," he hissed, then continued on, this time slashing things out of his way with the machete I'd so graciously given him. What did he expect me to do? Say I felt like a low-life, worthless piece of shit when I got out? No way. I was stronger than that.

After a few more minutes of silence as we trudged through the forest, we finally came to a giant hole in the ground. When I say giant, I mean giant. It looked like a crater, some extra water from the forest streaming down its edges. At the bottom was a dark blue pool.

"Down there," he said. We all peeked over the edge.

"How do we…" Ryker began. We were all wondering. Mavril rubbed his hands together, the stickiness of them creating an awful gooey substance.

He knelt down and put both of his hands on the wall of the hole.

Then, he swung his legs over. The thought flashed through my mind that maybe he really was going to kill himself.

But his hands stuck like glue to the side.

"New question," Ryker said. "How do *we*—" He pointed at the group of us. "—get down."

"Easssy," Mavril said. "You can jump."

"Yeah, right," Frost chimed in.

"The pool is deep at the bottom like a well. I've ssseen many Shufflersss do it before," Mavril said. I peeked over the edge again. I'd jumped off of planes, bridges, buildings, buses, and all of the above, but nothing from this high. My mind started doing the calculations...

"You're just trying to get us all killed, aren't you?" Frost asked Mavril, glaring at him accusingly.

"Shh," I said as I got lost in my thoughts. Frost looked at me kinda funny but kept quiet. "Possible," I said, not really realizing I'd said it.

"What?" Ryker asked, confused by my statement.

"It's possible," I said. I backed up. Immediately, Frost and Ryker held my shoulders, preventing me from running forward.

"Are you sure?" Ryker asked.

"You have three seconds to get your hands off of me." Their hands both flew off of me with remarkable speed. They were still hesitant though, I could tell. It was possible... and expected... but there was still some room for error. If the pool wasn't as deep as I calculated for instance. Or if my rusty insta-math calculations were off.

I ran at maximum speed and leaped off the edge of the hole... I was going forward for just a moment… until my stomach dropped to my feet. I was falling down – all the way down – with nothing to stop me. A bit of panic swept over me and I scolded myself for not accounting for the fact that it would be *absolutely terrifying.*

For just a few more seconds, I was suspended there, floating through the air, hoping that my math was right…

Then I hit the water.

20
Alex

    I approached Zahra's office. The door was slightly ajar. I heard Zahra talking to someone, and I stopped by the threshold to listen, trying to be as quiet as I could so that she didn't hear me.

    "Tell me where she is," Zahra commanded to the other in her office.

    "Zahra, please, you remember when I came to you. I wanted refuge from her, not an interrogation every other day. I know she's insane and I've had absolutely no contact with her. I understand it all now. I… I was naïve," the voice said. It was a scared, quivering female voice.

    It was Ella.

    I needed to know what exactly was going on, so I took the chance of being caught and peeked through the crack of the door. Ella was sitting opposite of Zahra's chair, silent tears streaming down her face. She looked lost... remorseful, maybe. Something like that. Zahra's pistol was to the side of her head.

"I am not joking, Ella. I know that you know where she is. I know you have been spying. I have no reason to keep you alive if you do not help me, Ella. Do you want to end up like her?" Zahra croaked. Ella shook her head. "Then tell me. Be a leader for once. I will not punish you if you tell me now."

I had to act. If I didn't, Zahra might kill Ella. As little as I knew about Ella, I felt the need to protect her. She wasn't accepted by the others, but I didn't care. She was too... special. But was I really going to try and oppose the leader of the group...

Yes.

I burst through the door, deciding I would. I hit the pistol out of Zahra's hand as fast as I could and kicked her hard against the wall. The force of the kick was more than I expected, sending her crashing through the wall. I took Ella's hand and pulled her up.

"What do you think you're doing, kid!?" Zahra screamed at me, furious, as she recovered. I'd never heard her cuss or use slang before. Bad sign.

"You're turning into her, Zahra. You're turning into Macki," I said philosophically as I exited back out to the hallway, pulling Ella with me. I slammed the door shut to bring my point home.

"What *are* you doing?" Ella asked, still shocked.

"I'm doing what's right," I told her simply.

"Alex, you don't understand."

"She has no right to be threatening your life like that."

"But... she does, Alex. No, it's true I don't know where she is. But I don't deserve to be here. I had my chance a long time ago and blew it."

"Don't say that. You're strong. You got past it. It's been a while since 'a long time ago,' if you haven't noticed. Things change, people change. You do deserve to be here just as much as everyone else. Especially Zahra."

"Thanks," she said weakly.

"It seems like a lot of people here live in the past, anyway. Otherwise, there wouldn't be this mess. They need to get over it."

She looked at the floor, nodding, reassuring herself.

"Yeah… yeah, I guess you're right." She still had a pained look on her face. I wish I could've just wiped it away, made her smile.

I just wanted her to smile.

--

I stood at the ready, one foot planted firmly behind me, ready to burst forward.

"I believe in you, Alex. Let's aim for five seconds this time, okay?" Logan said. I nodded, determined to meet her expectation.

I raced forward (as I had done so many times before with no result), picking up speed, and (at what I thought was the right moment) flipped…

Into a tiger, my claws tearing up the grass as I landed. I roared just because I could. I felt fantastic. My body buzzed with a mix of excitement and adrenaline. I looked back at my torso to make sure I was really what I was envisioning. I saw the bold black and orange stripes, and it confirmed my thoughts. I shook my head out and pranced over to Logan.

I could see her excitement, too. I nudged my head to her hand. She realized what I was trying to do and scratched it.

"I think you made it past five seconds," she told me, smiling. I decided to show off a little bit, so I pranced around a bit more then rolled in the grass. Finally, I realized I was starting to lose energy really fast, so I ran again, leaped, and landed back as my human self in front of Logan.

"Well, what do you think?" she asked me. Psht. Seriously?

"It's just... just..." I began, struggling to find the right words.

"Indescribable, huh?"

"Completely. I didn't think I could do it. Scratch that, I didn't think it was *possible*."

"You know, it took me fourteen months of intense training to go for five seconds, and I was considered exceptional. So you doing *that* in just a few weeks? It's truly incredible, Alex."

"Wow. Over a year? For a few seconds?"

"I was pretty excited."

"What was it like to become a Shuffler?" I sat on the grass, tired but beaming.

"It begins like a simple cold. Runny nose – a cough, maybe. It progresses until you're bedridden. Then, the worst part happens. You start hallucinating. All kinds of crazy stuff. You see people that you've lost, you feel like you live in your memories – which, most of our human memories aren't exactly... pleasant. People around you think you're going crazy. They realize that you're probably going to die, so they just try to forget about you. Eventually, you black out and go into a coma-like state.

"Then, you wake up and Macki or one of the Core members picks you up and brings you here or wherever they're traveling to next. Macki's job was to find the people whose bodies could process the formula. It would kill over ninety-nine percent of people right off the bat, before the switch even began to take place if we weren't careful. But then over ninety percent of those people weren't strong enough to make it all the way through. There's no way Macki could predict those people. I've seen them try to change thousands of people, and, as you can see, not many of them made it."

The doors to the greenhouse opened and I was both delighted and surprised to see Ella striding in. I found it strange because no one ever interrupted any of my lessons.

"How's he doing?" Ella asked Logan.

"Fantastic. But I need more time," she replied.

"Zahra's calling a Core meeting."

"Okay."

The three of us made our way over to the doors. I exited first, but not before I heard Logan leave Ella with a warning.

"You know I can hear your heartbeat when you're around him," Logan whispered. "Be very careful, Ella."

21
Macki

The thought finally occurred to me that jumping off the edge of that cliff might not have been the best idea.

I dragged myself the rest of the way up onto the edge of the pool. The water was so cold, it stung and I knew my leg had to be broken. Like I said, it was possible. And I did it... so... one point for Macki. I looked to the side and saw Mavril scurrying down the wall. When I'd landed, I was sure I'd blacked out, so why not add a concussion to the list of things I deserved for being such an *idiot?*

Mavril finally made it down and put his hand down for me to grab. I grabbed it... then pulled him down into the water. He fell all the way in then surfaced, a shocked look on his face.

"Bull*shit* you've seen other Shufflers make that,"

I told him.

"Now I've ssseen one," he said with a slight smile. I was about to punch him in the face when someone appeared above us – another Serpent. She looked at both of us like she was going to say something... then ran away when she got a good look at our faces. I tended to get that reaction a lot. Mavril slid out of the water. I pulled myself farther up onto the rocky side and looked down at my leg. I couldn't see any bone right away, so that was good. I grabbed one of my throwing knives out of their sling around me and cut off the bottom of my pant leg so I could see it better.

I felt around my leg, trying to find where it hurt most. Ah, there it was. I turned my leg on its side and saw that it was already starting to swell. Thank God it was only my fibula. It should heal within a day or so.

"Are you okay?" Mavril asked looking down at me. God, he was so freaking tall.

"I'm fine. Help me up."

Hesitantly, he put his hand down. I grabbed it... and shoved him into the water once again. He surfaced.

"Okay, okay. I get it," he scoffed.

"If you lie to me ever again, I might just mold and make a meal of you, hear me?"

"Yesss, Macki."

"Good. Now this time I really need help up." He did nothing, his arms folded as he got out of the water for the second time. I shook my hand in waiting. "Hello? Anybody home?"

He grunted and grabbed my hand. This time, I let him pull me all the way up so that I was standing. I favored my hurt leg as I walked around a little bit, trying to get a feel for the pain. It wasn't unmanageable.

"Now, are you going to tell me how to really get down here or not?"

"Sure. You don't."

What? "What do you mean?"

"I mean that no Shuffler has ever been inside this Serpent base."

"None? Like zero? Should have added this to my travel plans earlier..." I looked at him and his tongue flicked out again.

"I didn't think you'd actually do it," he said. Yeah, *thanks*.

"Well, I did." I looked up back to the top of the hole and saw my four measly followers standing there, peering down. I gave them a thumbs up. "All good!" I yelled up.

"Macki, I have to asssk," Mavril said. "Could you pleassse just keep thisss to you and me? I don't want to go marching in there with a gang of... of... *Shufflersss,*" he finished.

"What? Why?"

"It'sss jussst... it's dissshonorable." His tongue flicked out again a few times.

"Ahh... fine," I said. "Stay up there! I'll be back!" I yelled up. Ryker made a thumbs up to let me know they understood. "Let's get going, then. Chop-chop," I said to Mavril.

"After you," he told me.

"Hmph," I said as I passed him, my leg beginning to feel decent enough to put my full weight on it. Not saying it felt that pleasant, but it was usable.

We walked under the canopy of wet rock. There were no lights, so it got really dark really fast. Mavril took the lead and led us over toward what looked like a wall. When I got closer, I noticed that it wasn't a wall, but, in fact, a boulder.

He stopped and looked down at me.

"One problem," he said.

"Yesssssssss?" I said, trying to imitate him, accompanied by a full snake charmer-like move. I sucked, by the way. He glared at me.

"We have to move this boulder."

"Why? It's not like a Serpent could actually do that, right?"

"No, we're not ssstrong enough. That'sss why I need you."

"Oh. Is this… is it supposed to be there to stop you from coming in?" I asked.

"Yesss," he said, looking down with shame.

"They really hate you, don't they?"

"Sure ssseemsss like it," he said under his breath.

"No problem then. Welcome to my world." I put my hands out in front of me and pushed the stone to the side.

It was bigger and heavier than I thought it would be, but it moved with relative ease. When the opening was big enough to fit Mavril and me, I stopped pushing on it. I leaned on it for a moment, catching my breath. He walked past me and into the room beyond. I followed, limping slightly. Everything was dark. There was a long, seemingly naturally carved hallway that twisted and turned, finally leading us all the way to the great room.

There were at least a hundred Serpents scuttling around the giant room, a big stone dome high above them. All the way up were rooms with gas lamps hanging in them – bedrooms. There looked like there were thousands, lights illuminating each one like stars among the darkness. On the bottom floor, there were torches and gas lamps lit all around to keep it semi-light.

As I was taking in the scenery, everything

stopped. All of the Serpents were staring at the pair of us. Someone came forward out of the crowd. She was tall like all of the others and, well, snake-like. But her eyes were black and gray, her scales shimmering black. Her long black hair was pulled back into a series of braids. For a snake-human, she was pretty hot.

"How dare you come here," she scolded, getting right to the point. "Both of you."

"Erin," Mavril said, "we appreciate the warm welcome."

Ooh, Mavril had game. She still slapped him. Hard.

"Whoa there," I said, pushing her away. I felt like such the odd one out, it was almost nauseating.

"And you," she said, looking down at me, her eyes seemingly staring into my soul. "What the *heck* are *you* doing here?"

"Uh…" I began, "I was invited by a friend." I pointed at Mavril. "And I wanted to see you, of course, I mean after our last meeting… you're pretty hard to resist."

She looked at me, shocked and offended.

"Everyone," she said to the crowd of Serpents, "go to your rooms. There's nothing to see here."

After a moment, the Serpents took off, sliding across the ground to their respective walls. And much like Mavril had done in the cave, they wiped their hands together and climbed. The entire fleet of them climbing looked quite… amazing. Within seconds, they had all disappeared within the depths of their rooms.

A few Serpents stepped up and stood next to Erin like guards. They all had machetes hanging around their waists.

"We'd heard you'd both broken out," Erin began, "but we weren't exactly expecting a visit."

"Heard anything from the Ndege?" I asked.

"Yesss. Lauren said you forsssed her into keeping the Ndege neutral."

"Ah, ah, ah, I did not force anything upon her. She decided for herself."

"I'm sure you didn't make it an easssy choissse," Erin scoffed.

"I have a similar deal to make with you," I said.

"Oh, do you? Like you're in any posssition to make a deal?"

"Actually, I am. You see, I'm a Shuffler, if you forgot. You're a Serpent. Who wins?"

Erin looked away. "There are hundredsss of Ssserpents here. Not even a Shuffler could take usss all on and win."

"Oh, but I'm not just a Shuffler," I said, stepping toward Erin. "I'm Macki."

She laughed. "You've got a big head for being only a child."

"Child? I'm older than you." Serpents aged at about half the speed of a normal human, just like the Ndege. So they could be pretty old, but I knew for a fact that Erin wasn't close to my age. She turned completely serious.

"What do you want, then?"

"I want you on my side."

"We don't pick sssidesss, Macki; that's our peassse policy."

"Peace policy? What happened to the bloodthirsty Serpents that wanted to fight for what they believed in? Huh?"

"They disssappeared along with your buddy over there." I'd almost forgotten Mavril was next to me. He was being so quiet. I wondered why. When he was leader of the Serpents, he knew how to command people. He knew how to fight. But most importantly, he knew how to *win*.

"Well, you can either help me or be hurt by me. Your choice."

"You can't do anything to usss."

"Try me."

Erin looked again over to the side, thinking. "Picking sssidesss could mean the end to my rassse depending on how much stuff you get yoursssself into, Macki, you undersssstand that right?"

"Of course," I said, beginning to pace around. "That's always a concern, but I would never let that happen."

"Why should we trussst you?" one of her creepy, slimy, snake-human thingies asked. He spit in disgust.

"Because you have no other option."

"How about we do this the old-fashioned way?" Mavril finally chimed in.

"No, I refuse," Erin said.

"Because you're weak?" I said.

"Because I'm not an idiot."

"Come on," I said. "We could handle a little Mavril-Erin action, couldn't we?"

Erin gulped. She hadn't expected this. Her friends looked up at her in anticipation.

"Fine," she said as she unsheathed her machete. Mavril took his out as well.

"Fight!" I yelled overenthusiastically. They both glared at me, unmoving.

"Erin, are you sure you can—" one of her goons began.

"This'll be easy," she said, cutting him off. She pushed him lightly out of the way. We stepped away from Mavril and Erin, leaving them to their business. Was I nervous? A little bit, considering I could be left down here by myself with no way to get up and out of the forest. But even if Erin won the duel... she wouldn't make it to tomorrow.

They circled each other, slinking around on their weird feet. Finally, they charged at the same time, machetes raised. There was a *clink* as they hit each other in mid-air. Mavril kicked Erin down with all of his strength and she went flying across the ground. She popped back up smoothly and some of the scales around her stomach were mangled and falling off, but she came at him once again. They went back and forth with blocks and kicks and swings of their blades. I could tell they were both expert fighters, despite Erin's anti-violence bullshit. I glanced up and saw heads all peeking out from their rooms, watching the fight progress.

Erin slashed Mavril's arm, making him too slow to block once again. Her blade sliced across his stomach, creating an enormous gash. Dammit...

Without even thinking, I was in my white tiger mold, standing defensively in front of a dying and bleeding Mavril. He collapsed. I stood face-to-face with Erin. She smiled. She knew if I attacked, it would be over. The other Serpents drew their weapons and stood by her side.

"Don't be ssstupid," she said. I looked back and saw Mavril still on the ground, holding his stomach, hand drenched in blood, his breathing picking up speed with every breath.

"M," I heard behind me. Not now. "She's right. Don't be stupid," Asime said. "They were doing fine before you showed up."

I *needed* them. I felt a hand on my fur and growled at Asime. He recoiled his hand and stood there, willing me to just give up...

No. I didn't give up. I followed through.

I ran straight at Erin and leaped, clawing her to the ground. She tried to push me off of her, but I was too heavy. I raked my paw across her throat... and her eyes went blank within seconds.

Everyone looked down at me in complete shock. I heard some Serpents crying, some screaming out. I'd just crushed their symbol of peace. I jumped and molded back into my human self with one easy flip.

I looked down and saw blood on my hands — Erin's blood.

What... had I just done?

I had nothing to say. I didn't know what to say. What *could* I say? Thoughts started flying through my mind.

"I have to... I have to get out of here," I said as I ran back toward the tunnel that brought me into the room. I ran down it and molded back into my tiger form, which is how I felt the most comfortable. I ran out to the room with the giant hole and barreled into the pool.

The water was freezing, but it felt good. I needed to calm down. I molded back into my human form and stayed underwater, just looking around at the darkness of the water. I stayed under for a while, not wanting to come up and face what I'd just done. When I got riled up, this tended to happen. I killed someone I wasn't intending to lay a finger on. Just like with Asime.

I killed the leader of the Serpents. I just... I just killed her. The thought needed to catch up to me. She was their symbol of peace and the Ndege's symbol of peace. And I'd just finished her off so easily. This really wasn't my place, was it?

I came back up with a splash and was surprised to see that I had an audience. All of the Serpents stood watching me.

I pulled myself out of the water. I was strong, but... hundreds of Serpents coming at me at one time... well... I didn't know if I could do it. Was it the end?

I stood there, soaking wet, searching through the crowd for nothing in particular, wondering if it would by last images of the world.

Then, in unison, they all got onto one knee, heads down. It looked like... it looked like...

I gulped. Were they really bowing down to me?

One in the front looked up at me.

"You've killed our leader," he said quite nobly. "You... you have our ressspect." His voice wavered a bit when he said it, like he was unsure if this was what they were supposed to do or not.

"I, uh... I..." I stammered.

"You get to choose a new leader for us sssinssse you are not a Ssserpent," he told me.

"I can do that," I said. It would, of course, be Mavril. But, wait... what about... I cleared my throat. "That kid, what's his name..." I began. Some of the kids looked up at me, confused. "The Serpent-Ndege." A few gasps swept through the crowd.

"I don't know if that countsss exactly," the Serpent said.

"It's either him or me forcing you around. Choose one," I said, gaining my confidence back.

"I guesss..." He looked around. "Him."

"Send someone to get him immediately," I said. "You," I told the guy in front, "are in charge until they bring him here, got me?" He nodded.

They always nodded.

22
Alex

Every time I brought my arm around to strike the small shield Ella was holding, the stone was a different weapon. I'd been strengthening up, and I was surprised how much I could do without feeling totally exhausted. I barely felt anything at all.

"Stop," she told me. I stopped. I'd been going at it for a few minutes, transforming the stone to every weapon I could think of from a spiked riot shield to a broom handle.

"You're doing great," she congratulated me.
"Thanks."
"Do you want to spar now? Against me?"
I'd heard that Ella was one of the best Shuffler fighters ever. I knew I should have been more cautious, but I was overly confident after mastering my weapon.
"I think I can do it."

"I'll be right back. I need to get my weapon." She exited the practice room, shutting the metal door behind her.

I talked myself up. Yeah, I could do it right? I could be some good competition. Like Falcon had explained earlier, it showed true strength in the Shuffler world when you can win a fight without seriously injuring or killing your opponent (especially since it was hard to create them in the first place). Wow, I realized how much I wanted to win this fight. I mean, this could prove to everyone that I was worth a damn.

Ella walked back in with her weapon of choice. It was a nasty-looking barbed chain that she had wrapped around her hand. I realized why the skin on her hands was so tough. She stood across from me in the circular room.

"Ready?" she asked.

"Ready," I told her.

"Your move."

I took a deep breath in, strategizing before just going. I whipped around a long, black sword. Ella slashed it away then brought the chain back around at my feet. I barely jumped over it in time. I went after her with everything I could throw, turning weapons every couple of seconds. We went back and forth with attacks and blocks. Back and forth and back and forth. It went from blade, to chain, to shield, to throwing knife (which I brought quickly back to my hand after I realized I'd missed), to staff, to chain, to sword...

I felt the barbs of her chain sink into my ankles. It was wrapped around my legs several times. I fell backward, but before Ella had the chance to let go of her chain, I tugged it toward me as hard as I could, the barbs pricking my skin. She tumbled forward, landing on top of me. We were looking right at each other – body to body. My heart sped up. A thought flashed in my mind of Kaley, but I quickly reasoned with myself that I probably wouldn't see her ever again, so I'd have to move on eventually.

I pressed my lips to hers and put my hand on her hip. After a few moments, I pulled away. I brushed her bangs out of her face so I could see her sparkling lavender eyes better. Wait. What did I just do? The thought slapped me in the face.

"You didn't have to stand up for me today, Alex," she confessed.

"I didn't… but I wanted to," I told her truthfully. She smiled. I kissed her again. We repositioned ourselves so that we were sitting up against the wall. She slid off my shirt.

I knew Ella held a lot of dark secrets, but she was just so alluring. There was just something about her that I'd been instantly attracted to. I was glad we were together.

I was glad she was getting a second chance.

--

I was in my room, and I'd finally personalized it a little bit. I hadn't gotten to get anything from the house, so I didn't have any pictures or anything. I painted one of the burnt-red walls with a giant American flag mural. I wasn't very artistic, but Pilot had helped me with the stars, which were the hardest part. On another wall, I put up a bunch of athlete posters, movie posters, and pictures of my favorite bands. The last wall I left blank. I didn't know why; I just did. Maybe because I was waiting for new things – for things from my life as a Shuffler.

I was experimenting with the stone, seeing what exactly constituted a "weapon." I tried a crow bar. I flipped it in my hand, really feeling its weight. I thought again. A stapler formed in my hand. It was a pretty lame weapon, but, hey, whatever worked. Oh... I thought of a good one. Black fire shot out of a blowtorch.

Falcon startled me as he entered my room without bothering to ask permission first. I shouldn't have been surprised; it was typical of him.

"Feeling the need to catch something on fire, are we?" he asked.

"Just trying to figure out what this thing can do."

"Oh, sure. You know what I think we should do? We should go out and have us a good time."

"I have training."

"Please, Alex. You're not going to turn into an old fart like Phoenix, are you? I know this great place in town that'll let us drink until we pass out."

I stared at him. Was he serious? With everything going on?

"Not tonight, Falcon," I heard coming from the entrance to my room. The curtain was flung open and Pilot walked in with Quinn next to him. Quinn was wearing a sleeveless shirt, so his entire tiger tattoo could be seen. It was in black ink and designed like those Asian drawings with the thick, clean brushstrokes reaching all the way down his arm. It was awesome. I noted that maybe I should look into getting one sometime.

After my brother was safe, of course.

"Aw," Falcon pouted. "Come on, Pilot." He made a pouty face like a little kid. Pilot shoved the side of his head. Not in a mean way, but a stop-being-immature-Falcon kinda way. I felt bad. He had been only thirteen when he was changed into a Shuffler. Wouldn't it be hard to live like that? I thought it would be.

"You're going to help us clean up later," Quinn said, a slight accent on his words. German maybe?

"Clean up what?" I asked. Quinn smiled. Pilot looked at the ground, blushing.

"Seriously!?" Falcon jumped up, scaring me about half to death. He went over to Pilot and shook his shoulders. "Took you long enough!" Pilot looked up, half-smiling.

"Wait, I'm lost," I said. I was lost a lot around here.

"He's going to propose to Logan," Quinn whispered to me, cluing me in to what Falcon was going all crazy about.

"Holy shit! You're gonna be engaged!" Falcon exclaimed. Immediately, he got two *shh*s from Pilot and Quinn.

"Don't tell the whole place. I haven't done it yet!" Pilot said, trying to get Falcon to quiet down. We all laughed after Falcon settled down.

"Well, let me see it!" Falcon whispered, still a little too loudly. Pilot put his hand in his pocket and pulled out a shining ring.

"Oh, man. That's sick," Falcon said. It really was a nice ring. Shiny, but not over the top. The diamond sparkled magnificently. Not that I'm into rings much, but… it really did look nice. Pilot dropped it back into his pocket.

"How are you gonna do it?" Falcon asked him.

"We set up a piano down in the greenhouse," he explained.

"A piano? Really?" Falcon scoffed.

"Hey. Considering her situation, I think it's very appropriate."

"Oh. Yeah. I guess you can't really *look* at something cool…" Falcon began, trailing off when he realized what he'd said. Pilot ignored him, his face turning serious.

"Considering everything that's going on... I thought it must be the right time. I mean, we don't know what Macki's planning exactly, but I could... I could die, you know? And I just want her to know how much I love her before Macki's chaos is shoved up our asses. Do I make any sense here, guys?"

I nodded and so did Quinn. This was the first time I'd actually thought about... dying. I'd never even met Macki, so she seemed like a pretty distant threat. Sure, I heard the news about what she did to humans and stuff. I also heard the rumors. But that's all it seemed like – talk. I felt safe here. I felt comfortable. Could one girl really take all that away?

"You're not going to die," Quinn told Pilot, putting a hand on his shoulder. "None of us are going to die. Whatever Macki's planning – if anything – we can beat it. Look at us all. We have the upper hand."

"Why is that?" Falcon butted in again.

"We have a team. We're a family. Macki doesn't have that. All she has are some passive followers, a dead boyfriend, and some messed up brain chemistry," Quinn said. Pilot nodded and looked up.

"Yeah. You're right, Quinn." He paused, thinking. "Alex, can I talk to you for a moment?" Pilot asked me.

"What about me?" Falcon asked.

"You? You can wait downstairs. Go," he told Falcon plainly.

"Fine," Falcon said, sticking his tongue out. He hopped down.

"I'll wait with Falcon," Quinn said, then turned and jumped out after him.

Pilot turned to me, his unusual gray hair and eyes catching my interest once again.

"The Core just met," he began. "We have some

news about your parents." He coughed.

"Really? What is it?"

"They, uh… they sent a distress call from Tokyo. It came from a cell phone. We tried calling back, but… but it seems it was destroyed."

"That's it?" I asked.

"That's about it."

"Are you going to, like, do anything about it?" I looked up at him, anxious to know the answer.

"We discussed for quite a while. Phoenix, Logan, Quinn, and I are going to go find where it came from. Then maybe, just maybe, we'll get some clues on where to find Macki."

"Isn't Falcon going to be angry?"

"We don't have time to worry about Falcon. We're leaving tonight. After I, you know, do my thing." I just nodded. I had no words. He smiled and grabbed my shoulder with a tight grasp. "I'm sure they're fine."

I think he thought I was more concerned than I actually was. I mean, they were my parents, sure, but… I really didn't know them at all. I was sure Pilot knew them better than me even.

"Okay. All right," was all I could put together. "Anything on Joey?" I asked.

He shook his head solemnly. "If we find Macki, we'll find him, too, I'm sure."

I nodded. "Okay."

"Are you good?"

"I'm good."

"Great." He let go of my shoulder. "Now," he said, his voice jittery, "I have someone to propose to."

We both walked to the edge of my room and jumped down next to Falcon and Quinn. I landed in a crouched position. My strength and resiliency was increasing like crazy.

"Go, Pilot!" Falcon yelled, throwing double fists

into the air. Pilot saluted, a grin spreading across his face as he got to his feet and walked toward the greenhouse.

I thought about Kaley for a moment. I'd thought I was going to marry her. For the longest time, there hadn't been a doubt in my mind. Or hers.

But now… but now…

So much had changed.

23
Macki

Even though I'd thought that I was beyond actually feeling romantically attached to someone, my heart still sped up and I felt high every time I looked at my sexual partner for the night. It was like playing with a toy. It wasn't serious in any way, shape, or form, and I knew I would never remember this person after the night.

My back was up against the bar as we made out. She was quite pretty – medium-height, Asian, eccentric eye shadow, tall heels, a shiny dress – and I'd been drawn to her right away. After all of my years, I was never picky about gender. I was a bit drunk, but not as much as I'd normally be in a club like this.

I had something to do later in the night that I couldn't be drunk as a skunk for.

There were lights flashing everywhere, Japanese music blaring, dancers trying to seduce the crowd. But all I could think of was what a fantastic kisser this girl was. Damn. She gave me chills. She kissed my neck and I slowly traced my hand down her spine. Not to brag or anything, but I'd had a lot of experience in the area of sexual relationships. Most of the partners I'd been with since Asime died were pieces of junk. They were all around my "appearance" age and just didn't know how to do anything decently.

But this chick was something special. Her hand slid down to my chest as we began kissing lip-to-lip again. As much as I wanted to enjoy my time at the club, my eyes wandered the crowd looking for Frost and Ryker. Bull and Humvee weren't much for these kinds of places, so I told them to go find (and steal) some cool wheels in the city and bring them to the hotel we were staying at. Yes, we had actually rented a hotel room. Like normal humans.

A mosh pit had formed and there was some serious grinding going on between everyone. I really didn't expect to see Frost (she preferred a more private setting) and I figured Ryker was probably in the middle of the lot, so I gave up looking and focused back on my girl.

Wait. No. It couldn't be. My eyes were playing tricks on me. No, they weren't. My instincts knew something was up. I pushed the girl away a little too violently. She stumbled back but didn't fall.

"What's wrong?" she asked me in Japanese. I leaned forward, kissed her on the forehead one last time and walked into the crowd, trying not to stick out and startle my stalker. I slinked past the people to where I'd seen someone that caught my eye.

Nothing. They must be somewhere… I scanned the crowd again. There. I saw the back of a man shaded by a hat pulled down covering most of his face. He was wearing a thin vest and capris. He was heading toward the exit. I followed a distance behind him, not wanting him to notice that I was onto him. He left the club and went out into the dark Tokyo streets. If I followed him, it would be easy for him to see me, but if I stayed, I'd lose him for sure.

I put my hands on the cold handle of the door and prepared to push it open… when I retracted my hands. The man's eyes had been an unmistakable tea green. I knew for sure then it had been Jesse. He was watching me. When he wanted his presence to be known, he'd confront me, I was sure. Why not wait and let him come to me? Hopefully on a night when I had less plans.

So, I left the door with a smile, excited to soon be challenged again by two as experienced as Karen and Jesse, and went to find myself another shot for the road.

--

I kicked the door open into the alley. Alarms were going off in my wake, and I heard sirens rapidly approaching the facility. They wouldn't do any good. Everyone inside was already long dead. I unzipped my backpack as I walked down the dark alley and put a tube of yellow liquid carefully inside. Most of the people I had killed were the after-hours security team members because it had been around three AM when I'd gotten there.

I put my backpack back on my back and grabbed my black, masked helmet off of the seat of a sleek, black motorcycle Bull had picked up a few hours ago. Can you tell that black was my favorite color? Didn't think so. I didn't need the helmet for any reason other than it made me feel pretty cool. I mounted the bike and took off into the streets of Tokyo. It was too easy, and I enjoyed the air as I rode, twisting my way through the crowded street.

I saw something out of the corner of my eye, so I looked up to the tops of the buildings to my left. There was nothing there, so I turned my gaze back to the street. I heard the tires of a few cars spin out and swerve. Two cars wrecked in front of me. I evaded the trouble and continued, not seeing what everyone was being so weird about. Oh… damn. Jesse stood in the middle of the street, Karen on the sidewalk. I was advancing too quickly to stop properly before I hit him. If I did hit him, I was sure he'd throw me off easily, which could leave me severely injured in the middle of the street.

I jerked the handles all the way to the left, and then shifted my weight to the ground. I hit my side hard on the asphalt and pushed the bike out in front of me, letting go of it completely. I was up and running before I could see what happened next.

I shoved people out of my way as I sprinted down the sidewalk, looking for a good place to get to higher ground where I could properly fight. I found the right building and jumped, latching onto the closest handhold I could find. Karen was at my heels. She grabbed my ankle, but I shook her grip away. I climbed as agilely as I could, reaching the top and pulling myself onto the roof in record time.

I stole a look back to see how close Karen was to me when I felt hands grab me and I went soaring through the air. There was a little shack-like entrance on the roof with a door. I slammed into it, my body horizontal in the air, and bounced to the ground. Karen and Jesse stood above me, their expressions filled with pure rage. Karen pulled out one of her hatchets from a holder strung across her back and swung it around. Jesse threw my cracked helmet off to confirm my identity.

"It's over," he declared once he saw it was really me.

"I don't remember you two looking this shitty," I retorted. Jesse kicked my stomach as hard as he could, and I coughed.

"Give us our son, Macki," Karen demanded.

"Yeah... about that. I left him with a sitter. A very trustworthy one, I promise," I taunted them. Jesse grabbed my collar and threw me up against the already-dented door.

"We're not playing," Jesse said through gritted teeth. They seriously couldn't have thought that they were just going to waltz up to me, and I was going to give them back their son. At least call in some goddamn backup. Idiots.

"I am," I explained. "I think I'm winning, too." I smiled cheerfully. Jesse shook me violently.

"Not anymore," he told me.

"Oh really? I disagree," I responded. A chainsaw revved behind Jesse. Frost was holding her machine gun to the back of Karen's head. Karen immediately swung around, bringing her hatchet up at Frost's head. Frost ducked, and brought her barrel down so that it was touching Karen's foot. She shot a few rounds. Karen grimaced, removing the weight from her injured foot. That gave Frost the opportunity to hit her with the butt of the gun upside her head. Karen fell to the ground on her hands and knees. Frost hit her again, and she was out.

Jesse wasn't ready to give up yet. He charged at me, pulling out a knife he used for short-range battles, as opposed to his slingshot. He tried to bring the blade down on me, but I blocked his arm. He kicked at me, trying to knock me off-balance. He succeeded, and my foot fell backward just a hair.

He stabbed at me once again, and because I was off-balance and it took me longer to respond, the blade sunk deep into my shoulder. I grinded my teeth, trying to control the pain and not let it control me. Ryker threw Jesse away from me, and with Frost's help, they battled him to the ground, Ryker's chainsaw held just above Jesse's face, both of them spitting crude insults at him.

I grabbed the hilt of the knife embedded in my flesh and pulled the blade out, letting it fall to the ground. A chill radiated through me and I shook my head to one side violently. Then, I took a deep breath, straightened myself up, and walked over to where Jesse was lying, Ryker's chainsaw nearly touching the skin of his nose.

Jesse actually dared to open his mouth. "They already know where you are. They're going to find you, Macki."

"Aw. Way to ruin the surprise for me."

"You—" he began, but I cut him off.

"Take these idiots back to the hotel so we can have a nice little chat. We can discuss how the hell you two found me," I explained to him.

Before Jesse could say any more, I kicked his head with the toe of my boot, and he was out.

24
Alex

Quinn, Falcon, Maverick, and I stood in Pilot's room. We were all anxious to know how everything went down, and if he'd actually done it. I was sure he had. I mean, they were in serious love and had been dating for, like, ever it sounded like. But I changed my mind when I saw him.

We stood around Pilot. He was sitting on a couch, his hands on his knees supporting his head, which was facing the ground. I don't think he'd even noticed we were there – his mind was undeniably somewhere else. I saw a tear drop off of his face. Something was up.

"Pilot," Quinn said, shaking the young man. Pilot shot up, alarmed, wiping the tear away. He blinked himself out of his reverie.

"Dude, cool your beans," Maverick said. Falcon

hopped over and grabbed Pilot's shoulders, shaking them.

"So did you propose or not!?" Falcon asked, not getting the obvious hint that Pilot was having a hard time.

"I… I couldn't," Pilot confessed, sitting back down.

"Weenie," Maverick sneered. Quinn gave him a nasty glare.

"What!? I was really looking forward to getting wasted tonight in celebration," Maverick said.

"Em?" Quinn asked Pilot sincerely. Pilot nodded.

"I can't lose Logan like I did Emily," Pilot said.

"You won't," Quinn assured him.

"She just…" We were all staring at Pilot as he spoke. "It was perfect. We played the piano together and she said she loved me. I had my hand in my pocket, and I was going to pull the ring out. Then, she asked me what I looked like and I told her I looked how I was twenty years ago. And…" He ran his hand threw his hair and laughed nervously. "She said she didn't think I looked like a donkey because of… because of… never mind. It's hopeless. I just… I just… choked."

It was hard to keep up with what he was saying, but I'd gotten most of it. Someone tugged on my shirt – Falcon. He motioned toward the hallway. I nodded. He tapped Maverick and motioned the same way he did to me.

"I'm enjoying this," Maverick said too loud. Falcon put an arm around his neck and started dragging him out, our sneaky exit now compromised.

Falcon pushed Maverick out of the room and he landed on his side with a satisfying *thump.*

"Ouch!" Maverick yelled as we landed next to him on our feet, leaving Pilot and Quinn to sort things out.

"You need to learn when to stop being such a jerk," Falcon told him. He really did.

"Hypocrite," Maverick said back under his breath as he got up off the ground, rubbing his arm like it was hurt. I heard two voices down the hallway and turned to see who it was.

"We have to go. Like now," Phoenix said.

"Calm down, Phoenix," Zahra said. Phoenix was decked out in fight gear – a black and yellow long-sleeve (one of Macki's inventions – they made Shufflers even tougher), a knife around her leg, and she was putting some things in a little holder around her wrist – preypins. They looked like a cross between a nail and a needle. They automatically opened after they embedded themselves in something – usually Shuffler flesh. She'd shown me how they worked after training once. Luckily, not on me.

"Where are Pilot and Logan? They're not getting it on again in the practice rooms, are they?" Phoenix boomed.

"Shut up!" Falcon sneered.

"What? I don't care if they hear me." Falcon rolled his eyes and walked up to Phoenix. He whispered into her ear.

Her jaw dropped.

"What!? He did what!?" Some heads poked out from their rooms, seeing what all of the ruckus was. Falcon whispered again. "Now of *all* times." Falcon grabbed his sister's shoulders, keeping her from storming into Pilot's room. "Let me talk to him," she said.

"No way, Nix, cool down first."

"Yeah, bitch," Mav chimed in.

"Shut your face," she said, pointing a finger at Mav. Falcon let go of her. She crossed her arms.

Someone jumped down next to us – Logan. Her steel staff was out in front of her to help her stay balanced from the fall. Once she landed, she put it back in its sling across her back. She was in the same sort of shirt that Phoenix was in, only hers was ice blue and black, matching her eyes. Her hair was up in, whatever that braid is called, French maybe? Yeah, that's it, a French braid. She also had a knife around her leg like Phoenix, with sleek black pants. Her eyes were lost, as always. She walked over toward Phoenix.

"I have to go. Good luck," Zahra said stiffly as she turned to leave.

"Love you, too, Zahra," Maverick said with a cheesy grin and wave. Zahra looked back and glared at him but ultimately continued on her way, her robes swaying behind her.

"Where's Pilot?" Logan asked.

"I'm here," he said, looking down at Phoenix from the edge of his room. I'd never really noticed his necklace before. It had a strange symbol on it, almost like a half-moon with some extra lines. I made a note to ask him later about what it meant.

"Get dressed," Phoenix commanded, pointing toward Pilot's room. "We have to go." Quinn shuffled over to his room, and Pilot disappeared into his.

"How are you going to get to Tokyo?" I asked.

"Pilot's flying," Logan answered. "Royal Air Force plane," she explained.

"So he really does fly?" She laughed.

"Yep."

"Yeah, he flies, but apparently it takes him two hours to get all prettied up," Phoenix said, tapping her foot.

"Be nice," Logan said as she hit Phoenix lightly. "We have to spend a whole plane ride with you."

"Lucky you," Phoenix retorted.

After a few moments of us all staring around awkwardly, Pilot jumped down. He was in the same style shirt, but his was, of course, gray. He'd pulled his hair back into a little baby ponytail and had two pairs of metal nunchuks in special holders around his waist.

"I can always go upside down and see who throws up first," Pilot said looking over at Phoenix.

"That was a fantastic idea on my part," Mav said excitedly.

"Hey, that wasn't fair. Clearly you tried harder with me," Phoenix said.

"Oh, of course, Phoenix," Pilot said with a smile. Quinn jumped down next to us.

"Finally," Phoenix said.

I noticed that Quinn's pink eyes looked even brighter with his shirt on. He looked a little... uncomfortable. He kept pulling at his collar as if to loosen up his shirt and kept moving his feet around. Now that I thought of it, I'd only ever seen him in sleeveless shirts. Maybe that was all. Maybe it wasn't though. Hm.

"I'm sorry I won't be able to finish training you," Logan said, "but it was nice working with you, Alex." She smiled. Pilot came over and put his arm around her.

"We should be back soon," Pilot said. I looked over and saw Phoenix and Falcon saying their goodbyes... which consisted of Falcon standing there ready for a hug for like thirty seconds before Phoenix finally (and very awkwardly) complied.

"Be good," Phoenix told her brother, "and defend this place, okay? No more sleeping on guard duty, you little runt." She tousled his hair and shoved him playfully. He smiled. "Let's go," Phoenix said. The group walked away, Pilot with his arm still around Logan. Quinn swung his bolas around a bit. Phoenix stood tall – the leader of the group. They turned a corner and disappeared out of sight.

I looked back at Falcon. He was frowning. Not a fake frown. A real frown. Almost like he was going to cry, but he didn't. He realized what he was doing, stood up straight, and walked over to me with a smile.

"We can hang in Mav's room," Falcon said, pointing to a room on the ground level.

We walked over to it. It was disgusting. Even for a teenage boy, it was absolutely repulsive. Half-eaten food was everywhere, along with cigarettes, dirty clothes, and some stuff I didn't even want to mention. The smell about made me keel over alone. Mav plopped down onto an old, ratty couch. He had his own TV, and it was playing some daytime show in the background. Falcon sat down next to him and put his feet up on a pot from the greenhouse turned upside down.

"Are there any football games on?" Falcon asked. Maverick looked at Falcon seriously (a rare occurrence) with his sparkling green eyes.

"Falcon, you know I never miss a game. Do you see any athletes running around with fabulous uniforms on that screen?" Maverick said. Falcon shook his head. "Then no, they're not on right now." Falcon shrugged. I stood against the wall.

"Has she always been like that?" I asked, genuinely curious. "Phoenix?"

"It's gotten worse with age."

"Were you serious when you said you were in your sixties, Falcon?"

"He definitely was," Mav said.

"Yeah, pretty much," Falcon agreed.

I heard footsteps coming down the hall. I peeked out of the room. It was Ella.

"Could I talk to you for a moment, Alex?" Ella

asked. Maverick and Falcon looked out at her, eyebrows raised.

"Piss off, Ella," Falcon commanded. She stared at the ground, avoiding Falcon's glare.

"Oh. Things got serious in those practice rooms, didn't they? A little R-rated material going on, hm?" Maverick asked excitedly. My face got hot and I'm sure it turned bright red. "Goody goody, tell me evvvvverything."

Ella looked at me.

"Later," I told Maverick as I walked toward Ella.

"Be careful, Alex," Falcon said quietly, almost so I couldn't hear. "She's not who you think she is." Why were people so hung up on this?

I was glad to get out of Maverick's room. Ella and I strolled down the hall. She led me around a few corners until we got to a room with double doors – the Core room. She opened the door and we walked inside.

Around me were raised platforms arranged in a circle. It reminded me of a courthouse, with old wood that creaked under our weight. There were ten spots – one for each member of the Core. I looked up and saw the sky. It was dark out, the stars shining right through the glass dome at the top.

"What's up?" I asked Ella as I looked back down.

"I have to leave," she said. No.

"What? Why?" I put my hand on her arm and she shrugged it away.

"I'm not safe here."

"Sure you are."

"No, Alex, I'm not," she said, her voice the most forceful I'd ever heard.

"You can't just… you can't just… leave."

"Well, Zahra's left me no choice. Everyone

wants me out. Or they'll–"

"What, kill you?" She nodded. It started to finally sink in. "Where will you go?"

"My hometown probably."

"Where's that?"

"Russia."

"Won't you get lonely?"

"I'll find something to do."

"I can… I can go with you, can't I? Just the two of us?" She shook her head and looked down.

"You're naïve, Alex."

"Naïve about what?"

"Everything. Try not to get yourself killed." She walked away. I stood there, arms out in confusion. I'd never heard her talk like that.

"So that's it?" She nodded and kept walking. "Wait." She hesitated, then stopped. I walked up behind her and put my hands on her shoulders. She turned around finally and I rubbed her cheek with my thumb. We stood there in silence for a moment as I made sure to take in all of her features. Her eyes, her blonde hair, how her bangs fell over her face. My heart started pounding and I kissed her, letting myself be taken away by it as I put my hands gently around her neck. I silently gathered my courage and pulled away.

"I love you," I said. She looked up at me.

"I love you, too, Alex. I do. I just… I have to go." What else could I say to get her to stay? I really meant it. I finally began to see it. She was leaving. And I was staying. That was that. So, I took her chin in my hand, tilted it up and kissed her again. But I could tell she felt hurried, so I backed away.

"Bye," I said shortly.

"Bye," she said. She left. And I stood there in the middle of the Core room, looking up at the sky once again.

What was this madness?

25
Macki

I looked out my window at the dark sea churning beneath us. It was wonderful, really, all of that unexplored territory just begging for someone to jump in and get swallowed up by whatever lay beneath the surface. The plane shook a little bit – turbulence. I'd "so graciously" hired a pilot and a co-pilot to fly us to... well... I was still trying to figure that out. We were heading east, though. That's all I got.

I sat across from Karen and Jesse, who were both chained pretty damn tightly to their seats. Next to me was Frost and across the way were Humvee, Bull, and Ryker. Bull looked like he wanted to rip something apart. Apparently he didn't like water very much.

"So..." I began. Karen and Jesse barely looked up at me. They probably felt pretty bad. I was sure they both had fairly severe concussions and Karen's foot still had a few bullets stuck in it. "How did you find me again?" Jesse looked up, the space around his light green eyes glowing a sickly red. It reminded me of my father. A chill went up my spine with the thought of him.

"Why would we tell you?" he asked weakly.

"Well I don't know why *you* would. But I see that Karen has a habit of sharing secrets, huh, Karen?" I said. Jesse turned his head to Karen, confused.

"What are you talking about, Macki?" she said, her head still down.

"How did I know you had a kid? Hm?" I asked. I was trying to stir the pot. Duh. Karen put her head up.

"I sure didn't tell her," she reassured Jesse. He went back to glaring at me.

"Oh, maybe you didn't... but you did make a mistake."

"What was that? Coming to visit you? Macki, I felt bad for you. After four years of you being locked up in that little pit, I came. Did anyone else come to see how you were doing? No. Did Ella? Did Ryker? Did Frost? No. They were all too scared. Sure, when you finally got out they flocked back to you like moths to a light, but that wasn't after a long internal debate within each of them. They were unsure, Macki. Everyone was at some point. But I got off my ass and came and tried to talk to you. Not that you wanted to have a decent chat with me. I tried, Macki. That's all I'm saying." Her French accent pulled through as her words got faster and faster.

I looked at Frost. Her eyes were wide. I smiled at her. She relaxed a little bit but not much.

"You visited her?" Jesse asked. Karen nodded. She was starting to tear up. Boo-hoo.

"She saw that I was pregnant. I don't know how, but—" she began.

"I know people," I said.

"Obviously not," she retorted.

"I know how to get what I want when I want. That's all," I said plainly.

Jesse turned to Karen again. "Why didn't you tell me, K?"

"I thought she'd forget. Or never get out." We sat there in silence for a moment while I let that sink in for Karen and Jesse. "I'm going to murder you," Karen said, suddenly getting angry.

"Hey there—" Frost stood up and raised a fist at Karen. I stopped her hand.

"Settle down, Frost," I said. God, I sure had a bunch of hotheaded followers. "Well, that escalated quickly. How do you plan on doing that?"

"The very, very slow way."

Frost sat down, still uncomfortable.

"Ooh. Fun." I clapped and smiled in fake excitement.

"I'm serious."

"So am I," I said seriously. I crossed my arms and sat back.

"I am extremely tired," I said, laying back and closing my eyes. I hadn't slept in… oh, I didn't even know. Most nights, Asime kept me up. Or nightmares. Or both.

"Screw you," I heard Jesse say. My eyes popped open. I leaned forward toward them.

"You don't know what the endgame is here, do you?"

"We die," Karen said blatantly.

"Well, yes, but the big picture?" I asked.

"Creating a Shuffler army to take out Zahra and the others," Jesse said. Ryker and Humvee's conversation went dim. They looked over at me. Everyone was wondering what the hell I was concocting.

"Nope," I said to everyone's utter shock.

"Macki, then what are you..." Frost said, trailing off.

"That's what everyone thought was going on, yes?" I asked the group. They all looked at each other, then nodded hesitantly.

"You see, my friends, we are not the bad guys, even though everyone thinks we are. Including ourselves," I told them all.

"What's going on then?" Karen asked. "Planning to kill off all of the humans? Trying to kill... Alex?" She shuddered when she said the name.

"No. None of that nonsense. Simply... I'm... I'm trying to create something that'll... that'll..." I couldn't say it. I couldn't. Everything came rushing back to me. You see, I used to hallucinate my sister Samantha first. And when Asime came along, he'd... well, I remember every night he'd hold me as I cried. I was so... so angry and sad and confused. He'd stop me from killing myself. He'd calm me down when the urge came to mold unexpectedly. He'd tackle me if he had to and hold me down until the craziness passed. He'd do anything for me. Anything.

I looked at the room, still stuck in my reverie. I felt something wet on my cheek and I wiped it off as fast as I could. I didn't *cry* anymore. And especially not here. They all looked at me with expectant eyes.

"Never mind," I said. I looked at everyone then stood up. I slinked past Frost and took off down the aisle. I was getting anxious again. I knew the urge to mold would soon follow, so if I was going to rip everything to shreds, I preferred it not be by two people I actually did want to kill.

"Never mind?" Asime said. He followed me down the aisle. I got to the galley and searched for some ice. "This is your chance to tell them, M. Tell them how much you're hurting."

"That would make me look way too vulnerable," I said back quietly so everyone in the plane didn't hear. He stood next to me. I finally found the ice drawer and with shaking hands, I grabbed a glass and scooped some into it. "Hey, how about you help me rather than lecture me. Make yourself useful for once."

"You need to learn," he said.

"Learn what?" I said a little too loudly for my own comfort.

"How to control it."

"Oh, I've only been trying for, what, the last hundred-fifty years?"

"Tell the pilot to take you back so you can see Kai. He'll help you just like he used to."

"Kai is probably dead," I said as I pulled out a water jug and poured it in the glass. Some of it spilled, my hands too shaky.

"We both know he's not."

"You know nothing. You're dead, Asime. *You're dead.*" I chugged the icy water. "And if you don't help me, I'm going to attack everyone on this plane within the next few seconds."

"Stay calm," was all he offered.

"Oh, thanks, Captain Obvious," I said sarcastically. I was about to lose it. I was about to lose it. I was about to lose it. Molding was the only thought going through my head.

I dropped the glass and it shattered. Oh, no. It was coming.

Ryker appeared in the entryway.

"You okay, boss?" he asked me in German.

"Yeah. I'm fine," I said with as straight of a face as I could muster. "Just go sit down." He nodded and disappeared. I felt like I was about to burst.

"Do it for me," Asime said. I looked into his dark eyes.

"I'm already doing this for you."

"What?"

"If I were a normal Shuffler... I wouldn't need you in the first place."

He looked hurt. I didn't care. Then, he was gone. And I was left alone, gritting my teeth in an attempt to contain myself.

It didn't work. Within the next second, I molded. I attacked everything I could, but tried my hardest to stay conscious enough to stay in the small space. Bull, Ryker, Humvee, and Frost all got up and watched me in horror, unsure of what to do.

Finally, I molded back.

I lay on the floor and closed my eyes, wanting to ignore the mess I'd made. Just imagine if there were people around.

Just imagine.

26
Alex

I'd barely opened my eyes before Falcon burst in. He flipped my hammock and I fell to the ground. What a pleasant wake up. As I got to my feet, he started talking a mile a minute.

"There's two Serpents at the door – at the Terrene. We don't know what's going on. I mean, Serpents at the *Terrene*. Seriously. Anyway, we need to get downstairs. Grab the stone and let's go." After rambling all of that off, he turned toward the exit. "Let's go!" he told me.

I scooped up the Onyx stone off the table by my hammock and followed him. Luckily I'd figured out early on to just sleep in my normal clothes. The Shufflers around here had a habit of flipping my hammock at any time. I rubbed my eyes, trying to get them to focus through the fog of just waking up. Falcon jumped down. I followed and almost fell over when I landed. My foot hurt too. I guess I landed wrong. There were Shufflers running down the halls, some with weapons. Falcon had his grenades around his waist.

Falcon took off running. I did the same, hoping it'd wake me up a bit. For a little guy, he sure could run. The gap between us got bigger and bigger as we went around corner after corner. Finally, he slowed down as we came to the entrance of the vestibule.

We walked in and looked up through the bulb to see two… well, two snake people standing there. I'd heard about the Serpents, but never imagined I'd ever actually see one. They were both taller than me, super skinny, and freaky as heck. They stood there, their tongues flicking out every once in a while. The dude was blue with scales to match. The chick was a burnt orange color with black, white, and orange scales.

We stood around with a few other Shufflers, just looking up at them. All of us had weapons. I scanned the Serpents to see if they had any weapons on them, and it didn't look like it. Why would they come…

Zahra entered. All of the Shufflers made a clearing for her so she could stand directly under the bulb.

"Open it," she commanded the Shuffler manning the controls. He did as she asked and the bars and fiberglass bulb brushed away into the side of the hill.

"Zahra," one of them hissed, "may we have a word with you?"

"If you think I am going to let you in here without stating a good reason, you are wrong," she replied.

"We are merely messsengersss," the other said. "We have a messsage from Macki." A few gasps shot through the Shufflers.

"I thought you were neutral now," Zahra said, her voice as dry as usual.

"We have a new leader," the blue one said.

"Who? Why did I not know this?" Zahra asked.

"We came to tell you that asss well. But it'sss a sssmall matter," the blue one explained.

"Who?" Zahra grilled.

"The one Macki sssaved – Brit."

"Brit? Never heard of him."

"He'sss part Ndege, part Ssserpent."

"Bull," Falcon piped in. I looked over at him. He was angry. "You would never allow anyone that was part Ndege to be your leader. Let alone be part of your little clan or whatever you call it."

"It wasss not our choissse," the orange one snapped.

"Then whose was it?" Falcon asked.

"Macki," they both said.

"Back to the point," Zahra said. "What is your message for me, Serpents?"

The Serpents smiled. Not happy smiles, but devious ones.

"Macki requessstsss a showdown," the blue one sneered. Zahra looked over at me, wondering. Zahra didn't act like she hated me, but I knew she had to after I rescued Ella. We typically avoided each other anyway.

"With who?" she asked. I started to panic a little bit. If he said me…

"You, Zahra." I relaxed. I was so glad it wasn't me. I mean, sorry Zahra, but honestly… I might as well just roll over and die in front of Macki. "At the plassse you first sssaw Asssime."

"I am sure she has some rules," Zahra said. "What are they?" The whole room was focused on

Zahra. They all knew what this meant.

"She doesss," the orange one conceded. "Bring anyone with you and she'll kill Karen, Jessse, and Joey, and declare war on you. Sssame goes for if you're not there within the next forty-eight hoursss." Zahra looked down, thinking, a stumped look on her face. "Only one of you will sssurvive," the orange Serpent finished.

"How do I know she is not going to have any friends with her?"

"She will come basssed on the sssame conditionsss as you," she said.

Zahra took a deep breath.

"Is that all?" Zahra asked, not bothering to look up at them.

"Yesss," the guy said.

"Then leave," Falcon chirped. The blue guy bowed his head slightly, and they turned to leave. They started running faster than anything/anyone I'd ever seen. Their feet seemed to slide across the ground. Zahra still had her head down, staring intently at the floor.

"Party's over. False alarm," Falcon said to the room. Everyone gathered their weapons and flooded out. The glass and bars came back over the opening.

Zahra still stood there.

"What freaks," Falcon scoffed. There were only five of us left in the vestibule – me, Falcon, Zahra, Maverick, and the kid manning the control pad. We stood there in silence.

"What are you gonna do?" Falcon asked Zahra. Zahra didn't move. Even Maverick was quiet, waiting for a response.

"Tell Phoenix she's in charge when she gets back," she said, still looking at the ground.

"But what about—" Falcon began.

"Just tell her for me," she said. "Open it up,"

she told the dude at the control pad.

"You can't be serious," Maverick said. Zahra looked over at him.

"What other options do I have?"

The room went silent. We all knew what the outcome of this might be… our leader may not come back. With that, Zahra hopped out of the vestibule and walked out into the hills.

We all watched her as far as we could. No goodbye. No good luck. Just…

Gone.

27
Macki

My feet dangled over the edge of the ravine. Far below (a few stories), there was a river rumbling down the canyon. Not too far away was the waterfall, and I could feel the moistness radiating from it. I swung my legs around a little bit, looking down at the folds in the river's flow. Behind me was the rainforest that I'd spent like five billion hours trekking through. I'd stepped on a snake, too. That was pleasant. Luckily, I was fast enough to catch it so it didn't bite me. Otherwise, we would have had a problem.

I flew to Africa last night.

I came alone.

Why did I request to fight Zahra? Basically, I just wanted to take her out so the whole Terrene turned into a bumbling mess of idiots. Zahra wasn't my favorite person, but she did keep everything in order there.

Not too far from me, a bridge swayed over the canyon. It'd been years and years and years since I'd last crossed it. This is the place where Zahra had first met her brother (since she could remember). I remembered the day well. Asime had been bothering me to go back and see his family even though he still looked like he was twenty-something. I'd stood at the edge of the bridge with my arms crossed, waiting to see this "little sister" of his. By little, I mean like almost thirty years younger.

I hoped he didn't show up while I was here.

I stood up.

"Well, hello, old friend," I said.

She held her pistol to the back of my head – obviously close enough to kill me in an instant.

"It is over, Macki," she said, sure that she was going to finally end it.

"Why does everyone tell me that? And Jesus, Zahra, would you at least look at me face-to-face? Talk about bad etiquette." I turned around to face Zahra, adjusting the pistol so it was square in the middle of my forehead. God, I'd forgotten how tall she was. Why did everyone have to be so tall?

"After all these years, you are still playing games. Like a child."

"I am a child, aren't I? A teenager forever?"

"If by forever you mean the next few seconds, then yes." Always so headstrong.

"I've been waiting for you to kill me for a long time, Zahra. If you think my fun's going to stop once I'm dead, you're wrong. It'll always be a game for me. You know though, if your damned brother wouldn't have been such an ass, you'd never be in this mess, Zahra," I insulted.

Yes, I was intentionally trying to provoke her,

but she was so full of hate and disgust, she didn't realize it.

"Do not talk about Asime like that," she scolded.

"Why not? It's not like he's going to hear me. So, are you going to kill me or what? It's weird when you just stand there staring at me. Go on." I put out my arms like I was welcoming my imminent death. She didn't respond. "Oh, I get it. You can't, can you? Like you couldn't twenty years ago? You never know how to quit when you're ahead."

"Because you are always there to ruin it. It may seem like I am ahead, but I never am with you."

"Sorry I'm just so freaking awesome. End it. Now. Come on. Do it, bitch." Her finger tightened on the trigger. I raised an eyebrow. One more insult and she was done. "At least you won't have Macki guts all over with that pistol of yours. Never liked it dirty, did you?" She pulled the trigger. I stood there, still as stone, staring into her emerald eyes...

Then reached out my hand and opened it.

"Bet you wish you had the bullets now, don't you?" I let the bullets fall to the ground. "It seems like you're just insisting to continue playing my game, Zahra." I pulled one of my throwing knives out of the sash around my body with lighting speed and threw my arm up at Zahra's face, intending to cut it. Really, it was just to get the ball rolling. I had enough of talk. She stopped my attack. I smiled. She ran away from me and molded into a giant black cat.

Then, she circled back toward me, teeth bared.

"Game on, sister," I said as I cracked my knuckles. I took off sprinting along the edge of the clearing and molded.

I tackled Zahra, and it sent us both tumbling. She tried to bite at my fur, so I shoved her off of me.

We both got up and circled each other. I shook out my head. She attacked first, trying to swipe at my face with her paw. I jumped out of the way and tackled her once again, tearing in the air with my claws, trying to catch onto something solid. I came up dry, so I untangled myself from her and flipped back into my human form, pulling out a throwing knife.

She was back on her feet, staring at me and I threw a knife at her. She dodged, and it went sailing off into the canyon. I immediately pulled out another knife like a machine. I twirled it in my fingers. She charged at me. I jumped and planted my hands on the back of her coat and pushed myself off, flipping and landing behind her. The fight was getting nowhere. I turned back around to face her, but I felt the cat run into my legs, knocking them out from underneath me.

I ended up on the ground, and in the split-second I stayed there, she had already come back over and taken a swipe at my face with her paw. I felt her claws dig deep into the flesh of the side of my face. I kicked her off from over me and got back on my feet, my face creating puddles of blood wherever I stood. She molded back into her human form. She was smiling wickedly, proud of the mark she made on me. I wiped blood out of my eyes.

"Um, ouch," I said.

"You really deserved that one."

"Did I? You know what you deser—" Before I could finish my comeback, she had already charged at me, a medium-length blade in her hand. She came at me ferociously. Swipe. Dodge. Swipe. Dodge. I kept moving backward until I was on the edge of the canyon. She swiped at me again. I had nowhere to dodge to…

So I dropped off the edge.

I barely grabbed the edge of a rock jutting out

from the side. It jerked me violently upward, gravity wanting to carry me all the way down. Zahra brought her blade down to hit my hand... but she only hit the rock as I'd swung myself up. I came at her with vicious strikes, going as fast as I could without sacrificing too much control. She was quick... but not quick enough. And I was much stronger. I finally got a crescent kick in to the side of her face. She stumbled backward, which was the opportunity for me to really take control. I punched her in the face. Then elbowed her. Then kicked her in the stomach, and she hit the ground. I stood above her and smiled.

"A little rusty since our time in the arena, huh, Zahra?" I asked her. She tried to get back up, but I reached down and wrapped my arm around her neck. She coughed and struggled, desperately trying to escape my firm grasp.

"This... will be the end of you," she choked out.

"Fair enough," I said nonchalantly before she went unconscious. I still didn't let go. Pure hate controlled me now. My thoughts reeled. My memories of the both of us played in my head.

We had been such a good team, and it turned into this. Into us fighting to the death in a place we both considered sacred. Why didn't I listen to Asime on this one? I let go. I didn't want to kill her. I really didn't. But it felt so good. It felt so freeing. I hated her for imprisoning me. Yet the game I played with her was so, so addicting. How conflicted I was.

I took out one of my knives. This would finish her for sure (if she wasn't gone already). I motioned down, but then I stopped. *I stopped.* Then I got up and stood above her body. I guess it would be a surprise whether she made it or not. And, oh, how I loved surprises.

Now... what to do with her?

28
Alex

It was late out. Since Logan, Phoenix, and Ella (sigh) were gone, I had to switch trainers. Hand-to-hand with Falcon, weapons with Maverick, and molding... molding I did by myself. I actually preferred it that way. Logan was a great teacher, but I'd gotten the hang of it enough that it was fairly easy to do without any instruction. It was crazy. The only molds I'd tried were a tiger, a gorilla, and a cheetah. The cheetah was pretty wicked. Today I'd been training – mostly with Maverick; although he seemed out of it ninety-eight percent of the time, he was an amazing fighter. We sparred almost all day long. He'd told me his favorite weapon was a pitchfork. "You can use it as a staff or as three blades," he'd told me proudly. But he hadn't used it against me. He did use a few other weapons though – one of the staffs like Logan's mostly.

They had a freaking arsenal here.

Needless to say, I was exhausted as usual.

Falcon and I walked over the English countryside back toward the underground Terrene. We'd spent the night at a high school party over in one of the neighboring towns. Falcon drank. A lot. But he assured me that it was "hard to get completely hammered because of the chemicals and stuff in our bodies." Yeah, I had to watch out for him.

It'd been an okay party with a bunch of English girls and such, but nothing special. Falcon had an absolute *blast*, though. It made sense. He was stuck in a thirteen-year-old's body forever. He hadn't hit his growth spurt before he was changed, so he was short even for a teenager. It was one of the only places he could really fit in. Well, kind of. I still heard him being called out because of his height. He didn't seem to notice too much, which was good.

On the way there, we ran most of the way – me as a tiger and Falcon as a lynx – but now he was too drunk, so we had to walk. I was concerned even about that, the way he looked.

"How much longer?" he asked. Like I knew.

"I don't know," I said. "We're going the right way, aren't we?"

"I think so," he said.

"Great." He tripped on a hill and fell over. He rolled onto his back and I stopped walking.

"I think I'll just crash here," he said, closing his eyes. I grabbed him in an attempt to get him back up.

"No, let's keep going," I said.

"Come on, Alex, just let me sleep."

"No," I said. Staying out all night didn't seem like a good idea to me. Even going out at all tonight was probably a really, really bad plan.

"Why didn't they choose me to go with my

sister?" he asked, looking up at me from the ground. It was the most thought-out question of the night.

"Uh…" I said, "Why would I know?" Falcon shrugged a little too exaggeratedly.

"I don't know. It's just… every time, it's *always* her."

"Maybe she just wants to protect you," I said, recalling our conversation.

"Well, I wish I got some excitement in my life every once in a while. It's bad enough as it is."

There was a silence between us as Falcon stared up into space.

Then Falcon got up, like something had changed instantly. I didn't see or hear anything of interest. I started walking again and he put a hand in front of me, motioning me to stop.

I squinted into the distance and finally saw the shape – it was of a boy probably around my age. He was shorter than me but taller than Falcon, with a backpack. That's all I could make out.

"Who is it?" I asked in a whisper.

"Spyro," he said, concentrating on the boy. "Where are you goin', kid…" he trailed off.

"Maybe he's just going out to party."

"No," Falcon said, "he's leaving. For good."

"How do you know?" I reasoned. He turned to me.

"I just know," he said with the most terrifyingly seriousness I'd ever heard from him.

"What do we do then?"

"We're gonna follow him," Falcon said as he started walking over the fold of the hill in front of us. He was still a little wobbly. I didn't know what to do.

"Shouldn't we—" I started as I followed him.

"We don't have time. If my hunch is correct, he might lead us right where we need to go."

"Where's that?"

"Macki," he stated. Macki? With just the two of us? Was he crazy? Or was the alcohol really getting to him in some funky way...

I grabbed his shoulder. He turned to me, and I knew just by his face that this was exactly what he was just talking about. Excitement. A chance to do something better than his sister. He wasn't going back to the Terrene tonight. I withdrew my hand from his shoulder, and he continued on at a brisk pace. I followed closely behind. He looked back at me.

"You have the stone, right?" I nodded as I picked it up out of my pocket. "Whoa there, not now. For later." I nodded again and dropped it back in my pocket.

Falcon always carried at least one grenade, so I knew he was at least partially armed. I had a really bad feeling about all of this, but at the same time, I was a little excited. I felt confident enough in my fighting abilities to not be terrified of confrontation now.

We trailed the shadow all the way to the town we were just in, and it was quite a walk. We made sure to stay at a safe distance so we wouldn't be seen (yes, like in all of those ridiculous spy movies). Eventually, we came to a train station. It wasn't very busy at this hour, so Falcon and I had to be especially careful as we got even closer to Spyro. We hid behind the side of the station. A train pulled in, screeching on the tracks. I peeked around the corner and finally got a good view of Spyro.

He was probably five-eight, with dirty blond hair and a super skinny build. He wore a faded brown shirt with a necklace like the one Pilot had. He looked down at his necklace and ripped it apart, throwing it to the ground.

"Damn," Falcon whispered under his breath.

"What?" I asked.

"I was right. He's going to lead us to Macki."

Did I want him to be right? Maybe. But there were all those others who'd left, too, and by this time, Macki could have built up a miniature army. I thought of Frost and Ryker when I first... *encountered* them and imagined what facing tens or even hundreds of them would be like. My optimism fell a few points.

The train's doors opened and a few people filed out. Spyro hopped on one of the back cars. Falcon grabbed my shirt, pulling me with him and shoved me up to the train.

"You're sure about this?" I asked, standing on the steps leading up into the car. All he did was nod. "Okay," I said, trying to muster any remnants of faith I had together. I walked up the stairs and into the car with Falcon practically breathing down my neck. I'd never seen him like this. I didn't know if anybody else had either, but it was kinda freaky. There were a bunch of open seats, and we grabbed up two of them. I sat by the window.

And off we went. Limited weapons. No money. No army. No plan.

I just hoped fate would be on our side.

29

Alex

We watched from across the street as Spyro got his hotel room key for the night. It was light in there and really dark where we were. There weren't any street lights or anything. We were in Spain. Until a while ago, I had barely been out of my own *state*, so being here where they spoke a different language and everything seemed unreal. We'd followed Spyro all the way across the English Channel to France. When we got to France, he'd rented a scooter and made his way all the way to the Spanish-French border. It had been tough to follow him there, and we'd thought we'd lost him completely on multiple occasions, but we always ended up finding him eventually.

The weirdest part was riding with Falcon on a two-seater scooter. Yep. Also considering he was a pretty awful driver. I was sure we were going to hit something or another. After we hit a chicken (that was nowhere near the actual road), I took over the wheel.

When we got to the border, Spyro hopped on a bus that took him all the way here – to Spain. Through all of this, Falcon still seemed like a totally different person. He was focused on following Spyro, and he was going to do it no matter what happened.

When Spyro was finally gone, we gave it a few minutes. After that, we walked across to the hotel. A little bell rang as we entered and Falcon automatically scanned the room to make sure Spyro was gone. He was. I walked up to the front desk.

"Hola," she said. Oh, crap. I should have paid attention in Spanish class. We were in a tiny, quaint, town guarded by giant hills, so my hope of people speaking English was quickly squashed. *"¿Qué necesitas?"*

I stood there like a complete idiot. Falcon came up next to me and leaned against the counter.

"Necesitamos dos cuartos para esta noche," he told her. I nodded. Considering that's all I could do. They exchanged some more phrases in Spanish and finally Falcon pulled a wallet out of his pocket. I looked at him, confused.

"How did you get that?" I whispered, turning my head so that the woman didn't hear.

"Lazy people on the train," he said nonchalantly as he pulled out some Euros. He handed them to the lady and she gave him two keys in return. He waved one key in my face and dropped it into my hand. We headed toward the stairs at the other end of the room.

"Here's the plan," he said. "I asked her to give me a room facing the street so one of us will keep watch until Spyro leaves. You know how Shufflers are with their sleeping habits – or lack of them – so we have to stay really alert, okay?"

"Why'd you get two rooms then?" Falcon blushed.

"I didn't want her to think… I mean…"

"That we're gay?"

"Yeah, that." It was strange that that seemed to bother him so much. I figured he wouldn't care what humans thought. I was already starting to lose sensitivity to things like that. The stairs creaked as we walked up them, taking three or four at a time. Once we got to the top of the stairs, there was a long, carpeted hallway. Falcon went to the first room and unlocked the door. The place seemed ancient. But in the cool way, not the creepy way.

We walked into the room, and it was pretty small. The twin bed barely fit between its walls, which were covered in dark, peeling, flowery wallpaper. Two wood panels covered the window facing the street. I pulled them apart, and was happy to see that we got a clear view of the front door. Falcon flopped onto the bed.

"You tired?" I asked him.

"Nope," he said, "I've never felt more awake."

I thought for a moment.

"Say we find Macki and all of her minions or whatever. Who do you want to kill first?" I had a hunch he wouldn't say Macki. There was one name I'd heard him bring up a lot as being some big bully – Ryker. He seemed to have kindled quite the hate fire, although he never talked about him when Quinn was around.

"Ryker," he said, confirming my theory. I stayed silent, waiting for him to continue. "He's the one that always used to tease me. Real asshole he is."

"Why don't you talk about him when Quinn's around?"

"Quinn's his older brother. He tried to be a babysitter for Ryker – when he was at the Terrene –

199

but obviously that didn't even work out. He's always so optimistic that Ryker will 'change' and all of that bull. Reality is that Ryker's always followed Macki and always will. He'll always be an evil meathead, too."

I sat on the edge of the bed, keeping my eyes trained mostly on the street below. Spyro just got here, but, hey, you never knew. Falcon sat up.

"I'll take first watch," he said. Even though we'd been chasing Spyro for over twenty-four hours straight, I didn't feel tired or exhausted like I had when I was training. I felt ready to go. Ready to fight.

"I don't think I'll be able to sleep anyway," I said. He looked at me.

"Then stay up." I glared at him.

"Really? How logical."

"Hey, your stupidity left me no choice." I laughed and he smiled. That was the Falcon I knew. We both sat there looking out the window for a moment.

"So tell me more about this Ryker dude."

"Ryker. Hm. Well, he has the best mold of all of us." I remembered. Of course I did. His mold was some random hot lady. But if you really think about it, what good would it do against, say, my tiger? Not much.

"I guess that's true," I said.

"He's not the strongest fighter, though. Not very quick on his feet. I beat him a lot when we sparred, but he was pretty unfair. I remember one time specifically, it was me against him, Bull, and Humvee."

"What happened?" If I dared to ask...

He looked right at me with an embarrassed look on his face.

"I woke up hanging upside down naked in the cafeteria."

"Ooh," I said. That sucked. Major.

"Everyone came in for breakfast and there I

was. I had no way to get down, so until someone actually cared enough to help me, I was left there for the whole Terrene to see."

"Who helped you down?"

"Jess."

"My dad?"

"Yes."

Sometimes I still forgot my dad was anything... special – a Shuffler in the Core. He just seemed so... so distant still.

"Phoenix wasn't at the Terrene that day," he continued, "but she did have quite the talk with Ryker. Like that did anything. God, I hope she's okay." He looked away from the window and took a deep breath.

"I'm sure she is. Have you seen her fight?"

"Way too many times. It really does get old after a while."

"Hm," was all I said.

"You ever had a real girlfriend?" he asked me. I guess it was time for questions. I didn't mind. It was going to be a long night anyway. I scooted farther onto the bed and sat against the wall.

"I did, yeah," I said, thinking of Kaley once again.

"Was it... was it as nice as it sounds?"

"For me, it was. She was one of my best friends."

Falcon looked down and started swinging his foot back and forth.

"Sometimes I wish I was normal," he said to my surprise. I thought he loved being a Shuffler. It sure seemed like it. "Just to... to try it. See how everything would turn out. Stay in one place with a wife and kids and stuff. It just seems so simple."

"Compared to this, it is."

"Yeah. At least you got sixteen years of it. After

a while, it'll all fade together. You'll get your stories mixed up. You won't know what year it is. You'll lose count of your age. That's how it works. You should grow to be in your twenties, though – appearance age I mean. That'll be good."

"Is that when Asime stopped growing?" He nodded. "Did you know him?"

"No. None of us did. Well, that's not true. Your parents, Macki, Logan, and Zahra did."

"Logan did?"

"It's a long story."

"I see." There was another silence.

"Hey, Alex," Falcon said, suddenly perking up.

"Yeah?"

"There's one thing I don't get about humans."

"What is it?"

"How do they forget?"

"Forget what?"

"Their lives. Things that happen. That sort of thing."

"Oh, uh… eventually you just have to suck it up and keep going. Why?"

"We all have issues with letting things go. There's so much… pain among us. That's the one thing I really hate. Shufflers can't let go of their pasts. And it hurts. It seems like Macki used us all for a reason. I just haven't figured out what it is yet."

"Maybe she thought it'd be easier to control you."

"Maybe. But she seemed… so nice about it when Phoenix and I changed. It just makes me wonder…" I looked down, thinking about that a little bit. Were we all here for a reason? Was this all Macki's plan? I couldn't even think about it much or my brain was going to explode. "I guess we'll see."

"Yeah," I said.

Not that I was particularly ecstatic to see what Macki had in store for us.

30
Macki

The white-hot sun stared down at me, making the air hanging around me feel like an oven. I kept my head down, staring at the wisps of sand skating around as I trudged over the cracked, dry ground of the Moroccan desert. I regretted not picking up a dune buggy or a… or a camel or something. Wow, I really sucked at finding any sort of useful transportation. Any human would have keeled over hours ago. Finally… finally! I saw some tents in the distance.

I ran, molded, and ran some more. They'd made it to the camp. I was so happy to share the news about Zahra. Once I reached the first open pea-green tent, I molded back and walked the last few feet toward it… when Frost stood in front of it, her Uzi in hand. Her hair was black with all kinds of vibrantly colored streaks.

"What's your business?" she asked. The rake from Zahra was still healing across my face, and I was actually wearing sunglasses. Not to mention the cloth I had over my mouth and nose to protect it from the sand. My hair was wrapped into a short, black braid. Oh... yeah, I didn't look like myself.

"Move, dimwit," I snapped as I tried to push past her to the shade of the tent. Ahh, I was so close. She stepped in front of me, pointing the Uzi right at my chest. I smiled. Everybody, I give you Frost. I made it my own personal game to get past her without getting shot in the face or revealing who I really was. Test the security a bit. She poked me with the barrel.

"What's your business?" she insisted.

"I'm looking for Macki," I said, getting all giddy inside.

"Who are you?" she asked. Not nicely.

"Someone," was all I could come up with.

"Hey, Ryk!" she yelled over her shoulder. That was the perfect opportunity to shove the gun offline and kick Frost hard in the chest. She fell backward, the wind definitely getting knocked out of her. Before she could raise her gun again, I stepped on her wrist and pried it out from her grip. I took out the ammo and dropped it to the ground.

"Really? That's all yah got?" I asked. She looked up at me, shocked. She tried to move, but I put more weight onto her wrist and she squirmed in pain. I heard more feet coming toward us. Ryker and a team of five of my Shufflers came around a tent, all armed, of course, with their weapons of choice.

"Ryker, help," Frost cried – a little too sensitively for my taste.

"Get off of her," he said as he revved up his chainsaw. I stepped off.

"I don't want any trouble," I said with my hands up passively. Frost scrambled to get up. I kicked her Uzi farther out of the way. Then, I started laughing. Like *legitimately* laughing. I doubled over, putting my hands on my knees. My stomach started to hurt from cracking up so much. Apparently no one else thought it was funny as they approached me slowly.

I looked up once again, some tears falling down my face in pure hilariousness.

"You guys…" I squeaked out. They looked at each other so uncomfortably confusedly that I wanted to just slap all of them like fifteen thousand times. "That *sucked*," I said as I pulled down the cloth covering my mouth and nose.

"Jesus Christ, Macki," Frost said, agitated. I took off my sunglasses and stepped under the tent and out of the sun. My body instantly felt rejuvenated. I threw my neck back gently and it cracked. Then I looked at everyone.

"We could have killed you," Ryker said, embarrassed. The others dispersed back into camp.

"There's no *way* you could after that little demonstration."

Ryker's cheeks grew pink. Ryker and Frost both walked under the tent with me. Ryker turned off his chainsaw and dropped it to the ground with a thud. I wiped my glasses clean on my shorts then hung them on my shirt.

"Well… hi," Frost said sheepishly.

"Hi," I said as I folded my arms. I swayed back and forth a little bit, transferring the weight from foot to foot. Even that little bit of fighting got me amped.

"How's camp been?" I asked.

"Pretty boring," Ryker said honestly. I nodded.

"I can see how that could happen," I agreed.

"How was… you know… fighting to the

death?" he asked with a smirk.

"It was fun," I said.

"Is Zahra dead?" Frost cut in.

"That's for me to know," I said cryptically.

"You should have brought her back," Ryker said. I looked at him curiously.

"Why?" I asked with a slight smile. I had an idea of what he would probably say...

"So I could cut her up into tiny little bitch pieces," he said with a proud grin. I started pacing. I felt really anxious... uh-oh.

"Ah. I see. That definitely would have been more fun," I said and looked down. I was getting really antsy. "Well, we'll have a talk about security later. I have to go... do something," I said as I walked off. My thoughts started racing as I stumbled across camp, shoving a few Shufflers out of the way as I went along. I twisted my way through the rows of tents until I was at the other end of camp. I looked out over the desert. With a moment's hesitation, I took off running. I hated this feeling. I had to mold. I had to. I ran up to my maximum speed then segued into a round-off back-handspring. When I landed back on the ground, I was my favorite four-legged creature.

I ran around aimlessly. I felt the need to attack, but there was nothing around, so I clawed at thin air.

"What are you doing, M?" I heard from behind me. I swiveled around. I didn't respond. Obviously. I was a tiger.

I looked over at him. He had his arms crossed. I shook out my head and roared as loud as I could. Finally, I started running again then flipped, landing back as my other self. My thoughts quieted down. The jitters were gone. I felt better.

"You know how I get," I told him.

"Macki... why would you... why would you do

that to my sister?" he asked with a waver in his voice. I looked at him. I actually thought about what I'd done to Zahra again. It seemed too easy, but was she really gone? Like… for good?

"Asime—" I began.

"After everything. After changing her because you felt so awful about me. Weren't you supposed to protect her? Protect my little sister for me? What happened to that?" I just looked into his eyes. They seemed dead. That made my heart sink a little bit. If I'd ever loved anyone, it had been him. I couldn't sleep now either. Not because of nightmares… but memories. Good memories. I missed them so much sometimes I wanted to just rip my own heart out. God, I sounded pathetic…

"She betrayed me," I said.

"Because you gave her a good reason."

"What? Are you joking? I told her you never left and she used it to condemn me as mad. I told her I had trouble not molding sometimes and she called me rogue. I told her I killed you and she… she called me a murderer. That's the truth," I told him.

He looked at me, trying to find the truth in my eyes. Then, he put his head in his hands and exhaled.

"What?" I asked him. "Can't handle the fact that your little sister lied about me and got me thrown in a cell for twenty years? Huh?"

"M," he said. We were inches from each other. I looked up at him. He took my hands. God, why did he do that? He smiled. "I love you," he said. He opened his mouth to say something else, but then he stopped. I wiped a tear from my face quickly, hoping he wouldn't see it. "No, don't cry."

"I miss you," I said, not completely believing what I was saying. It just came out. Bleck.

"I haven't heard you say that for quite some

time," he said.

"That's because I try not to think about it. No help from you." He laughed.

"I see how it is." I pushed him away. "Whoa there."

"You're dead," I told him.

"I'm aware of that."

"You shouldn't be doing this to me. It's torture."

"Doing what?"

"Being here," I said. "You shouldn't be here because you make me want to… you make me want to… just shrivel up and die because I can't take it anymore."

"Me being away?"

"You being dead. Yes. Exactly. Obviously we can't be together."

"Yes, we can-"

"No. Go away," I said getting suddenly angry. "You're a glitch – a screw-up. I never should have taken the formula before I knew what the unfortunate side effects would be.

"Why do we always go through the same thing?" I didn't answer. I just shut up.

"Silent game?" he finally asked. I nodded and headed back toward camp.

"Mackinley!" he yelled at me.

"What!?" I yelled as loud as I could back at him.

"I know what you're doing," he said. I stared at him.

"Good," I said as I stormed off.

Excuse my mood. I did have feelings every once in a while, and it usually didn't work out very well.

31
Alex

The darkness seemed endless. Out in the middle of the desert, there weren't many places to hide, so we followed directly behind Spyro. It was fairly cold out, actually. I'd heard that was what happened in a lot of deserts, just hadn't experienced it. We'd crossed over from Europe to northern Africa – Morocco, specifically. I was starting to get more and more anxious. We had to be getting close.

The shadow of Spyro led us on. Wait. I looked over at Falcon. He grabbed my arm and pulled me down to the ground.

There were more shadows approaching – three more. Only two looked human. The last one was a wolf. Spyro stopped moving, waiting for them. They held a torch that illuminated their faces. Two were in dark clothing, and the third was in a fiery red shirt. The wolf molded into a girl with a tan complexion and dark features. She looked rough. One of the boys standing in the pair was Asian and probably in his late teens. His eyes were like nothing I'd ever seen − bright yellow and shaped like a cat's. He sure seemed like he was the one in charge.

"Once you join Macki's army, you're hers forever. Are you sure this is what you want? Are you willing to die for our leader?" the boy asked. Spyro nodded hesitantly. I could see the fear in his eyes.

"You're sure, Spyro?" the girl asked the boy. He nodded again, more confidently this time. The third boy − a redhead − had blood red eyes. He looked like what I would imagine a vampire or demon to look like. Legitimately.

"Exodus, put out the torch," the cat-eyed boy commanded. Exodus − the girl − dropped the torch and stomped the flames out. Now we were in complete darkness once again.

"There really were more at the Terrene," Falcon said to himself unknowingly, mesmerized by the scene playing out in front of him. Exodus's head swung around, hearing Falcon.

"Lucifer, Valkyrie, there's someone over there," she alerted the boys, pointing toward us.

"What do we do?" I asked Falcon, panicked.

"Run," was all he said as he got up and sprinted farther into the desert. I followed him. I looked back and saw that a black wolf and a Great Dane were chasing us.

"Split up, don't let them catch you. Kill them if you must," Falcon said. He took a hard right, and myself a hard left, running in opposite directions. I wasn't sure if it was the right decision to split up already, but Falcon was much more experienced than I was, so I listened to him. *Kill them if you must* rang in my head. Could I really kill someone?

I didn't have time to worry about it. I was breathing hard, sprinting as fast as I could. The wolf was catching up to me, so I jumped, landing as a horse. After a few moments, I heard an explosion – it must have been one of Falcon's grenades. I hoped he was okay. He carried specialized, high-powered grenades that could easily blow a Shuffler into a thousand tiny bits.

I decided to mold back into myself and turn to fight Exodus. I ran a few more steps in my human form then turned, bringing a black sword around to face the wolf. The wolf stopped as fast as it could, backpedaling so it didn't run into my blade. It flipped backward nimbly into Exodus. She pulled a black composite bat out of a sling on her back and flipped it in her hands, preparing to rip me to pieces. She attacked, swinging her bat with amazing speed, but nothing I couldn't handle. In a matter of seconds, I flipped her over and she was lying on the ground. I was glad to see Falcon run up.

"Do I kill her?" I asked, staring at the girl on the ground.

"Yes," he said. I'd always thought of Falcon as a loose cannon and had never imagined him in a situation like this – directing me to kill a Shuffler. I gulped. Could I?

"I don't think—" I began, finding myself unable to pull the trigger. All of a sudden, I saw Valkyrie's yellow eyes bouncing in the darkness, his long katana to my throat.

"Falcon, you move, he dies," Valkyrie explained simply. Falcon stopped immediately, hands by his sides.

"I think Macki would be quite disappointed if she didn't get to kill you herself," Valkyrie said to me. Exodus hopped up, positioning her bat so she could swing it at Falcon's head. I didn't see any shame in her expression.

"Put your hands up, jackass," she ordered Falcon. He pulled his hands up slowly.

"You, too," Valkyrie added, motioning toward me. I complied, following Falcon's lead, unsure if he had a plan or not. I sure didn't. "And drop the stone."

I looked at Falcon for support again before I dropped it. He shrugged, revealing to me that he had no plan. I dropped the stone. Valkyrie kicked it away. I guess he didn't know much about it.

"Good. Now get up," he dictated. I got up slowly, not wanting to provoke the blade. "Exodus, kill the runt." Exodus smiled.

"My pleasure," she replied. She cocked the bat back... I had to do something. In one, swift movement, I hit Valkyrie's wrist and felt bones crack. The katana dropped. I kicked Valkyrie hard before shoving Falcon out of the way of the bat and catching it mid-swing. I put my hand out, willing the stone to come to me, and it flew to me. I swung at Exodus with a newly formed staff and it connected, sending her to the ground unconscious.

I saw Falcon turn just as an arrow soared past his face. Like guns, arrows only worked on Shufflers at point-blank range. Spyro stood with a bow, but he wasn't close enough to do any damage. I wondered why he even shot it. He dropped the bow and ran.

I turned my attention to Valkyrie, who crawled backward as I approached. I turned the stone to a spear in my hand. I hesitated. I had to kill him. I *had* to. I closed my eyes and threw my spear squarely at Valkyrie's chest. I didn't want to see it sink through his flesh. I opened my eyes, and (to my horror) the spear was going right through his heart. I couldn't believe I'd done it.

I knelt next to him as he died and pulled out my spear, his insides making a very unpleasant noise as I did so.

"Macki will win, Mono," were his last words. They exuded a lot of confidence for a dying boy. I watched as his eyes turned a shade darker in his unmoving body. His eyes were bugging me – they were still open. I turned away, unable to look at him anymore. Falcon held Spyro by his collar behind me. The boy was shuddering under Falcon's intense grasp.

"What do you think you're doing? Huh?" he asked.

"I... I didn't want to. Macki threatened me, I swear," Spyro uttered, trying to make himself sound as innocent as possible.

"We'll see what the Core has to say about this," Falcon spat at him. He shoved Spyro to the ground.

"Whoa there," I said. Hm, I wondered... "Falcon, we could use him."

"What?" he asked as I walked closer toward him, still trying to shake the image of Valkyrie out of my head.

"He can spy for us."

Spyro got up from the ground slowly, looking at us with wide blue eyes.

"He'll go and tattle. Maybe we should just kill him."

"No, no, no," Spyro said in a shaking voice, "I'll help you. I will."

"Why would we trust you?"

"I'll do anything you ask. I just don't want to get hurt," he said. Wow, what a wimp. Falcon looked at him, contemplating.

"Fine," Falcon said as he kicked up some sand. "Do you know how to get to wherever we're going?"

"Yes," Spyro said. "I can lead you there if you

want."

"All right," Falcon said, "And we can also have ourselves a wonderful little chat about loyalty and dignity, hm?" Spyro nodded.

"What about Exodus?" I asked Falcon. He looked to the ground.

"You guys go on ahead. I'll catch up with you."

"What are you going to do with her?"

"I'm going to kill her, goddammit," he said angrily.

"Oh," I said. "Okay, let's go, Spyro." I didn't want to be around for that. We walked away. And the thought really sunk in…

I just killed someone.

32

Macki

I looked out at the desert. Behind me, I heard loud, booming music, shouts, and the bustle of feet shuffling around. It was party time around here. And me? I was being a stick in the mud. After my conversation with Asime today, I was still... I hated to admit it, but I was pretty upset. How could I be so vulnerable? I wasn't *vulnerable*. I didn't *love* anything or anyone. I *never* needed him. All of my walls had crumbled around me earlier. When I finally realized what I was doing, he'd already gotten me to say that I missed him. Bastard.

I sat back in my chair, leaning it against a support post. I crossed my ankles and told myself to shut off my brain. It was time to celebrate. Zahra was finally gone. My formula was nearly complete. Finally.

I put my head down and looked at the sand skating around my feet. I heard footsteps, but didn't care to look up. It was probably just "security" roaming around. I had to keep a few people sober, didn't I?

The footsteps slowed to a stop. I realized that they weren't normal footsteps. They were quieter, softer. My heart sped up in excitement.

"Been a while," a voice said. I looked up with a smile on my face.

Ella.

Her lavender eyes were so colorful compared to the dark void behind her. They were the perfect purple. Not too dark, but not so light that they looked like they belonged on an Easter egg. I chuckled and uncrossed my feet.

"It has," I said. "I almost thought you weren't coming." She glared at me.

"Of course I came. Why would I go anywhere else?"

"You make a pit stop then?"

"Yeah. I went the long way."

"Let me guess," I said. "Russia?" She nodded with a bashful look on her face. I got up, one of my knees cracking as I did. "Here, I'll show you around."

I brushed past her toward my tent. I walked through the rows until we got to the center of camp. There was a whole crowd of Shufflers jumping up and down, dancing, going completely crazy. Pretty much everyone had some sort of alcohol in hand. I spotted Ryker in the very middle of everyone with a bottle of something raised above him.

We walked around the group. Someone stumbled and fell right in front of me. I didn't bother giving him a hand up and hopped over him.

The music was interesting. All of that "electronic" stuff or whatever. I led Ella all the way around to the other side of camp where my own tent was. I lifted open the flap and held it for her. She ducked in and I walked in right behind her. I closed the tent flap. Unfortunately, it didn't keep out that horrid music.

My tent was just how I'd left it earlier. It was larger than the others, of course. Frost had set up a table on one side for all of my papers and lab stuff. How thoughtful. My bed was in the corner, the mattress lying on the ground because I hated that space between bed frames and the ground. It just gave me the creeps. Don't judge.

I didn't realize that asking them to drag everything into the middle of the desert would be such a chore. I'd given everyone the coordinates, so they'd know where to rendezvous and most of them had found their way. I still hadn't seen Valkyrie, Exodus, Lucifer, or that one kid... whatever his name was. He was a weak addition, but I figured I could get him to serve some purpose. It was one less Shuffler that Phoenix (who I assumed was the leader) didn't have. Hell, maybe I could get all of my Shufflers back. Hm. Never thought about that. Except for Phoenix and Falcon and... well... the rest of the Core. Never mind. Bad plan.

Ella ran a finger over my papers in the corner, skimming over them.

"I don't understand," she said. She picked up a piece of paper.

"What?" I asked. She looked at it curiously. I leaned against the table. She turned it toward me.

"I thought you hated your symbol now," she said as she turned the paper toward me. It was a page completely covered in my symbol.

"Nah. I figured I already have a tattoo of it, so why not embrace it?"

"I see," she said as she put it down. "When do I get one?" I laughed.

"You should be glad that I didn't let you get one last time you asked."

"Hey. That was the first and only time I've ever gotten drunk. Give me a break," she said.

"But you were hilarious."

"I'm sure I was. Considering I don't remember it." There was a silence as we both thought about that night. She opened her mouth to say something. Then shut it.

"What were you going to say?" I asked smugly.

"What do you mean?"

"Right now. You were going to say something." She blushed.

"Fine," she conceded. "I was going to ask if you remembered Mexico City."

"Uh… kind of. Why?" I asked. I had only a few sparse memories of the event. "Wait, that's the time you dragged me out of the Gulf because I'd passed out there, wasn't it?"

"Yeah. Is that all you remember?"

"Uh, yeah. I think so. I was super drunk." I paused, really thinking about it. "Wait…" I said, some pieces beginning to come back to me. I shrugged. "We made out. That was nice. Why do you mention it?" I smirked.

"I uh… I just…" she stammered. I noticed that she was shaking ever so slightly.

"You liked it, too, didn't you?"

"I was just thinking… you know… I didn't want to mess with you and Asime."

Was this really happening? Could all of my emotional barriers come down twice in one day? I contemplated. I really did. If I took her hint and… and we like… became a "thing," I'd be vulnerable again. I couldn't do that, could I? I could just brush it off...

"Shh," I told her, putting a finger silently to my smiling lips. Then silence.

"What?" she asked.

"He doesn't need to know. Or he can, I really don't care." I sat down on the bed with my arms out. "Come here, sweetheart. Let me tell you a story."

She started shaking more. Like a Chihuahua. I knew how sensitive she was. And how much she put on herself. She had issues with shame. Sometimes just saying "hi" to her could make her panic. It must have taken nothing short of a leap of faith and a damn good dose of courage to get her to tell me what she had. I'd take it from there.

She sat down next to me and I put my arm around her shoulders.

"There's a girl," I began, "that loves two people, hm? A beautiful, strong, wonderful girl. Any guesses who that is?" She hesitated before she responded.

"Me?"

"Yes," I said. My smirk didn't fade. "You love Alex... and you love me, hm?"

"Yes," she confirmed. "How did you know that?"

"That's a story for a different time," I said. "Let me tell you something." I looked her right in the eye, my lips centimeters from hers. "I'm going to blow that idiot out of the water." I let my words hang in the air for just a moment before I pressed my lips to hers. She slid over the bed until she was sitting backward on my lap and undid my crappy remnants of a braid.

"I need to ask you something," she said as she finished fumbling with my braid.

"Anything," I said.

"Why didn't you tell me to leave?"

"I've always protected you. I always will."

"Zahra nearly killed me. Alex saved me."

"Do you know why Alex just happened to be walking down that hallway?"

"No."

"It's because Cheshire told him to."

"You planned it. You... you saved me." I nodded.

I felt her fingers run through my hair as we started kissing again. I put my hand on her hip and trailed her shirt up her side...

And let me say something.

I was *ecstatic*.

I felt that rush, you know, that I never thought I'd ever feel again. Screw my emotions. Screw my walls. I had to stop and live every once in a while. And this was a good start. It felt so right. So natural. So... beautiful. *Beauty*. Something I had forsaken for many, many years.

Not anymore.

33
Alex

If I had to imagine what Macki's Shufflers were doing, I would have guessed training or something of that nature. But when we arrived at the outskirts of their camp, I quickly realized that they were, well, partying. In the middle of the desert. Curious. Anyway, we'd sent Spyro to go into camp and tell us where everyone was – meaning if there was any security and where Macki was. He walked back toward us, checking over his shoulder for any followers. Falcon had also picked up Valkyrie's katana, so he swung it around a little bit, getting a feel for it. Not gonna lie, it made me a little nervous.

"So?" Falcon said.

"There is security. About four or five guys walking around camp," Spyro reported.

"Are they armed?"

"Yes."

"Damn."

"What about Macki?" I asked.

"I believe she's in her tent. I didn't see her anywhere around camp," Spyro said. "She's with Ella, too."

"Ella's with her?" I asked.

"Of course she is, dimwit. I told you all along," Falcon sneered in overconfidence. I looked down, not wanting to meet Falcon's merciless glare. "Oh, boo-hoo," he added unsympathetically. "What about Karen and Jesse?

"Ah," Spyro said, "they're on this side of camp. I didn't look inside the tent though. There's a guard right outside it."

"Who's the guard?"

"Bull," he said. Awesome. Falcon kicked at some sand, thinking.

"Either we cut a hole in the tent and go behind or we distract Bull. Any preference?"

"The first one," I said immediately. That sounded like a much better plan.

"Okay. Spyro, you can come keep watch for us," Falcon said.

"I don't know," he said. "What if we get caught?" Falcon glared at him.

"Then we're screwed," Falcon said bluntly as he set off toward the camp. I had to jog to catch up. Spyro was next to me. Once we got closer to the camp, we ran in a more crouched position. Falcon slowed down and let Spyro take the lead. If we found my parents... this would be the first time I'd see them in six years. And even then, I didn't remember them that well. Finally, we walked around the back of a tent. It was tan and fairly tall. My heart started beating faster both in anxiety and adrenaline.

Falcon lifted up the katana and raised it above him. He made a long cut down through the material. Spyro looked around nervously.

"We're gonna get caught," Spyro whispered.

"Shut up," Falcon snapped back at him as he stepped through the hole. A light bulb in the middle of the tent flickered, making the sides of the tent dark. Immediately, I saw two shapes in medium-sized cages. They were lying on the ground. One was a woman with light brown hair and light yellow eyes. The other one – a man – that was across the room had short hair and green eyes.

There was only one problem.

They looked like they'd been beaten to death. Blood was splattered all over. Their wrists were bound tightly behind their backs as well as their feet. The cages had extremely thick bars and the biggest locks I'd ever seen. But, through all of that, I recognized them as my parents.

"Shit," Falcon said a little louder than he should have. He raced over toward Jesse and knelt next to the cage. "Jesse," he whispered forcefully, "you okay?" My dad coughed and turned over. My heart sunk to my feet. He looked terrible. I felt like throwing up.

"Falcon?" he asked through an obvious haze.

"Yeah, yeah," Falcon said as he reached a hand through and touched Jesse's shoulder. Jesse recoiled at first then relaxed.

"You shouldn't… be here," he said weakly. I stood there, petrified. I looked over and saw my mom starting to stir. I forced myself to make my legs move. I had to go see how she was. I had to. I made my way over toward her and crouched so I was at her level.

"Mom," I squeaked out.

"Alex. Go," she said. "She wants you."

"What? What do you mean?" I asked,

perplexed.

"Go," she commanded. I turned back to Falcon and Jesse.

"Do you know their plan?" Falcon asked my dad.

"Protect Alex," he said. A chill ran through me.

"We need to get them out of here," I told Falcon.

"No," Karen said. "Leave," she insisted once again.

"Merry Christmas," Spyro said, peeking in. What?

"What? Is that code for something?" Falcon asked. Spyro jumped in through the hole.

"Yep. Someone's coming," he clarified.

"Dammit," Falcon said as he sprung up. I was up within a second too. "Hide." We all looked around for a spot. All at the same time, we ran over to the darkest corner of the tent. I heard someone open the flap and march in.

"Oh. Well that's no fun," I heard a young, female voice say. The three of us were frozen. Falcon mouthed a word to me... Mac... Marker... *Macki*. Jesus Christ.

"What?" my mom spat at her.

"You're still here," she said. "I thought you'd have thought up some insane plan to escape. No? God, you look awful." There was a bang on one of the cages. "You know what..." she began, "something seems off." I heard her walk toward us. What would I do if she saw us? Run? Fight? I told myself to make a decision because it seemed inevitable...

When she stopped.

"How about we get you out and have some fun?" Macki said.

Okay. Now I was seriously ticked. More than

I'd ever been in my life. Did I mean anything to Ella? And what about this, this Macki character? And my parents. They were locked up here and obviously tortured. I had every reason to just go after Macki now and shut down any plans she even had. I could just rip her throat out. I was strong enough, right? *Right?*

I fell forward a little bit. I was going. Like now. But Falcon grabbed me and shoved me back. He shook his head. Then he put a finger to his lips, motioning me to shut up. Well you know what, Falcon, you can just go and shove your own...

Finally, I stopped. It was useless. Who was I kidding? Finally, I heard Macki and Ella walk out, the tent flap closing behind them. I was going to be sick. Seriously. We stumbled back into the center of the room.

"God, that was close," Spyro said as he exhaled. Apparently he'd been holding his breath the whole time. He looked almost blue. I still had fists made.

"Merry Christmas?" Falcon said.

"It was the first thing that came to mind," Spyro said simply. Falcon glared at him.

"Never mind," he said as he put his palm to his face. Jesse was now sitting up against the edge of the tent. He looked a little more alert. Karen still looked the same.

"That was a close one, guys," Jesse said. He coughed again.

"How do we get you out of here?" Falcon asked.

"It's no use," he said.

"What? What do you mean?" I said.

"Alex," he said, staring at me, "you need to listen to me. Get out of here and don't come back."

"We can't just leave you," I said.

"You have to. We'll be okay," he tried to

reassure me.

"No," I said firmly.

"Alexander Gabriel Keefe, I need you to listen to me right now. Go."

"But… but…" I began.

"Go," he insisted.

"We better go, dude," Falcon said.

"Why are you siding with him?" I snapped.

"Because he knows what he's doing." Falcon grabbed my shoulder and led me toward the hole in the tent. Spyro jumped out in front of us.

All of a sudden, I spun around with a fist aimed at Falcon's face. He put up a hand and caught it.

"Don't fight with me now," Falcon said. "Bad plan." He shoved my fist down.

"Fine," I said reluctantly.

"Bye, Jess," Falcon said. He saluted him. Jesse smiled oh-so-little.

"Bye… Dad," I said, unsure of what to call him. I happened to catch a tear fall down his face. I felt like I was betraying him. But there was nothing I could do. We walked out of the hole in the tent and back into the desert.

I was not going to disappoint them.

I wasn't going to let their suffering be for nothing.

I was going to fight.

34
Macki

It was still hot as hell. That didn't change. I sat in my tent, my sash of throwing knives set out in front of me. I slid one out of its holder and studied it. I got a little lost in it… thinking… Damn. I almost forgot I had stuff to do. Karen and Jesse sat across from me, both bound to chairs and gagged. They looked a little bit better than they did the other night. I'd sent Frost to hose them down this morning. Jesse's lip probably had the biggest gash.

"So…" I began, "which one of you is going to tell me who was here?" I looked back and forth between them. Karen had her head down.

Jesse squirmed a little bit. With a swipe of my knife, I cut his gag off.

"We don't know," Jesse said, spitting out a wad

of spit-soaked cloth.

"Oh, please. Spare me the bull, would you?" Jesse looked over at his wife with concern.

"Why," he began, "why would you do this to us? We're not your enemies."

"How my times do I have to tell you, you insufferable creature, that I am not your friend?"

His lip quivered. "You're a monster," he said. "A wonderful, pleasant, moral person degraded into a shell. That's what you are." He stared at me, not letting his gaze falter.

Okay, I had to admit, that did hurt a *little* bit. Just a little, though.

"You know what…" I started, my knife swinging expertly around my fingers. "Maybe I will just kill you both." I contemplated. I very well could. Alex and the others wouldn't know it, so they'd think there was still something at stake. Hm. I reached forward and lifted up Karen's chin so she was looking at me.

"Get your hands off my wife," Jesse spat at me.

"You don't like that?" I asked with a smile.

"No, you creep," Jesse said.

"You like this?" I said as I held my cold blade sideways and put it up by Karen's face. I started lightly tracing her features with it.

"What do you want?" he asked urgently.

"I want names."

"Fine," he said. "Just put your knives away. I'll help you."

"I don't need help. It's strictly extraneous input." Jesse looked to the side and thought, trying to get his game plan figured out. I sat back in my chair and crossed my legs. "Take your time," I said. "I have nowhere to be."

"Please, Macki. Let's be civil about this."

I stood up. "Civil? *Civil?*" I pointed a finger at

him. "Do you think throwing me in a hole for twenty years for doing absolutely *nothing* wrong was civil? Sorry, I just want to return the favor." I started pacing, my hands folded behind my back.

"That was wrong," he said. Wait, did he really just admit it?

"What?" I said in disbelief.

"It was wrong of us."

"Are you seriously telling me this now?"

"Yes. Look, Macki, we were scared. We took precautionary measures, but obviously it was too premature." I looked at him, my jaw hanging in shock. Karen nodded her head a little bit, but kept her eyes trained on the ground.

"Now. Do you really mean that or do you just want me to leave you alone?"

"I really mean it," he said immediately. A little too quickly. I could see right through it. Obviously. I sat back down. I did wish someone understood. I could get any member of the Core to admit what they did was unjust, but probably none of them this easily.

"Names," I said, getting back to the point. He looked away before he opened his mouth to speak.

"Falcon," he said, his green eyes blinking. "Falcon and Pilot." I sighed.

"Okay, we can do this the hard way."

"What? I told you the names," he told me. Yeah, right.

"I found a cut in the tent. Neither of those two carry any type of blade."

He looked at me, planning his next words carefully. "They stole it," Jesse said.

"From who?"

"Valkyrie."

"Why would they get it from Valkyrie?"

"They killed him." I sat back once again. The

logic was there.

"That's why he's not here? He's busy being dead?" He nodded. "What about Exodus and Lucifer?"

"I'd have to conclude that they're dead as well. They're not here... are they?"

"No," I said. "Good lord." I thought again. Falcon and Pilot? Plausible. But... not the truth. I swung my knife around and put it next to Karen's lips once again. It was going to be like carving a pumpkin. I would make delicate, slow, precise cuts until I was satisfied with how she looked, which would probably take a while. I smiled.

Karen finally looked up at me, defiance in her light yellow eyes.

When her fist came around and hit me in the face. It took me a second to recover, which was just enough time for her to grab one of my knives and bring it in front of her defensively. I didn't have time to think about how she did it, but I was pretty impressed.

She came at me with expert speed and precision. I dodged the first time. Ducked the second time. The third time, I dodged, then grabbed her arm. I jerked it toward me and she fell over the chair. I kicked the chair as hard as I could and she went flying backward, crashing over my mattress. The knife fell out of her hand. I grabbed two more of my knives. I threw one and she barely rolled out of the way in time. I threw a second one, and it met the skin of her leg. I held the third one. She groaned in pain as she tried to get up.

I walked over to her past the shreds of the chair and picked her up by her shoulders. I threw her across the room and she snapped my table in half, falling through it and tumbling through the fabric of the tent. Damn. I'd have to get a new one later. I followed her out, not getting my speed up over a leisurely walk. I knew she'd be down for a while. I peeked my head through the wall and saw her lying there helplessly. Ryker had been keeping watch (despite his quite nasty hangover) and stared at Karen with wide eyes.

"Just having a nice chat," I said. "Why don't you take her back to her cage? She's been quite naughty," I told him. He just nodded. After a moment of letting that sink in, he came over toward us and wrestled Karen up, even though she didn't have much fight left in her. That had been tricky, but, eh... nothing special.

I walked back in toward Jesse, who was desperately trying to copy his wife. Nah. Not gonna happen. He saw me and stopped wriggling. I pulled my chair over and flipped it around, sitting on it backward. I stabbed my knife into the wood of the chair back.

"Tell me the truth or I'm going to leave right now and take out all of my anger on your lady."

"Macki, come on..."

"No," I said. "You have a choice. Now choose. If the next thing you say is not an accurate name, I'm leaving."

He opened his mouth like he was going to speak... then didn't. "Falcon," he said.

"Okay, I buy that."

"God, I can't say it," he said.

"Then send it to me telepathically. Come on, doofus, tell me. I've waited long enough." I waited a few moments in silence. I was done waiting, but-

"Spyro," he said.

"Spyro? Are you joking?"

"No." I slapped my knee.

"I knew that kid was a loser."

"Can I go now?" Jesse asked.

"Yeah," I said at first. "Wait... no."

"I told you. We had a deal."

"Don't get me started about deals," I said coolly.

"Whatever. Just… please," he said as he looked up at me again.

"Say it."

"What?" he asked, seemingly perplexed.

"There was a third."

"A third? I only saw two." I zoned out a little bit, staring into space.

"Tell me. Now."

"I didn't know–" I leaned over the chair, getting as close to him as possible without touching him just to make him feel uncomfortable.

I whispered, "It was Alex, wasn't it? He was here?" I smiled ever so slightly. He was freaked. I heard him gulp, sweat gathering on his brow. I sat back down and I just stared at him. Alex. Alex had been here on my turf. And I hadn't even known it.

Or had I?

35
Alex

Falcon and I had been running in our molds for the last twenty miles. Finally, we'd made it to the Terrene and up to Falcon's room. Phoenix had been jabbering since the vestibule, but Falcon had been pretty unresponsive. Until now.

"You did what!?" Phoenix yelled. Falcon and I stood against a wall of his room. Logan was sitting in Falcon's old chair in the corner, her staff held in front of her.

"I'm sorry?" Falcon said angrily. He waved a finger in her face. "Phoenix, I saved your ass. If I wouldn't have gone… who knows what would have happened."

"Well we still don't know what's going to happen, do we?" she retorted. "You could have gotten yourself *killed*, Falcon. Does that register with you?"

"I didn't though. And actually… we. Kicked. Ass. Especially Alex, he was a beast." He smiled smugly, knowing that he was pushing his sister's buttons.

"Thank you," I added, playing along. I didn't usually like getting on Phoenix's bad side, but it'd been my first real fight, and I thought I deserved some recognition.

"Welcome," he said smoothly, glaring at his sister.

"Guys! God, you're so immature," she said, throwing up her hands. It was a lame insult, and we knew we'd won.

"FYI, I'm only eight years younger than you, Phoenix," Falcon pointed out.

"Exactly, thirteen doesn't count as mature," she countered.

"Who needs maturity anyway?" Falcon suggested, shrugging his shoulders.

"Ridiculous. Absolutely ridiculous," Phoenix said. She began pacing anxiously in front of us.

"We need to call a Core meeting. Like now."

"Who cares about the Core now? It's pretty much disintegrated," Falcon reasoned.

"Fine. You're right. You know what, I don't know what to do. I don't," Phoenix said, frustrated.

"We need to fight," Logan said. I'd forgotten she was even there. We all turned to look at her. I'd pegged her as the pacifist type. It was strange. "We need to go. Take all of us. And take Macki out. If they don't have Macki, they don't have anything. It'll disintegrate all on its own. But if we just leave her… we can't expect good things. We can't let her strike first. And we can't let her go on too long by herself because she'll either build an army or think up some sort of other scheme. We only have one option. And it's not the most favorable or the most glamorous, but it's all we've got." Phoenix bit her lip.

"It's your call though, Phoenix," she finished. Phoenix stared off into space, deep in thought.

"You're right," she finally said. "You're absolutely right. Gather everyone in the Core room and I'll give them the spiel. Tell them to get into fighting gear and grab their weapons before they come." By the time Phoenix finished talking, she'd already jumped out of the room. Logan got up.

"Go ahead guys," she said.

"We're going... to war?" Falcon said hesitantly.

"Yes," Logan said.

"Just like that?"

"Just like that."

"But... people... people die in wars, don't they?" Falcon asked. Neither Logan nor I wanted to answer his question.

"Yes," she said. "People die."

Falcon looked down, almost like he was going to cry. Logan jumped down with a worried look on her face. Falcon and I were left in the room.

"What's wrong, dude?" I asked after quite a long silence.

"I can't... I can't think about losing my sister."

Ooh. What do I say?

"You won't."

"How do you know?"

"Because she wouldn't leave you alone. She loves you too much."

Falcon looked up. I thought he was going to say something... then he didn't. He just walked over to the edge of the room and hopped down.

"Everyone!" he yelled through the hall. "Get your fight gear, get your weapons, meet in the Core room!"

She wouldn't leave him, would she?

--

All of the Shufflers in the Terrene were squished inside the walls of the Core room. Phoenix stood proudly above us (I was assuming in what used to be Zahra's spot). I looked around. A lot of the Shufflers I'd never seen. They ranged in looks all the way from thirteen to probably thirty-five or so. In total... it was hard to say how many there were. It wasn't as many as I'd thought there would be, though. I finally understood why the Shuffler formula was so important and why Zahra had risked Macki being out again to keep the prospect of making more Shufflers.

These Shufflers here wanted to create more Shufflers, so they could build a new species and grow their power. They needed to be understood, and interacting with humans just wasn't going to cut it. They needed something to do other than just sit around and watch the days go by. If the humans found out, they would either attack them or try to create more of them, which would involve testing. Testing didn't sound fun. They didn't want to hurt anybody. They just wanted to feel accepted.

Falcon and Maverick stood on either side of me up toward the front. We all had those cool shirts on that matched each of our eye colors (gotta be color-coordinated in battle I guess) and our weapons. Now, these weapons were insane. They ranged from knives to chains to spiked riot shields to Phoenix's preypins. Some of them I couldn't even begin to describe, let alone know what they were called. Maverick finally broke out his pitchfork. It was stuck to his back in a special holder.

Phoenix cleared her throat, indicating for us to

shut up.

"I just wanted to get up here and brief you guys since, well, since Zahra isn't here. The one who created our race – the one whose only job was to maintain leadership of this race justly and sanely has gone rogue. You all know that, though. She's killed our leader. She's taken Karen and Jesse – both valued Core members – hostage and tortures them on a daily basis. These acts of hostility indicate to me and other members of our clan that Macki is looking for nothing but trouble in the future. Killing humans? Sure. Creating a Shuffler army? Probably. Killing us all? Most likely. It is because of precautionary measures that we take action today.

"Our plan is to ambush their camp in northern Africa. Get the element of surprise on our side and attack with full force. Show no mercy as you fight. These Shufflers are considered criminals. There is also a possibility of Serpent involvement. If they show any signs of hostility towards us, they will become targets as well. Just… as a word of advice. Let your hatred of Macki and all that she and her followers stand for take charge. Think of how twisted and disgusting her mind is. How much you want to knock some sense into her. Well, now you can. You have the power to end this. We have the power to end this.

"I realize that a lot of you think we should have killed Macki when we had the chance, and I think we now regret that decision as well. But if we can save the world, I think that'll about make it up. This is the time of the Shuffler. The time for us to show that we cherish happiness, love, peace, and don't want death, torturing, and suffering ruling this planet for a second longer." Phoenix then broke into speaking in a few different Swahili phrases. Phoenix had taught me the primary Shuffler sayings, and they were all in Swahili.

Everyone raised their weapons in unison.

"Until the end," the room thundered back in Swahili. For a moment, time seemed to stop. Then everyone put their weapons down and began filing out of the room. Everyone looked jazzed and ready for a fight as I looked around. I thought about Phoenix's speech. First of all, it was a damn good speech. I didn't know that she was capable of staying composed that long. I guess when it came down to it...

"Alex, Falcon," Phoenix said as she jumped down about a story. I turned back toward her. "We wanted to tell you our plan," she said.

"What is it?" Falcon asked.

"You are responsible for Alex," she told him. "Do not let him out of your sight. Lay down your life for his if it comes down to it. Most of all, no matter what happens, you mustn't let them capture him. You understand?

"I do," he said dutifully.

"Whoa, whoa, whoa – why would you make one of your best fighters protect me? Shouldn't he be the one battling people like Ella, Macki, and Ryker?" I asked. It didn't make sense to me.

"Ryker is a horrific fighter," Falcon chimed in.

"You're the most important thing we have, Alex. She has the formula. We have you," she said.

"But why even bring him if he's not going to fight anyway?" Falcon asked.

"If I fail, he'll be our last hope. If he fights to his full potential, he'll be stronger than any of us and hopefully Macki herself," she explained. "*If* he fights at his full potential. He's like a magical toddler or something."

Wait, me? I failed when Phoenix went full speed on me with a *staff*. And I was sure Ella wasn't trying anything near her hardest when we sparred. They were being ridiculous and hoping for something that could never be. I knew it in my heart – it wasn't me. Phoenix and Logan were the real deal.

"So you're going after Macki?" Falcon asked his sister. She nodded. "And if you die or break all of the bones in your body or something, Alex is supposed to go after Macki?"

"Both of you would in that case. And Logan, if she's not… busy I guess." Quinn and Pilot walked up behind us. Falcon turned his head to them.

"And what are you guys doing?" Falcon asked them.

"I'm going to act as a medic and Pilot's coming with me," Quinn said as he patted Pilot on the back.

"So that's it right? Protect the kid and kill the bitch?" Falcon said. Phoenix glared at him.

"I guess so," she said.

"All righty then. How 'bout we go, like, pray or something freaky spiritual like that?" he asked, poking me with his elbow.

"If you set one foot in Maverick's room, Falcon, I will disown you," Phoenix threatened.

"Gotcha, no drugs or booze before my impending death. Thanks for the pleasure, sister," he said, bowing sarcastically.

"Go blow yourself," she snapped.

"Phoenix," Logan said from across the room, signaling for the tall girl to cut it out.

"Whatever," Phoenix said. Falcon and I turned to leave the Core room.

"Oh, and Alex?" Pilot called after me. I turned my head back.

"Yeah?" I asked.

"You get to ride with me," he said.

"Sweet," I responded. "By mode of what?" I asked after I thought about it for a moment.

"My name is Pilot," he reminded me. Wha… oh. I smiled and nodded then left with Falcon. I had to spill my guts to him as soon as we were in the hallway.

"Have they lost it?" I asked Falcon.

"Quite possibly," he replied honestly.

"Do you think we'll have to go after Macki?"

"Phoenix… will get whooped by Macki. Macki may be small, and most of the time she's fighting, she's going half-ass, but when she goes full-force… she's a highly lethal killing machine."

"So we will?"

"That would be my unfortunate guess."

"We're screwed, aren't we?" I asked, wanting to get his true opinion. He was deceiving because he looked like a boy and he acted like one, but he was nearly an elder in the real knowledge he possessed. I had to give him some credit.

"Yes."

"Even with Phoenix and Logan?"

"Let me put it to you this way: Macki is the best fighter. Ella is the second-best fighter. If we come across Ella, I don't think we'll all make it through alive, but we still have a chance. If Macki and Ella are together… we're flaming toast."

I nodded, absorbing the information, despite how morbid it was.

"And… my family's probably all dead, right?"

He exhaled loud enough that I could hear it. "I don't know. The only reason I'd have a shred of hope is that Macki likes to play games. She won't shy away from using your family as game pieces. She might just be keeping them alive so that she can bait you or something like that." I nodded my head. He could have said worse. "I just hope we come across Ryker."

"What do we do now?" I asked, ignoring his last comment.

"Now? We're going to Maverick's room."
Sounded like Falcon.

36
Macki

"You know what, Spyro. Life looks beautiful, doesn't it? Out here in the middle of nowhere?" I said, my arm around his shoulders. He was already uncomfortable.

"Yeah… I guess," he said nervously. I looked at him with a smile and squeezed his shoulder. He did everything he could to escape my gaze, but finally he stole a peek. We stood at the edge of camp, looking out at the nothingness. Spyro reeked of guilt. It was really too bad. He was too weak. Too easily manipulated. Not a good fit for my team and me. I kind of wished I could just send him back to Phoenix.

But I couldn't do that. I knew better.

"How was your trip here?" I asked.

"It was all right."

"Some of the others complained about some of Phoenix's Shufflers trying to tail them. That happen with you?" He exhaled.

"Uh… no, I don't think so."

"Good, good," I said. There was silence for a moment.

"I remember when I picked you up in the States," I said. "You were a bumbling mess."

He forced a laugh. Spyro was the last Shuffler I changed before I was imprisoned. He was really a poor representation of my choices. I have no freaking clue how he made it through the process. He was so weak. When I picked him up, I was secretly hoping to put him out of his misery by killing him with the Shuffler formula. It was the least I could do. But, by some miracle, he made it through.

"I didn't really get to know you before I was, you know, thrown in a hole," I said. "Who recruited you to my side?"

"Exodus and Valkyrie mostly."

"Oh, really? That's too bad. They seem to be missing."

"Maybe they deserted," he said.

Nope.

"Doubt it. They were quite loyal to me."

"Hm. I don't know then. I haven't heard from them for a while."

"I see," I said as I looked back out into the distance. "Now, you stayed longer at the Terrene than almost everyone else on my side. Why?" I asked.

"Honestly?"

"Honestly," I said, trying to reassure him. He looked down, his bright blue eyes (like mine) staring at the ground.

"I was scared. You know, I heard things."

"Scared of what?" He knew he had to watch

what he said next.

"Well…" he started.

"Me?" I said. He nodded. "Ah."

"Not that I don't like you or anything, I mean I came. It just took me a bit longer to decide. I wasn't around when you went through everything with Zahra and such, so I had to figure it out by myself. And I did. I chose you."

Well, it was an honest answer. I appreciated that. I started to have second thoughts about my next series of predetermined actions…

He started visibly shaking, his teeth chattering together every once in a while. He blinked a little too rapidly. He was *terrified* of me.

"Any regrets?" I asked him.

"What?" he said.

"Any regrets? I asked again.

"Um… not really. Why?" He looked at me strangely.

"No reason," I said, nodding my head a little bit to myself. Okay, enough screwing around. "You hear that someone snuck in to see Karen and Jesse?"

"Yeah, it was goin' around camp," he said.

"You didn't happen to be around when that happened, did you?"

"I was at the party."

"Yeah right," I said.

"I was."

"All right, kid, we both know you're lying straight-up to me so cut the crap."

"I'm not… I mean… I, uh…" he stuttered. I took my arm off from around him.

I whispered, "I can kill you right now or I can give you a day to dwell on your impending death. Which would you like?" He looked at me with a horrified look on his face. Then he tried to dart off, but

I grabbed his shoulder and pushed him to the ground. He ended up on his hands and knees in the sand. He tried to get up, but I pushed him back down with my boot.

"I didn't mean to!" he yelled in a really obnoxious screamy-whiny tone.

"Face it like a man, you little jerk," I told him as he scrambled to get up once again. He got up and put his fists up defensively.

"You're really gonna do that?" He was shaking even more and bouncing back and forth a little bit. He looked like he was about to burst into tears. I threw a punch and hit him square in the side of the face. He was knocked off-balance but not all the way to the ground. He struck at me with a fist, but I easily dodged it then kicked him in the stomach. Not as hard as I could, but just enough to knock the wind out of him. Then I grabbed him by the back of the neck and he automatically tensed up.

"Please, Macki," he pleaded. To no avail, of course. I marched him to the center of camp. He was screaming. Shufflers came out of their tents and from hanging out to come and surround us in a crowd, wondering what was going on. I dropped Spyro and he fell to the ground.

"Everyone, this is Spyro. Spyro, this is everyone," I said to the crowd. "Spyro here thinks that he can go behind all of our backs and live to tell the tale. What do you think?" The crowd of my followers yelled back, saying "kill him" or something along those lines. That was exactly what I was going to do. "Anyone got a weapon?"

Spyro tried to run out of the circle of Shufflers, but my followers threw him back toward me.

Someone threw me a metal rod. It would work. Spyro was back on his hands and knees, now completely bawling. I hit him with the rod and he fell flat to the ground. The crowd cheered.

After a few moments, Spyro tried to get up again. He got to his feet then fell over again. I rolled him over with my boot and hit him in the stomach. More tears fell down his face, and he couldn't even muster a sound.

Finally, I hit him one last time. I barely felt it crash into his skull. His blue eyes became a deeper shade. He stopped squirming. I could feel the air around me die.

Spyro was gone.

37
Alex

With every step, my shoes squashed the bright white snow of the Alps. Being from New Jersey, I understood snow. And a lot of it. But I'd never been in mountains like these before. It really gave a whole new view of "snow." I turned my head and looked out at the vast array of mountains speckling the horizon. Wow. Just wow. I didn't want to ever look away. Especially with everything going on.

"Never been here, have you?" Phoenix asked over her shoulder as she trudged through the snow in front of me.

"Never," I said.

"Lauren didn't take you anywhere, did she?"

"Not many places. We stayed near home most of the time." She nodded.

"I see." The path we were walking on was cut

right out of the mountain. Logan and Pilot were behind me, also taking in the scenery. In front of me was a giant door. Phoenix rapped on it. I looked around again, getting lost in the breathtaking view. Pilot and Logan had talked the whole way up. Apparently they were good friends with the Ndege. My parents were as well. Phoenix thought it'd be better if the rest of the group stayed behind, and she was pretty much calling the shots now, so Falcon reluctantly stayed with the others. She didn't want me coming either, but I finally got her to change her mind.

A peephole opened and someone put their eye behind it, looking at the visitors.

"Phoenix," I heard from inside. They heaved the door open and it swung inward. The Ndege who opened the door stood out of the way and another one stood right in the middle of the long hallway. He was tall, with white-blond hair and pasty white skin. He half-smiled, and it gave him a sort of angelic presence.

"Welcome, Shufflers," the man in the hallway said. "We just received your message a few moments ago. Excuse us for not expecting you this quickly." He bowed his head then lifted it back up. Phoenix strode in.

"Hey, Mark," she said. "Where are Lauren and Rachel?"

"In the Pillar. I'm afraid that–"

"Let me just talk to them. We're in a bit of a time crunch," she said as she brushed past him. He looked a little discouraged, but still kept his half-smile. I walked past him as well, flashing a smile in greeting as I did. I looked back and saw that Logan and Pilot had stopped to talk with Mark. Pilot had his arm wrapped around Logan, and they laughed. Apparently someone said something funny. I was too far to hear what it was.

At the end of the hall were glass doors. Phoenix

held one for me.

"Thanks," I said.

"Are Pilot and Logan talking with Mark?" she asked. I nodded. "The amount of friends they have disgusts me."

I ignored the comment and walked into the room. It was huge with giant windows at the back displaying the white-topped mountains. There were also – hence the name – big pillars supporting the place.

In the center of the deserted room were two people – twins. Lauren and Rachel (Rachel of which I'd never met but was surprised to find looked almost exactly like Lauren). I quickened my pace as we walked toward them. A grin spread on Lauren's face.

As soon as we got to them, Lauren gave me a hug.

"Good to see you doing well, Alex," she said. After an abnormally long hug, she let me go and looked at me. "Seems you're growing up." I guess I did look a little older, because I was a hair taller and a lot stronger. Or maybe she was just saying that. Phoenix stood with her hands crossed and foot tapping.

"Why are you here, Phoenix?" Rachel asked hostilely.

"We, uh… we were going to request your help," Phoenix said quietly.

"What was that?" Rachel asked as she turned an ear.

"We need your help, goddammit!" Phoenix semi-yelled.

"Whoa, calm down there guys. We're all friends here," Lauren said. That was so her style. Always breaking up fights. I realized how much I'd missed her. I mean, she was basically my mom, sister, and best friend growing up. And I'd left her in one crazy whirlwind of a day.

"We can't," Rachel said.

"What do you mean *you can't?*" Phoenix asked.

"Lauren here made an agreement with Macki."

Phoenix looked at her, shock spreading across her face. "You *what!?*" Phoenix exclaimed as she made a fist.

"Phoenix!" I heard from across the room. Logan and Pilot had just entered. Logan was again trying to control Phoenix's rage. "Calm down," Logan said.

"I'm not your bitch," Phoenix said under her breath. Everyone chose to ignore that one.

"As I was saying," Rachel began, "Macki broke in a while back. I wasn't here, but Lauren was thankfully."

"She marched in and told me she'd kill Joey if I didn't give her Mavril. I told her to keep us out of whatever she was doing and she agreed. That was all," Lauren said gently.

"What about the part where you told her you'd remain neutral?" Phoenix snarled.

"We called a truce," Lauren said. "Look, Macki *was in our sanctuary.* I did what was best for the Ndege as a whole."

Phoenix sighed.

"It's okay," Pilot said. "We understand."

"Understand? If you guys needed help, would we help you? Yes. Even if we had a truce with Macki? Yes. You know why? Because if we have you in battle, we kill Macki. Therefore, she can't uphold your dumb truce. Now do you understand?" Phoenix said.

Lauren looked hurt.

"We heard about Zahra passing," Lauren said. "And we knew there would be a fight soon. We know you need help, but you won't find it here. We just can't.

Our numbers are dwindling nowadays." It was weird that Lauren was involved in this world, too. My head started spinning. She wasn't the woman I had known for all those years. She was a leader. A fighter. A *Ndege*. Ah, God, it was so hard to believe.

"What about my brother?" I asked. Lauren bit her lip. Rachel piped down.

"Why would we know?" Rachel asked. I looked back and forth at the twins.

"You just... you were always there for us, so I figured you might know."

"Sorry, Alex. I'm so, so sorry, but I don't know where Joey is." She rubbed my shoulder. Lauren knew this would piss me off. I had hope they might have known. But... but apparently not.

Why would Macki take him away from me? Who would do that? I thought of all the disgusting and vile things she could be doing to him, and I wanted to scream. They told me the stories about this girl. But none of those stories matched what I was going to do when I got ahold of her. For my brother. For all of the pain she already made me feel despite me never really being in her presence.

I wanted to see him again. See him smile and talk about what he dreamed of doing when he grew up. And create his own future. Live until he turned a hundred.

She would pay.

Yeah, she would.

38

Macki

"Welcome to camp," I told the group of Serpents at the edge of camp. Ryker, Frost, and Ella were on either side of me. There were seven Serpents, but I only cared about two of them. Amazingly, Mavril had survived. Serpents also had faster healing times than humans, so the worst of his gashes were healed.

The new leader of the Serpents was also in the group. He was the kid we'd found in the church. I'd heard through the grapevine that his name was Brit. Basically, he was a flying snake. Literally.

"That wasss quite the trek, Macki," Mavril hissed.

"Wonderful scenery isn't it?" I asked sarcastically. "Hi," I said to the kid. "Remember me?"

He nodded. "Of course," Brit said.

"Well, let's get to it then," I said. "We'd like to

request your assistance."

"Assistance? For what?" Brit asked. He didn't hold his *s* like the others did. I wondered how he'd settled into his new position. I appointed him, after all.

"We have reason to believe that we're going to be attacked by Phoenix and the other Shufflers sometime within the next few hours," I explained.

"How do you know that?" Mavril asked.

"You think I don't have spies over there?"

"Oh… didn't think about that." Duh.

"We can't do that," Brit said surprisingly. Oh, what had I gotten myself into this time? I laughed.

"Brit," I began, "maybe you don't understand the politics around here, but Serpents are supposed to be on *my* side."

"I'm part Ndege," the boy said. "I've heard about what you're like, and I don't want any part of it."

"I saved you," I told him. "I made you leader. Don't you owe me a favor?"

"I owe you nothing. We don't want to be dragged into something that's just going to get us all killed. This is between you and Phoenix. Not us and the Ndege."

"But we could really… frankly, we could use your help. It'll be a quick fight, I'm sure," I said.

"No. Goodbye, Macki," he said as he turned. I grabbed his shoulder and immediately the Serpent guards had five spears in my face.

"How about I just kill you and make Mavril leader like it should have been," I told the boy. "It doesn't have to be a drawn-out thing either. I can follow you and attack when you least expect it. Then you're done." One of them poked me with a spear. "Get those things out of my face, or you're all dead snakes." They budged a little bit but not much. "After all," I continued to Brit, "you're just a little screw-up, aren't you?"

Brit turned to me.

"I am not a *screw-up*," he said angrily. Wow, he was different than when I'd found him.

"But aren't you really? You don't fit with either clan."

His wings sprung out.

"You wanna play, Macki? I'll play." He ran at me. I didn't have enough time to react, so he tackled me. As he did, he grabbed me and we started going up toward the sky. Shit.

I squirmed against his grip as he kept going up and up, his wings thrusting upward violently. I watched as the group got farther and farther away, all of them looking up at me. Brit was slimy and it felt disgusting. If I jumped from this height... I wasn't sure. It was questionable.

"Fun, huh?" he asked, looking over at me.

"What happened to you? Get some sort of confidence booster or something?"

"Being made the leader of the Serpents might do that to you. Also, I'm on good terms with the Ndege now. Thanks to you."

"Yeah, thanks to me," I said. "What's your goal here? Are you trying to kill me?"

"No," he said. "You just need some sense knocked into you." And before I knew it, I was hurtling toward the ground. I'd done this once before, and it hadn't had a very good ending. And I had to be ready to fight soon as well. I closed my eyes, open air rushing past me. The anticipation about killed me.

Finally, I hit the ground. Everything was dark for a moment, and I was sure I was dying. My ears were ringing. My head felt like it'd been split open.

"Macki?" I heard through the haze. I tried to get up, but I stumbled and fell back down. I rolled over onto my back and tried to open my eyes. Ryker was above me, shaking my shoulder, but the picture was sparse. I couldn't feel my hands either, I realized. I tried to catch my breath. All of it seemed to have escaped me.

"What the hell did you do?" Ryker asked Brit, who'd just landed next to us. He had his arms crossed. Ryker grabbed him by his collar and shoved him over. I heard a fight break out. Frost called for other Shufflers to come and fight. I sat there helplessly. Ella came over from her tent and knelt beside me. A chainsaw revved. I tried to focus on her.

She helped me into a sitting position as I coughed and coughed and coughed.

"You okay?" she asked, biting her lip. I nodded. Or I thought I did. My head hurt really badly, so I couldn't be certain. She held me up like a ridiculous little baby. God, how could I have been so stupid? I mean, he was a *kid*. In actuality (not his appearance age), he was probably in his twenties, but eh. That's still a kid compared to me. What'd happened that made him such a stud? I mean, the wings were pretty cool...

Then I realized that he was like Alex – an oddball of nature, but... somehow stronger and faster. No normal Ndege could have carried me up that high. And no Serpent could have run that fast. Hm.

Ouch, ouch, ouch. Everything hurt. Ella picked me up so that I was on my feet, and I got a better view of the fight happening around me. A few of the Serpents were on the ground either knocked out or dead. Brit was battling it out with Frost and Ryker. Mavril... was nowhere to be seen. Interesting.

Ella put her arm around me and led me back toward my tent.

"How do you feel now?" she asked.

"Terrible," I said. She looked worried.

I'd been this close to death on multiple occasions.

This one just hadn't been in my plans for the day.

39
Alex

Pilot and I landed not too far away from the camp. We hopped out and immediately got out our weapons. I made the stone change into a long, black, shining sword. It was one of my favorites. It was hot out – a lot hotter than I'd expected. Well... considering we were in the middle of the desert, I probably should have expected it. Pilot and I had flown in an F-22, and it was one of the coolest things I'd ever experienced. I mean, we were flying to go to war, but it was still cool. Most of all, it kept my mind off things.

Now, I started getting nervous. Really nervous. None of it had really sunk in until I saw Macki's camp. It was way off in the distance, but I could still see it. The rest of the group came behind us on a jumbo transport plane piloted by some Shuffler I didn't know and Phoenix. I couldn't imagine having Phoenix chatter right next to me for almost four hours, especially since she hated flying.

"Come on, Alex," Pilot said gently. I'd never seen him flustered or upset, but I could tell he was holding back tears. It was painful to watch. I wanted to say something... but I couldn't think of anything. His gray eyes seemed to hang and looked darker than they usually were. Like a lot of us, it wasn't about him. It was about Logan. He couldn't protect her all the time and now was the time when he had to let her go and fight for herself. Not downplaying that Logan was an amazing fighter, but to Pilot... he was worried.

Logan ran up to us as the herd of Shufflers took off sprinting toward the camp. Phoenix nodded her head at me in goodbye as she passed and then she broke into a sprint, molding into a cheetah. She took off and within a few seconds, she was at the front of the group, leading us all toward war. It was no surprise that Phoenix was a big cat; those tended to be some of the strongest molds.

Falcon and Quinn jogged in Logan's wake as she ran up to Pilot. He picked her up effortlessly and twirled her around, her staff slung around her back. He kissed her.

"I love you," he said.

"I love you, too, Pilot," Logan replied.

"Be safe," he warned.

"You'll be with me forever, no matter what happens, babe. Remember that. Always," she reminded him. Nobody had the heart to tell them we had to go, so we just waited. Pilot put Logan down and squeezed her hand one last time. "Never forget," she said finally. Their hands unlinked and Logan came toward Falcon and me. Quinn stood with Pilot as we turned toward the camp and took off running.

I didn't know exactly what I was getting myself into, but I was ready to fight… and possibly die. Finally, we were within fifty yards of the camp. Quinn and Pilot both jumped next to me, molding into a rhino and elephant respectively. They were huge and looked extremely dangerous as they hurtled toward camp at top speed. I could see the fights breaking out in front of me. Animals clawed at each other and others went at it in their human forms with all sorts of weapons.

I looked over and saw that Logan was no longer next to me, but a bat flew above. Falcon and I were left together, running toward camp in our human forms. Finally, I decided to mold. I jumped and landed as a tiger. I roared. I was ready to find Macki. Find her and rip her apart. What she did to my parents… it was repulsive. And whatever she did to Joey, I was sure it wasn't pleasant. Also, considering all of the people she'd killed to make her stupid formula… she had almost killed Rachel, too. And sent her followers to kill Lauren. What kind of monster was she? From the stories I'd heard, she sounded like some sort of completely twisted byproduct of sheer madness. But she was going to be gone after this; I could feel it. I could feel myself ripping her throat apart like she deserved.

That was all she deserved.

We made it to the edge of camp and scanned the scene. I saw a polar bear rip another boy to shreds with a few swipes of his claws. Pilot and Quinn rammed through a group of Macki's followers. Phoenix and Logan were all the way across camp fighting.

Falcon turned to me. "Let's find Karen and Jess–" He was cut off as a sharp kick hit his chest. He flew backward. Ryker and Frost stood in front of me.

"Ooh, we get the Shuffler baby first," Frost said, seemingly giddy with excitement. She grabbed her Uzi out of the sling on her back. Ryker revved his chainsaw.

Falcon got up and came to stand right next to me once again.

"Hey, pygmy Shuffler, miss me?" Ryker played, grinning at Falcon.

"How about I shove a grenade up your ass and see how that feels?" Falcon retorted as he ran and tackled Ryker. They tumbled around in their human forms and then disappeared behind a tent.

That left me with Frost. She jumped and molded in a standing position and ran at me in her husky form. I was much stronger in my tiger mold, so I went after her. I tackled her and we rolled over. Oh, God, I was actually fighting. For my life. Too late to bail now.

We tumbled around a little bit and she finally got a good hold on my leg. I shook her off and she went flying, slamming into a broken tent support. Immediately, she was back on her feet in her human form. I molded back into my human form as well and changed the stone into a knife. I couldn't let her get too close with her Uzi...

I threw the knife and she dodged it. I held out my hand, and it came flying back to me. She pushed me over and pulled out her Uzi. She stood above me, the Uzi trained on my chest.

"Well that was no fun," she said. With one fluid motion, I hit her wrist, knocking the gun away. It fired and in another second, I was back on my feet with a chokehold around her neck. She struggled to try and pry my hands off, desperate for air. Finally, she used a counter-maneuver and hit me. I doubled over, but was quickly back up. That rapid healing thing really helped.

I brought my sword around at her and she dodged it. I brought it around and she dodged once again. I ran at her with full force and knocked her down. Then, I got up and picked her up with a bit of effort and threw her into a tent, sending it crashing.

She scrambled to get up, but was too late. I was standing above her, her green hair spread out around her. I stabbed down. She screamed. The blade went through more smoothly than I'd expected. I pulled it back out and it clambered to the ground, blood staining the long, black blade. Frost was still alive – barely – and struggling for breath, a hand over the heavily bleeding wound. I saw her gaze turn to stone just as I had seen Valkyrie's.

I hoped Falcon was handling Ryker okay, but I still couldn't see them. I waited for a moment – just a moment – in pure shock and adrenaline before I picked up the stone and rushed over toward where Falcon had been, the stone changing into a dagger in my hand.

That scream might just haunt me for the rest of my life.

However long that may be.

40

Macki

Well, absolute chaos was panning out in front of me. I'd known they would probably be coming today, but I still wasn't completely prepared. I was sure Phoenix and probably Logan would be coming after me any minute, but for the time being, I relaxed in my tent with Ella. It would take quite the amount of fighting if anyone wanted to make it over where I was.

The thing that sucked was that now I had something to protect. If I wasn't so damn courageous, I might have just left with her. Ella sat on my mattress and I sat next to her, inspecting my own boot. My ears were still ringing and whenever I turned my head, I saw spots. I'd wrapped my hands up to keep the bones somewhat in place. I was sure they were shattered from my fall earlier.

Unfortunately, Brit had left camp relatively

unscathed. And he was pissed. I had a hunch that someone was behind him, pulling the strings, but I had no idea who. Phoenix, maybe? No. She wasn't that smart.

"Should we go out there now?" Ella asked.

"Nah," I said as I picked a piece of dirt out from the sole. I looked up and she was smiling. "Why are you smiling?" I asked.

"No reason," she said and looked away sheepishly.

"What, am I that entertaining?"

"Yes, of *course,*" she said, somewhat sincerely, but with a giggle. Something seemed off about her today.

"What's up with you today?" I asked bluntly. The smile came right off of her face.

"I'm just worried..." she began.

"About?" I said, trying to get her to expand.

"Alex," she said and flinched just a bit like I was going to hit her or something. Which I would never do.

"Ah, I see. Same old, same old. It's okay to hope he's all right," I said, saying it more because I had to than I wanted to. She went over to the tent flap and peeked out.

"You're sure we shouldn't go?" She picked up her chain off of the table and swung it around a little bit, like she always did when she got nervous. I got up and wrapped her in my arms, my lips right next to her ear.

"If you really want to, you can," I said, like I didn't care what she did. She turned her head halfway toward me. "Or we can stay a bit longer."

She half-smiled and put her hands on mine. They were warm and made me relax even more. I had all I needed right here, didn't I?

Her face turned serious. "Macki, I want you to

go," she said.

"What?" I asked, looking at her from centimeters away.

"I want you to get out of here. Take the formula and run."

"Why would I do that?" This was my fight.

"Because you don't want to lose it," she said. "There's a big chance they're going to try and steal it, and I couldn't imagine that happening. You've worked so hard."

"Why do you care about my formula so much?"

"I know what it's for," she said softly. "Go."

I was a little shocked. I called the shots. I was the leader. *I* ran when I wanted to run. But this was not the time for that. She took my hands off of her and stepped away.

"Come on, Ella, I mean—"

"Go!" she said the loudest I'd ever heard her voice go. She was serious. But could I really run? It took a moment for me to calculate what exactly my thoughts on that were.

"We're a pair," she said, "and I want to watch out for you, too." My heart and my head were in two very different places. She started herding all of my papers together and shoving them in a battered backpack I had lying around. "That formula is everything for you. You don't realize it yet, but if you lose it... I'm afraid you won't be very happy."

"I won't let you get killed or captured," I told her. "That's my condition."

"Fine. You can watch from afar then. Maybe from a dune."

I started helping her pack all of my stuff, suddenly in a hurry. I had to show her I could listen to her, too. Wasn't that vital? She knew I cared so much about my formula, but how did she figure it out?

"If you're in any danger, I'm coming back."

"I have a few tricks up my sleeve as well," she told me. Finally, I grabbed my vial with its case on and put it in the backpack very carefully, in between the papers so that they padded it a little bit. I zipped up the pack. I had genuinely not expected this to happen. I slung the backpack onto my back and pulled out a throwing knife just in case.

She turned to me and grabbed my forearms. Then she kissed me. Not a hurried kiss. A nice, slow one. A proper one. When she pulled away, she stared right into my eyes. She was in strange form today... but I liked it, of course. She was taking control. Ooh, I got jitters thinking about it.

"I love you," she said. I was a little blown away. But could I say it back? Could I let myself be that vulnerable once again? Could I really... I didn't have time to think about it.

"I love you, too," I said, looking down, my cheeks turning bright red. She squeezed my hands and finally let me go.

"Go," she said and pointed out the back of the tent. Painfully, I turned away and walked toward the edge of the tent. I cut a giant X in it and hopped through. I was going to say something... but nothing I could think of topped "I love you." So I smiled at her. She shooed me away.

I took off running, my thoughts going five hundred miles per hour. I molded and kept running until I was on a dune a few hundred meters away. I could still see fine, but it would be hard for anyone to see me. I molded back and put my backpack to the side, making myself comfortable.

My heart about died.

Logan and Phoenix both approached my tent, which I knew had Ella inside. Oh, God.

I had to trust her though. I had to. It was just... so hard. I watched as Ella jumped out where I had, her chain wrapped around her hand. I had a good view, but if I needed to get down there... I calculated the time it would take. It was not good.

All of a sudden, I heard an extremely loud siren and covered my ears. I was wondering what the hell that even was... when Ella threw something out of the way. It was her. Why would she... Logan stumbled out of the tent and fell to the ground, covering her ears. Ella was a genius. She'd used the noise to *deafen* Logan. Her hearing was so sensitive, it'd probably completely blown her ears. So Logan was pretty much down and out. Phoenix stepped out and knelt next to her. Once my hearing came back, I really, really tried to focus so I could hear their conversation. And I could.

"Phoenix, Phoenix, are you there?" Logan asked. "I can't... I can't hear anything. Phoenix..."

"Logan, it's me, I'm right here. Can you hear me?" Phoenix said. Obviously she was hoping it would come back. But I didn't think it would.

"Phoenix?" Logan asked again.

"Yes, it's m—"

"I can't hear anything. Phoenix," Logan cried again. Phoenix grabbed her hand and drew Zahra's symbol in Logan's palm so that she would know it was her. After Phoenix finished the sign, Logan squeezed Phoenix's hand. Ella molded. I'd forgotten how *mystical* her mold was as she slithered around. It was an anaconda. The big-ass sorta snakes that you would not wanna mess with.

I knew Phoenix heard the slither. She spun around, but there was nothing behind her. She was going to look around in a whole three-sixty when Ella's chain wrapped around her neck, pulling her backward. Phoenix pried it off, a ring around her neck bleeding.

She got up and charged at Ella, who was standing across from her. Phoenix molded into a cheetah and launched herself at Ella, but she disappeared into another smaller tent. Phoenix pawed the flap open with her head and was about to step in… when Ella's chained wrapped itself around the cheetah's leg.

The cheetah jumped at Ella as soon as she caught sight of her. She disappeared again, the chain hanging lazily off of the cheetah's leg, following Phoenix like an extra metal tail. Phoenix molded back into her human self and unwrapped the chain. Her leg was left bleeding like her neck.

"Come out and fight me face-to-face, Ella," Phoenix commanded. She turned in a circle, looking for any sign of the Russian. Ella stepped out of another tent and stared at Phoenix with her lavender eyes. Phoenix ground her teeth.

The golden-eyed girl charged at Ella again, swinging a fist. They went back and forth with a series of blocks, hits, and strikes. No human would have been able to follow their movements like I could. Phoenix and Ella were pretty evenly matched. I started to get up to go help…

When Phoenix finally got the better. I panicked. Panic, panic, panic was all I thought. Phoenix threw Ella helplessly through a tent.

"You're a coward. And a murderer. And weak. I don't think you deserve any last words," Phoenix sneered as she drove one of her preypins into Ella's thigh. Ella screamed in pain as the steel wings opened and embedded themselves under her skin. I cringed. Phoenix wanted her to feel pain. I could tell. She picked up another preypin and aimed it at Ella's stomach.

I was already running down toward them in my tiger mold, my four legs moving as fast as they possible could. I kept watching, terrified, a feeling of dread overwhelming me. I never should have let her do this...

Ella slid out one of my throwing knives. I molded back and glanced at my sash. One was, in fact, missing. Phoenix's expression turned to terror for a just a millisecond before the blade sunk into her chest and slid through what looked like her heart. Phoenix's body dropped, but she was still alive. She looked down at the blade in horror and lay back in pain.

Ella sat hunkered on the ground, breathing hard.

"Phoenix? Are you there?" Logan asked. Ella gathered her strength and got up, standing over Logan.

"No!" Phoenix yelled at Ella in between deep breaths. She stood there, shaking. Phoenix had tears in her eyes, but couldn't muster enough strength to get up.

That had been way, way, way too close.

41
Alex

All of the death around the camp was really starting to get me. I felt sick. I'd never actually been in a war before, but I knew now that I had been and still was totally unprepared. Falcon had taken care of Ryker and left him unconscious at the edge of the camp. The fighting was starting to wind down. I'd taken out a few other Shufflers – three, to be exact – and each of their deaths haunted me. God, it sent chills down my back when I thought about them.

Falcon and I were together again near the center of camp. Everyone was either participating in the last few skirmishes around camp or... dead. I caught my breath as I brought the stone back to me. I was sweating buckets, and the air felt thick as ever as I tried to inhale. I stayed in a defensive position with both of my fists out just in case someone else decided to come after the pair of us. I saw Pilot protecting Quinn, who was helping a Shuffler who'd had his leg completely torn off.

"We need to go after Macki," Falcon said between breaths. We'd heard the buzzer. We knew that Logan would be deaf and blind, and that would leave Phoenix to go after Ella and whomever else they may have encountered. Falcon sprinted toward the other side of camp – where we figured Macki's tent would be. I followed behind him.

We got to the tent and burst inside.

"Holy shit," Falcon said. I looked up at the side of the tent. Macki's symbol was painted on the wall in dripping blood. After a moment of staring at it, tears started to well in Falcon's eyes. Somebody was definitely dead or dying. There was a giant rip in the fabric at the end of the tent, so Falcon jumped out of it.

"Phoenix! Logan!" he yelled. "Christ," I heard him say as I hopped out too. I looked at what he was talking about... it was Logan.

Logan sat near the tent, both of her wrists and neck slit. I panicked as I tried to stop the bleeding.

"Dude, help me!" I commanded Falcon, but his thoughts and gaze where elsewhere. I followed his line of sight.

Dear lord.

Falcon got up and walked slowly toward his sister, who lay on the ground not far away. Her eyes were closed, a blade sticking out of her chest. Falcon shook her shoulder and we both waited to see if she'd... if she'd made it. She stirred a little bit and her golden eyes blinked.

"Phoenix?" he said, shaking her harder.

"Yeah?" she said weakly.

"Stay with me, okay? Keep your eyes open."
She nodded slightly. Thank God.

With that, Falcon sunk back onto the ground and cried into his hands. A real cry. There was nothing beautiful about it. She was alive still, yes. But it was a lot to take in.

"Quinn!" I yelled as loud as I possibly could. "Quinn!" I yelled again, desperate for him to respond. "Stay with me. Please. Stay with me," I pleaded with Logan.

"Tell Pilot… yes," she said so weakly I could barely make out what she was saying.

"No, come on…" Her body went completely stiff. There was no heartbeat. There was no movement. She was gone.

For a moment, I just sat above her, holding her wrist, unable to bring myself to the realization that she was actually dead. A lot of people had died today, but it meant something so much different when I had memories attached to the deceased – when I could put a name to a face and it was connected with emotion. I took deep breaths, calming myself as it really sunk in. Then I thought of Pilot. All he had wanted was for her to stay safe – to be with him. He was willing to protect her, love her, and take care of her for as long as he'd live. How were we going to break it to him?

I snapped out of it. We were in the middle of a war, I remembered. I let go of Logan's wrist, and it dangled over her knee. Her icy blue eyes looked royal blue, but they were no longer shining like they used to.

I looked over and was surprised to see that Falcon had stopped crying. His eyes were still red and puffy, but he was looking at something else that I couldn't see around the tent. He got up and walked around the corner. I took one last look at Logan then ran over to him.

When I turned the corner, my jaw dropped.

Ella sat there, her leg bleeding from a preypin

embedded in it. She had propped herself up against the edge of a tent.

"You no-good piece of shit!" Falcon screamed. He ran at her, a fist raised and she braced. I was just going to let him kill her. She *had* killed Logan, and Phoenix was dying. She deserved punishment for what she'd done. Falcon was almost to her…

When someone pushed him over backward with the metal rod part of a titanium pitchfork.

Maverick.

He looked wicked, his eyes sparkling green.

"Maverick, let me at her," Falcon said, his hands made into fists, his eyes dry from all of the crying.

"You never woulda guessed," he said.

"Guessed what? Let me at her," he said again as he tried to brush past Maverick, but Maverick stepped back and put the prongs of his pitchfork right at Falcon's chest.

"Maverick," Falcon said. "Get. Away. From. Me." Falcon shoved the pitchfork away from his chest.

Maverick tried to stab him, but Falcon was too quick. He deflected it away from him and got Maverick into a chokehold.

"What the *hell* is wrong with you?"

"He's on Macki's side," I told Falcon in realization. He looked at me as he held his hands around Maverick's neck.

"Bingo," Maverick said with what little breath he had left. He kicked himself out of the hold and faced Falcon.

"You little…" Falcon began as he got into fighting position. I stole a glance at Ella and she saw me. She started to get up, then looked past me at something. She tried to make it inconspicuous, but I knew she'd stolen a glance at something…

I looked back and saw a shadow in the dunes, running from camp with a backpack. I recognized her. She was the girl from the pictures.

Macki.

I had to go. I had to.

I took off, sprinting toward Macki's fleeting shadow.

"What are you doing!?" Falcon yelled as he circled around with Maverick.

"I'm going to kill Macki," I said.

He said something, but I wasn't listening.

I was focused on one thing. And one thing only.

Kill her.

42

Macki

I ran, but it was no use. Alex was going to catch up with me sometime, so I slowed down. He stood behind me. I dropped my backpack carefully to the ground.

"Hello, Alex," I said.

"I don't know what makes you such an asshole, but it really works," he sneered. Exactly what I'd expected – angry as hell. I heard something flying toward me and flicked one of my throwing knives out of its holder at the shuriken he had thrown without turning around. They collided in midair and both dropped. Alex held out his hand and the black, shining shuriken flew back to him. It was a nifty little trick, but I'd been trained in defending against the many forms of the stone when Asime was alive.

"Well, you seem pissed out of your pants," I

observed. I turned around and I saw his eyes go directly to the scar of the rake across my face that Zahra had left so generously. I walked toward him slowly, swaying from side-to-side on the uneven sand, taking my sweet time. There was no rush, after all.

"Where's my brother?" he asked quite sternly. It was more of a demand than a question.

"He's here," I lied.

"What do you want, Macki? Asime's not coming back. Neither is Frost or Logan or any of the others. Grow up and get over it," he snapped.

"Oh, shut up," I said. "You know talking's not going to kill me." With that, he charged at me, the stone now a sword in his hand. He was swinging angrily at me, and I was able to disarm him in a matter of seconds, the sword dropping to his feet after a quick, hard strike to his forearm. "You'd much rather play the fun way."

He brought the sword back to his hand and came at me again, switching weapons with nearly every strike he attempted. My hands stung with every movement, but at least my head was clearer. He was quick and strong, but nothing I couldn't handle. It seemed like I'd overestimated him even after my injuries. What a shame.

He finally stopped with his weak attempts to win me over in close-range combat and leaped – molding into his admittedly awesome Bengal tiger mold. I molded into my own white tiger and attacked him.

It went much as the fight with Zahra and I had gone. We brawled and brawled, rolling around the room like idiots trying to scrape and/or bite each other. He molded into a rhino and came at me with all of his speed... but I jumped out of the way and he almost sent himself through a dune. This wasn't the turf I was expecting to fight on, and it was proving tough to really get footing on.

He turned around and molded into a jaguar. He kept attacking me, switching molds like crazy – gorilla, crocodile, bear, lion. He bit me once with his crocodile mold, and it made me wince, but it didn't slow me down too much. He was tiring out; I could feel it. I knew that molding like that took a lot of strength, and he didn't have much of it due to his short time in training.

After a while, he molded back into his human self (as did I) and again attacked me with the stone. He switched the stone around way too much. Well, too much for him. He wasn't exceptionally skilled with any of the weapons, so I once again got the better, and the stone came tumbling out of his hand and rolling across the ground. I pushed him over and kicked him hard. He slid across the ground, and his head went into the sand. I was upon him within seconds, a knife to his throat. So disappointing. He was so weak. Definitely not the ending that I was hoping for.

He reached out his hand and tried to bring the stone back to him, but he was out of strength. It merely rocked back and forth.

"I thought that'd be a better fight, Alex. I'm disappointed," I admitted with a sigh.

"You're never going to win, Macki. Never," he spat back at me. A lot of confidence for a dead boy. "You're a murderer, a liar, a cheat, and a disgrace to nature. You're crazy, too. Absolutely insane. But you know what, maybe you don't even realize it. What happened to the old Macki? The one nobody talks about any more because she was so nice and humble and generous? Huh?"

"That Macki died a long time ago," I explained simply. "Oh, and by the way I had such a *fantastic* time with your parents. Although they were quite the party poopers."

"You–"

"Goodbye now, Alex." My wrist twitched, preparing to slide across his throat...

But something threw me off of him and sent me flying away from the boy. I landed on top of a dune. Well, that hurt.

Someone let Karen and Jesse out.

I pushed myself off of the ground and onto my feet. A jaguar was racing toward me. I caught her and she bit into my forearm, but before she could do any major damage, I threw her off of me. As she rolled, she molded back into her human form.

Jesse attacked me next with his gorilla mold. He charged at me and we held each other by the shoulders, testing each other's strength. I was sliding back, sand collecting around my ankles. I had to move fast, or I was going to slip.

I put one of my hands around the back of his neck and kept the other on one of his shoulders and jerked him toward me as hard and as fast as I could, bringing him closer to me. I swiftly twisted my body around and flipped him over my shoulder. That brought him down long enough for me to roll out of the way. Karen was waiting for me. She had no weapon, so she would have to rely on her hands. Jesse molded into his human form, standing on the other side of me.

I thought about pulling out one of my knives, but decided I'd once again keep it classy and match the tools that my opponents had. They both lashed out with their own attacks, and I back-flipped out of the way so that I could see them both, my hands out in front of me – ready to fight. I smiled and challenged them with the look in my eyes. They came at me, swinging punches and kicking, using everything they had. My quickness was strained, but I managed to block most everything and finally got a kick around at Karen. She fell backward, so I had my chance to finish off Jesse.

I switched to the offensive and he kept up his defense pretty well. I thought for a moment that maybe I wouldn't get the better of him in time, but finally my luck turned. I elbowed him right in the face, giving me enough time to drive the heel of my palm upside his nose. It sputtered out blood and he took a step backward. I slinked around so that I was behind him just as Karen was coming toward us both. I put one hand on each side of his head.

"Bye, Jess," I said.

"No!" Karen screeched, clambering to save her husband. I twisted my hands violently, snapping his neck. I let his body crumple to the ground. Karen stopped running toward me. I smiled at her. She turned her head and looked at Alex, who had turned the stone into a hatchet. He looked weak, but I could tell he was regaining his strength – powering up, if you will. She ran toward Alex and stood in front of him protectively. She was finally stepping up to be a mother. She wasn't going to let anything touch her son… well, at least that's what she thought.

I charged at her. When I was nearly upon her, I saw Alex toss something to Karen – oh no. She swung the hatchet around and I felt the blade cut into my side.

She followed up by kicking me in the stomach. I doubled over. She punched the side of my head and I fell onto my hands and knees. She kicked the side where I'd been cut and I fell all the way over, lying on the ground. She raised a fist like she was going to bring it down at me with all her force. It came down and I rolled out of the way at the last second, springing to my feet. My lip was bleeding, as well as my side.

I was tired and hurt, but that didn't stop me from facing off against Karen one final time.

Again we went back and forth, and with my injuries, I'm sad to say we were pretty evenly matched. We both molded and attacked each other in our cat forms as well. When we molded back, I was done with her. I pulled out a knife and flung it at her. She dodged. I threw another. She caught it and threw it back at me. I didn't even have to move; it missed me by a mile. I threw another. And another as hard and fast as I could. Finally, one sank into her stomach, so she was unable to dodge the next one, which stuck through her throat. She gasped for breath.

I thrust her up, holding her by her neck against a dune. I thought about going into some long, epic speech about how she had been like a mother to me back in the day and then how she had betrayed me and how that was her payment, but I didn't.

"Good freaking riddance," I told her. I shoved one of my knives through her ribs to her heart. Her lips parted like they were going to say something, but they quivered, then stopped. I dropped her lifeless body.

"No," Alex said. Why did people always say that when someone died?

I turned around to face him.

He was holding my backpack.

"Phew. Well then. Where were we?" I said. I clutched my side; blood was seeping over my hand. He threw down the backpack. I cringed. I wanted to tell him to be careful with it. I started walking toward him, but he waved a finger.

"So what was your formula for?" Alex asked. "An army?"

I shook my head. "No. None of that nonsense."

"Then what?" he asked. He raised a foot above it. I bit my lip.

"It's for me." I scrambled. He dropped his foot a little lower.

"Obviously."

"No, not like that. Not like that at all. It…" He smashed his foot through it. I heard glass break. I sunk to my knees.

"No," I said.

"What was it? Huh?" he asked as he changed the stone to a sword and approached me. I just sat there on my knees. Ella was right. I did miss it. He put the sword to my throat, and I just let him. The metal was cool.

"It cured me."

"Of what?"

"Why do you even care? You're going to kill me anyway."

"I'm curious. What did it cure you of? Being a Shuffler?"

"My hallucinations and outbursts. That's all."

He looked at me, shocked. "Don't lie to me."

"Are you joking? Why would I lie to you? I've never been more serious in my life." His hands on the sword dropped a little.

"I'm going to kill you now," he said.

"Alex, if you're going to kill me, I want you to do it for the right reasons." I looked up at him. This was it. I was done. He was going to kill me now. "Kill me because I killed those scientists. Because I killed Spyro. But do not kill me because I'm crazy. Don't kill me because I was concocting some crazy formula. Don't kill me because of my name and the rumors about me."

"You didn't want a war?"

"Of course not."

"But why did everyone…"

"They just want to condemn me because I think

a little bit differently."

"You're not a murderer?"

"Not especially."

"A monster?"

"Here and there."

"A psychopath?"

"Also here and there. But not like they say." He looked dumbfounded. "It's more out of desperation than anything else. After I got out, I had to run, didn't I? They didn't accept me there. No matter what I did, it was going to look like a threat to them. And that's sad."

He stared at me for quite a while, thinking. "I'm going to ask you one more time. Where's my brother?"

"Oh," I said, "he's with the Ndege."

"*What?*" he said.

"I didn't want the little guy to get hurt now, did I?"

"He... you... what?"

"Sorry, Alex. I'm not the sadistic loony bird everyone thinks I am."

"I don't know what to believe anymore," he said. Finally, he dropped his sword.

"Rightfully so." I was about to cry. Damn. The silence was eerie after that.

"I want you to leave," he said.

"What?" I said. Was he serious?

"Go disappear."

"Why... what changed your mind?"

"I believe in second chances." I got up from my knees. He picked up the backpack and tossed it to me. "Disappear now."

"But—"

"Macki. *Go,*" he said.

And there I went, traveling in the desert. I couldn't believe what had just happened.

He let me go.
Bad decision.

43
Alex

The aftermath of our war was horrifying. Lifeless bodies littered the ground. Some were unconscious, I knew, but others… not so much. Thankfully, we had won. We were in the middle of camp. Quinn had been working extremely fast with a little kit to save as many of our Shufflers as he could. Phoenix was on the ground as Quinn worked to close up the gash in her chest. The bloody throwing knife sat next to her in the sand. Falcon was right next to them, trying to keep his sister awake. Falcon's leg was bleeding, too, with three wounds on his leg from the prongs of the pitchfork. He didn't seem to notice. All of his energy was focused on keeping Phoenix alive.

Pilot was next to them, watching over the procedure and helping Quinn when he needed. The two were speaking in German to each other. The rest of the camp was silent. Terribly silent.

I heard someone crying and looked over. A short, Middle Eastern dude wrestled with Maverick, who was (to my surprise) still alive. Apparently someone had talked Falcon out of killing him. He had burn marks on one of his arms from one of Falcon's grenades.

"She saved my life!" Maverick cried as the man led him toward the tent where we were holding prisoners. Then he started babbling gibberish through his tears, his head darting back and forth. Most of the other tents were in shreds, the supports inside them snapped into pieces. I'm assuming he was talking about Macki. That seemed to be a common theme around here.

Macki.

A shiver went down my spine. Macki. Macki. Macki. I couldn't think about her. I'd told Falcon and the others the truth... kind of. I left out the part where I *let her go* and in exchange said that she'd had me pinned down then decided to leave me there. How could I tell them the truth? I still couldn't believe it. My mind felt so burnt-out. Just done with everything. I couldn't take much more, but I had to stay alert.

I also thought about my parents. They were... they were dead. It all moved so fast; it was taking a while for it to catch up to me. Ella was nowhere to be seen either. Then, it hit me for real: what did I just do? I screwed up so bad. I just... I felt so bad for her. I knew Macki had given all of the Shufflers so much. She killed my parents, but I didn't know them really. Logan died, and I knew her, but not like I did my brother. Macki saved my brother. I guess my brain just bypassed all of that other stuff in the moment and thought for just a second that maybe she was a decent soul. Maybe she had decent intentions.

I mean… I messed up. So bad. So, so, so bad. Could I tell the others? Was Macki simply just protecting herself and those she loved? Or was she as sinister as everyone made her out to be? I wanted answers. I almost wished I could just sit down with all of the Shufflers and have a serious conversation with them where everyone told the truth. Too bad that would never happen.

When I really did try to put myself in her shoes, I came up with this: *we* attacked her. Not the other way around. The other Shufflers locked her up for no concrete reason. Her family was dead. Zahra hated her. Asime haunted her. She couldn't control her molding sometimes because of a side effect, not because she was simply trying to attack random people or things. Most of her best friends turned on her when she needed them most. Even my parents. How could she forgive them for that? How could she not become the monster everyone wanted her to be?

I thought about Joey again. I couldn't believe it – he was safe. I was safe. Lauren was safe. My real family was safe. And no matter what, I was going to fight to keep it that way. Therefore, if keeping Macki alive proved to be a horrible decision, I would hunt her down and kill her without a second thought. If it was a good decision, I would let her be. It was not my place to kill her just because I could. Although, I was still angry about the whole Ella thing, but I couldn't let that cloud my judgment.

But still… maybe I was just a good, old-fashioned idiot, or maybe I was overthinking it way too much.

I looked back over and saw Pilot walking up toward me. My stomach flipped. I almost wished he hadn't made it. Logan was *so* special to him, and he'd already lost the first love of his life.

"Hey Alex, have you seen Logan?" he asked me. I could barely listen to what he was saying. It sounded distant, like I was hearing through a haze.

"What?" I asked.

"Logan. Have you seen her?" he asked again. How should I tell him? Should I just show him? Should I... should I make a speech about how brave Logan was? Should I tell him how she died and what her final moments were like? I just looked at him. I didn't want to say anything, but I had to.

"I... I'm really sorry, Pilot," I said. I turned my head to look at our makeshift graveyard with bodies lying next to each other in rows. They were all covered in sheets or whatever we could find. He took off running toward it.

A lot of survivors turned their heads to watch him. When he got to the bodies, he ripped the sheets off, going down the line until he found Logan.

He didn't want to believe it was her. He started crying. Not crying – *bawling*. It wasn't just sadness, it was pain, and it was hurt. Just like it would be if it were physical. It was like a piece of him was dead – like he and Logan were one soul, not two. Logan's body had been cleaned a bit, and now the wounds were just deep slits in her skin.

"No, Logan, please no, no, no. This can't happen. Please. No. No, Logan, no. Please no..." Pilot pleaded. He dug his fingers into his scalp, pulling on his hair, and his tears created a stream flowing off of his chin. I'd never seen anything like it.

"No, Logan, no," he said. With shaky fingers, he pulled a sparkling ring out of his pocket. "I... I was going to propose. No. You didn't... you didn't even get to see the ring. No." He held her limp hand delicately and put the ring on her ring finger. "See... it fits great.

It's beautiful. You're beautiful." He actually let out a short-lived chuckle accompanied by a brief flash of a smile through the tears. "Please, Logan, please… this can't be happening again. Not again. No. Please…" He wouldn't let himself see the truth – the fact that she was dead. It was like his mind was prohibiting him from thinking it – accepting it.

"That's it," I heard from behind me. Falcon hopped up, favoring his injured leg as he strode toward the prisoners' tent. He stepped up on a broken crate and looked over the crowd of survivors.

"Are we really going to do this again?" Falcon asked the crowd. Everyone looked at him. "Lock up all of these worthless pieces of shit so that they can break out again and let this happen all over again? Really? You know what, I have a suggestion." He pulled out a grenade from around his belt. "How about I chuck this in there and see what happens?"

A few hooted in approval. I was conflicted. If I told him to stop, they might think I was a traitor, but if I didn't…

Falcon pulled the pin off of the grenade with his teeth and tossed it toward the tent. In a rush of adrenaline, I took off running and molded into a tiger, jumping toward the grenade. Right before it landed in the tent… I batted it away with my paw. It went flying off into the desert. I roared.

When I finally turned and looked at everybody, they'd all stopped whatever they were doing. No one spoke. I guess they saw my ferocity and knew that I meant business.

I molded back into my human form.

"That's enough," I commanded.

"Oh, so now Mr. Hero's gonna tell us what to do. Sorry to steal your stage, master," Falcon retorted and bowed sarcastically. I'd never imagined getting into a fight like this with him. And, honestly, I didn't think I was a hero at all. My parents had died trying to protect me. I didn't like Falcon playing on my pride like I had some huge ego.

"Don't you see? You're turning into your own enemy," I explained.

"You're the one glorifying the enemy, Alex," Falcon said.

"No. Without these Shufflers… we only have remnants of a race. I suggest not madly killing them off now due to the fact that we have no formula. The one Macki was making wasn't the Shuffler formula, so there is no formula right now. And if there is going to be one, she's going to have it. Understand?"

I saw some nods.

"They fought us, though. They're *enemies,*" Falcon said.

"Well…" I thought of how to respond to that one. "I didn't say you have to be nice to them." Judging by the way the crowd reacted, I had a suspicion that they would rethink slaughtering them all.

Everything was going to be okay. Not great.

But okay.

44
Alex

Phoenix had taken a few weeks to recover.
Quinn said it was a complete miracle that she was even
alive. The Terrene was just plain depressing. The lights
seemed darker. The halls seemed aimless. The
silence... the silence reminded me of the battlefield.

I'd been left on my own the last couple weeks.
Falcon disappeared into the hills on the way back and
no one had seen him since. Pilot locked himself in a
room as soon as we got back. Quinn took care of
Phoenix and other injured Shufflers. I guess after my
little display, people didn't want to be around me.

And after all of this, we still hadn't gained
much.

Namely, Macki was still alive.
Macki was still alive.
I couldn't get it out of my head. I felt constantly

jittery. Everyone was suffering from insomnia. The prisoners of the battle were locked in the small cells of the Terrene and guarded 24/7 by at least five of our Shufflers. Ryker was in there. And Maverick. It was weird to think that they were still around.

It felt so... so empty.

But my brother was with me, so at the same time, I felt content. I felt victorious. I wasn't really victorious, though. None of us were.

I sat in the greenhouse on the overgrown grass by the river with my eyes closed. I took a deep breath and tried to relax. I hadn't wanted to let Joey out of my sight, but Lauren said she'd take care of him for a few weeks while the Shufflers at the Terrene figured out a game plan.

It's okay. Phoenix was alive. Falcon was alive. Macki had (almost) no followers left to roam the outside world. Ah. Everything's going to be fine.

But Macki was still alive.

My eyes popped open. The thought interrupted my peace once again. What was I thinking? My breathing sped up and I made fists. No, I couldn't lose it. I couldn't lose it. I had responsibilities now that I'd made such an enormous decision. And one of those was not going crazy.

I got up and looked around. No one else was in here with me. I looked down at the ground and remembered Logan sitting there. It seemed like ages ago. The thought of her last words began to creep into my mind, and I shoved it away. I couldn't go there.

It was dark and gloomy outside, rain pattering on the clear top of the greenhouse. I walked toward the door. I could have molded and been there within a few seconds, but I felt so depressed, molding sounded horrible. The last time I'd molded had been at the camp. Yeah... Falcon wouldn't even look at me after that. And I felt awful about that, too. Was I going crazy? I betrayed my own friend's much more experienced judgment and walked away from it like I had some giant ego. What a jerk.

I opened the door and walked into the earthen hallway. I was so tired and hungry, and everything ached. Mentally and physically. I moped down the hall toward the Quarters hallway. When I got close, I started hearing yelling. Not normal yelling – the type of yelling that gives you chills because there's so much energy being put into it.

The Quarters hall looked empty and I looked around for the source of the noise. I already knew who it was, though.

Phoenix yelled out a string of curse words. The ground was littered with scraps of wood and a ton of other stuff.

I jumped backward just as something hurtled toward me. It landed in front of me with a thud – a full couch, the fabric ripped to shreds with stuffing floating around it. Phoenix kept yelling, but it didn't deafen the sounds of her ripping things apart and banging on the walls. No one would ever want to get in the middle of that, I was sure.

I looked around at what else she'd thrown down as I stepped over it all. I was getting out of here. Phoenix this angry? Dear lord.

Then, everything stopped. A tall shadow loomed above me as I looked up slowly toward the third story of cubicles. Phoenix's eyes were bloodshot both from lack of sleep and crying. Her knuckles were bleeding, the blood dripping to the floor. Her hair was disheveled, and she was in only a sports bra and shorts. She was shaking violently. I was going to say something, but... what would I say?

"She's not here," she said through chattering

292

teeth. I felt so uncomfortable, and I was truly scared for my life. I mean...

"Who?" I asked meekly.

"Logan. She's not here to stop me."

"Maybe," I began, "you have to learn to stop yourself, Phoenix." Tears started streaming down her cheeks. "I know you're upset, Phoenix, but look... look what you've done to yourself."

She held out her hands and they shook uncontrollably, blood pooling at her feet. Her breathing continued to slow down, coming back to a normal level. She looked at her hands, horrified.

"She's not here," she said again. I was speechless. Phoenix turned back into her room and sat down. I lost my view of her. Should I go? Stay? What–

"Phoenix," I heard from over my shoulder. Falcon stood at the end of the hall. His hair was a little crazy, but other than that, he looked a lot better than I imagined he'd be. I hadn't even noticed him walk up. He took my shoulder and looked at me.

"I'll take it from here," he told me softly.

"I... I didn't know–" I started.

"Stop, Alex. It's fine. I can handle it." He continued past me. "She's gone, Phoenix," he said to her. "Now I'm here to take care of you."

Falcon jumped up to the second story and pulled himself up then jumped to the third, disappearing into Phoenix's room.

I watched my step as I walked through the pieces of furniture and other miscellaneous objects that Phoenix had thrown down. Finally, I got to the edge of the hallway.

Phoenix was right. Logan was gone. And she was always there to say Phoenix's name when she got out of control.

Macki was still alive.

I shuddered at the thought. She was probably out there, somewhere, making a new plot to take us out... or worse. No, she'd keep her promise. She'd disappear. Would she? Did she ever do things like that?

I doubted it. I'd been so, so, so stupid. And naïve, just like Ella had told me I was. Like a child. Did I really know the whole game yet? Or did I just think I did? I kept going back and forth in my mind. I could hardly stand it. One moment, I'd think I was doing something right by keeping her alive, and in the next moment, I had an uneasy feeling that I'd made a terrible mistake.

So many questions and not enough answers.

45
Alex

We were gathered at the edge of the hills, overlooking the indigo waves of the ocean. The moon was out and reflecting off of the water below. It was a chilly night with a light breeze. Each of us was holding a candle in a jar. They radiated through the darkness. Phoenix's remaining Shufflers were all there. There were hardly any of us left.

Phoenix was there. Her self-inflicted wounds were pretty much healed. Apparently Falcon helped a lot. I was so glad he was back, but he still hadn't said a word to me. Pilot finally came out of the room and was standing next to me.

I convinced the others that Macki was no longer a direct threat, so we were all able to relax for a while. Whether that was the truth or not... I couldn't say. I still regretted my decision. It never left me. I let Macki go when I could have killed her with one easy movement. *One.* That's all it would have taken.

But enough about what was going on. This was a night meant for us to mourn and grieve. There was a sense of solemnity hanging over all of us. We were here to remember what we had lost.

"For Zahra," Phoenix said. "Our leader and a good friend of mine." She released the jar and stepped back. Pilot stood slouched over, and I looked at his tired, depressed face that was illuminated by the light. He motioned forward but hesitated. Then he stepped all the way forward, gaining confidence.

"For Logan. My love. My best friend. My heart," he said quietly but proudly. He dropped it. He waited a moment before stepping back. Once he did, I knew it was my turn. I stepped onto the edge of the cliff. I thought about just designating my candle to my family, but at the last moment, I changed my mind. There were some other people that needed to be remembered as well.

"My parents," I said. There was still hope. "And a man. Mr. Asime Avi himself," I finished. I dropped my jar. I watched it as it hurtled toward the waves, the flame flickering. It was so beautiful on the dark backdrop, traveling silently through the air. It hit the water, and the glass shattered.

I felt a sense of relief and looked up to the stars.

No matter what happened here on Earth, the stars still seemed to shine.

--

Before I made myself known to Pilot, I watched him for a few moments. We were in the greenhouse. He was playing the piano, his fingers gliding fluidly over the keys. He was producing a beautiful tune – an original song he'd created. The Terrene was nearly deserted. There were only a few left – myself, Ishme (a former member of the Core), Pilot, and just a couple of others – along with all of Macki's followers that were captured at the battle. Pilot had been in the greenhouse nearly all day, every day for the past week or so. He didn't sleep and was improving rapidly. By the time I saw him, he could play anything I could throw at him.

"You're getting better," I told him. He stopped playing but didn't look back at me.

"I'm hoping Logan is listening," he said.

"She'd be proud," I encouraged.

"So what now?" he said as he looked back at me.

"Now… we leave the Terrene." Ishme was more like the leader now, so he instructed most of us to leave the Terrene. He'd been part of the Core, but he hadn't been as important as say, Phoenix or Logan. He was really nice, though, and it seemed like he knew what he was doing. Quinn would have led us, but he opted out. Phoenix and Pilot were having such a hard time dealing with the loss of Logan that neither of them were in the right condition to take on such a big responsibility. Akim – another member of the Core – was killed in battle.

"What?" he asked.

"I'm taking the prisoners with me. To keep an eye on them. Straighten them out if I can. You're welcome to come with us or…"

"I can go off by myself?" he finished.

"If you'd like. It's up to you. Falcon's in New York. I'm going to Romania. Quinn is back in Germany."

Pilot thought for a moment. "I think… I think I'd like to go off on my own for a while. Have some personal time, if that's okay?"

"It's great. You can relax a bit. Have some fun. Ishme said you can take the F-22 if you want."

"To get to fly again… sounds awesome."

I had one last thing to tell Pilot, and I'd been waiting for the perfect moment to tell him. I was going to be leaving soon, so I couldn't find any reason that that moment wasn't a good one.

"Logan… told me to tell you something before she died," I confessed. He perked up and searched my face for answers.

"What? What did she say?" he asked eagerly. I looked him straight in his gray eyes.

"She said… yes."

46

Macki

I hunkered down in a cave. My hands were covered in blood. The sand had inflamed my nose and eyes, so everything burned.

But I could barely feel it.

I had to admit, I was going a little bit crazy. My formula was gone. The formula that I'd worked so hard on that would take away Asime and make me... normal, more or less. Zahra was gone. Logan was gone. Ella was somewhere – hopefully. All of my followers were dead or captured. I had... I had lost.

Lost? Yes. I couldn't believe it.

But I really lost the most. In less than an hour, I lost all of my friends, my love, and my dignity – or whatever shred of it I'd had left. My heart ached. My brain hurt. I'd felt all of this before... yes, before. All of those years ago when my family was killed. And then again when they locked me up. Even then I'd had a little ember of hope, but now… now I felt done.

And what was I trying to do this whole time?

Attack the others? Make an army? Destroy the world as we knew it?

No. I was simply trying to help myself a little bit – something that I hadn't done for quite some time. They'd attacked me for no reason. I wasn't a threat. I wasn't crazy.

Until now.

"M, I know you're upset," Asime started.

"Shut up," I told him. "I don't need you around reminding that I failed, too."

"Alex knows the truth," he said. He did indeed. But what good did that do? "He let you live."

"Because he doesn't know who I really am!" I screamed at him as loud as I could.

"Who are you, then?" he asked calmly. I felt warm tears come to my eyes.

"Who am I? Who am *I?*" I asked. "I'm a waste of space."

"Babe, please, don't–"

"Shut up!" I yelled at him again, running my hands through my hair. I was in the corner of the cave, all curled up, tears forming little speckles all over my shirt after dripping off of my chin. "Why are you the only one who can make me feel? Why are you the only one, Asime!?" I screamed at him once again. I hardly ever screamed, and he knew it.

"M, you need to feel. Let me in."

"You're dead! I killed you! Why should I let you in!?"

"Because you love me, Mackinley." He looked hurt, his face looked sullen through the wall of tears.

"But… I don't understand. I just… I don't

understand. I can't feel love because you died. I can't feel pain because I've been through too much of it. I can't feel sadness because sadness is a weakness. I can't feel angry because I don't take anything seriously. I can't feel shame because I don't look back enough. I can't feel happy because nothing on this Earth will make me happy again. You know that leaves? Huh? It leaves jealousy.

"Jealous of, you know, all of the Core members. Zahra's sternness. Phoenix's drive. Pilot's civility. Logan's kindness. Quinn's intelligence. Falcon's juvenility. Maverick's carelessness. Karen's protectiveness. Jesse's understanding. And now Alex's power. That's all I had, Sime – power. And now I'm going to lose that, too. All of my 'friends' have been taken away from me. Why can't I figure anything out now? Why don't I have a plan? Because I've been labeled. Labeled as a traitor, as a fool, as insane. Insane for Christ's sake. Messy, sadistic, troublemaker. I cause havoc everywhere I go. So I stay in the shadows and pull the strings? Yeah, right. Not my M.O."

He went quiet for a moment. "You have all of that, M, don't you see it? You remember how you were with me. When I was with you all the time, right? You must not because, M, you were a great person. You *are* a great person."

"I'm a lunatic," I said. "I'm exactly what everything says I am. I'm crazy."

"You're not crazy."

"I *am* a monster, Asime. Look at me and tell me I'm not." I stared at him, his dark eyes like tiny muddy pools.

"You're not a monster," he said quietly.

"I'm missing something, Asime. My life is missing something."

"Me?" he asked after a silence.

"No."

"Then what?"

"Death," I told him. "I'm going to change the world as we know it. How's that for purpose?" I started laughing maniacally. "I'm going to kill them and I'm not going to make it out alive. I can't take this anymore."

"Macki, please—"

"Oh, shut up," I snapped. Was I going crazy? Sure seemed like it. But I was determined. The world will have never seen anything as vile and cruel and murderous as me. That's what they asked for after all, wasn't it?

Wasn't it? So watch out.

Macki's coming.

And I'm going to destroy everything they stand for.

ABOUT THE AUTHOR

Alina Simon is a novelist and screenwriter based in Los Angeles. In her spare time, she is usually researching something obsessively, philosophizing, or spending time with her family and friends as well as her two Chihuahuas, Taco and Bell.

Made in the USA
Middletown, DE
13 January 2023